The Habits of Falling Leaves

Orange Hat Publishing
www.orangehatpublishing.com - Waukesha, WI

The Habits of Falling Leaves

Benjamin R. Nysse

Orange Hat Publishing
www.orangehatpublishing.com - Waukesha, WI

The Habits of Falling Leaves by Benjamin R. Nysse
ISBN 978-1-948365-21-5

For information, please contact:

Orange Hat Publishing
www.orangehatpublishing.com
603 N Grand Ave, Waukesha, WI 53186

Edited by Lauren Lisak
Cover art by Lorene K. Lisheron
Flowing Autumn Leaves Frame Free vector © BSGStudio

I would like to thank my family, friends, and colleagues, especially those who took time to read and reread the manuscript and also listened to me go on and on about Craig and Abby.

I would like to thank the countless students who endured endless questions about all the things I could not know. A special thanks to DK, CC, LL and KH. Your contributions are too many to name.

I would like to thank Shannon and Lauren at Orange Hat for the opportunity to start this journey.

Mostly, I would like to thank my children, Will, Addy, and Lauren, for putting up with dad sitting at the kitchen table night after night.

Finally, to Terri, who remains my purpose and whose spirit is in these pages.

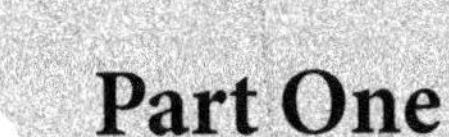

Part One

Abby: 18, In first college class. Texting with her best friend.

How's your first class?

The words appeared on my phone. It's Meghan. She's such a goof. At least I'm sitting a ways back. It seems like a lot of people have their phones out though.

Fine. I type back. But there's this guy looking at me.

Really? Is he cute?

I don't know. I'm not looking at him. I'm trying to listen.

No you're not. You're texting me...Look at him.

Why?

To see if he's cute.

Fine...He's pretty cute.

Did he see you looking at him?

I think so...Why?

Smile at him.

Why?

Why not?

Ok...I smiled at him.

Good.

Why?

Cause you never do things like that. It's time you started.

Thanks Meghan.

Not a problem. Now listen to your professor. cyl?

Sure.

Craig: 18, At home with his sister Claire.

"I remember the first time I saw Abby. She walked slowly into biology on the first day and sat down a few rows in front of me. It was like grace personified just sat down in front of me. I mean, there she was, this girl with hair, straight and dark, that fell almost down to her waist. It was incredible. She tossed it from side to side, covering her face and revealing it again. I don't know...it was like, really too perfect. Do you ever get the feeling that you just need to talk to someone?" Claire nodded slowly. "She wasn't like any girl I hung out with in high school. You know, I always went for the fit pixie girls with the narrow faces." Claire smirked and nodded again. "Abby's face was round, and she looked like someone who was in shape, you know, but not fit fit. God, I'm being so superficial. But then, she looked at me. Her eyes were amazing. They were light and framed by these long lashes. You know, lashes get me every time. After that, I couldn't stop looking at her. I kept waiting for her to turn around again. Then, she smiled at me. That's when I knew I had to talk with her."

"So, what did you do, Craig?" Claire asked.

"I found her in the Union and said..."

Chapter 1

"I don't really know many people around here, so you mind if I sit down?" Craig said as he stood behind a chair in the Student Union. He had already put his tray down and looked around to see if there was anyone who would recognize him.

Abby looked up and mumbled, "Ah, sure." She wasn't certain about what she was doing. She didn't know anyone either, so 'what the hell' she thought. 'Like Meghan said, I never do stuff like this.'

He sat down across from her, and they barely looked at each other. People bustled all around them, and he seemed distracted for a moment, still looking around. Their trays bumped together, and their bookbags sat on the table, creating a space between them and anyone else who might sit down. "I saw you in biology. That was a pretty lame first class. I learned most of the stuff on the syllabus in AP last year," he said, smiling and trying to get her attention.

"I didn't take AP classes at my school," she responded, just peeking up at him. "I don't know anything about biology."

"I can help you," he said confidently. "I'm Craig." He reached his hand across the table. His smile was big and toothy, almost as if someone told him to smile.

She couldn't tell if he liked her or was just making fun of

her, but she took his hand. When she looked up, she saw him clearly for the first time. She hadn't gotten a good look at him in class, just enough to know that he was cute. Actually, he was athletic and had high cheekbones and narrow, brown eyes. His dusty blond hair was curly, and he had a little scruff on his face. "Hi. I'm Abby. Thanks for the offer, but I need to learn this stuff on my own or I'll never get it. I can't afford to get a bad grade in anything. I want to get right into business school." Abby tried to sound annoyed, not knowing why this stranger was offering to help her.

Undeterred, Craig squeezed her hand gently and then let go. He responded, "That's cool. I can help." He liked the way Abby looked. He noticed her when she first walked into the classroom, and he had spent the entire class watching her instead of listening to the professor. She had that outdoorsy essence about her. Shades of amber streaked her dark brown hair, and freckles road across her nose down onto her cheeks. Her eyes were bright, glinting with blue or green or white, he couldn't tell, but he was drawn in. Craig thought she was pretty. She was not a girl you would whip your head around for on the path to class, but the more Craig gazed at her, the prettier she got.

"Where are you from?" he asked, looking directly at her eyes.

"Up north," Abby responded curtly.

"Cool, like around the Dells?" Craig said, starting to feel comfortable.

"No." Her eyes narrowed as she peered up at him. "Eagle River, up north." She pouted as she spoke that last part. People down here were always mistaking the Dells for up north.

Craig's expression softened. As she studied him, the rest of the room faded away. He never took his eyes off her. It was both disarming and comforting at the same time. She couldn't figure out what she was feeling.

"Oh sorry. I'm from Hartland."

"Where's that?"

"Waukesha County. Just outside Milwaukee." Her eyes stared blankly at him. "About forty-five minutes north of here. Right by 94."

She smiled and leaned. He thought he could look at that smile forever. And those eyes! He had never seen eyes like hers on someone with such dark hair. She reminded him of somebody, but he couldn't put a name to a face. He couldn't stop staring at her. It was like nothing else existed in the room.

Just then, two kids he knew from high school approached from behind Abby. Craig put his head down, hoping they wouldn't see him.

"McLean!" A slap came across his shoulder as one of the guys stopped right next to him. "Missed you again at practice, you wuss." The voice came from a huge guy with a gut. Abby thought the slap must have hurt.

"Yeah, sure." Craig managed a smirk and looked up.

Abby focused on him, not his friends. She was frustrated that he seemed to know quite a few people.

"Where you been, man? Since you quit, we've hardly seen you. You been hiding?" The other kid chimed in. He was also big and wearing a school football jersey.

"I'm not playing anymore, and I…" Craig paused, looking at Abby, then back to the guys. "I kinda met someone. This is Abby. Abby, these are my friends...teammates...from high school. They're on the football team." He took a breath and then continued, "We're eating, guys." Craig returned his eyes to Abby and shook his head a little. She faked a smile.

"Well, see you later. Maybe you could come to your senses and stop being such a pussy. If Coach will even take you back," one of the guys said.

"Yeah, ok man. Whatever," the other one said, and they left, shuffling through the Union, bumping into tables and grumbling to each other.

"Sorry about that." Craig pressed his lips tightly, his nose twitching a little. His face was red.

"I thought you said you didn't know anyone?" Abby said sharply, but with a wink she didn't think he caught.

"That was just a line. I really wanted to talk with you and couldn't figure out what else to say."

Abby's eyes softened, and she smiled again, this time almost chuckling. "No problem. You play football?" The room began to narrow again.

"I did," he responded, shifting in his seat and focusing on her.

"Those guys were really giving it to you. Why don't you play anymore?"

"I didn't like it. Not sure I ever did." He continued to shift uncomfortably in his seat.

"Really? Were you playing here?"

"I came for camp, but stopped." Craig was desperate to get off the subject of his football playing days. "You play sports?"

"I hike a lot. I like canoeing too, but nothing organized."

"Cool, I've never canoed. Maybe you can teach me."

Biting her lower lip and letting it roll out, Abby asked,

"What did you mean, I kinda met someone?" She was done with the small talk.

Surprised, Craig stammered, "I met you."

"We just met."

Again searching for words, Craig managed, "I know. But I meant it."

"Meant what?" Abby would not give up on the conversation. She was determined to get to the bottom of this guy's deal.

Sensing that she wouldn't let it go, Craig came right out with what he wanted to say. "I like you. I don't care about those guys. I met you. I would like to see you again."

"We have class together. We'll see each other every other day," she said hesitantly.

"What are you doing for dinner?" Craig began to clean up his tray.

"Not sure, probably eating with my roommate," Abby murmured, starting to get flush.

"Well...maybe I'll join you. If that's cool?" He became aware he was saying 'cool' a lot but couldn't seem to stop. While he was confident in asking the question, Abby's long pause made him begin to worry.

"I suppose," she said, letting out a long breath. "Don't you have a roommate?"

"Yeah, he's got practice all the time, and he's got a pretty serious girlfriend." Craig continued to pack up. "I've gotta get to class. I'll find you." He let the lie escape his mouth. Really, he just wanted to go and tell Brent about Abby.

"Oh. See you, I guess," she said, feeling a bit startled about the abruptness of Craig leaving. Abby turned her head as he walked away. She felt flush all over. For the first time since she sat down in the dining room, she noticed the sound all around. Trays were bumping, people were having conversations, and the nonstop busyness was unnerving her. The guy next to her was tapping on the table, seemingly unaware that there were other people sitting there too. Someone bumped into her and apologized. She was a bit overwhelmed by the crowd. Then, someone squeezed her shoulder, making her jump a little in her chair as she looked up. It was Craig. She let out a breath.

"I forgot to ask, where do you like to eat?"

"Ah, wells...Wellers...yeah, Wellers," she mumbled, looking at his excited face. Her vision narrowed again, and it was just him and her.

"Cool, so you eat at Esker?"

"Sure," Abby said slowly, then realized that she had just given him the name of her dorm, not the cafeteria. He obviously knew more about the Whitewater campus than she did.

"Ok, see you around five?" He squeezed her shoulder again. As he walked away this time, she watched him. He seemed so confident. Waving to a girl a few tables down, he stopped to wait, and they walked out together. The girl was skinny and blonde. Abby noticed her hand run down his back, but he didn't react. They were obviously familiar with each other. 'Who is this guy?' Abby wondered. He was like no one she had ever met. Most guys she had met in high school were so shy they couldn't get a sentence out. Craig was different. Right before he let go of the door he held open for the other girl, he looked back at Abby and waved.

Chapter 2

"Hey Craig, who was that girl?" Jen asked smiling, as she always did, and with a hint of sarcasm. They began to walk back to the dorms on the hill. "She was cute."

"Yeah, I think so. She's really nice." Craig looked Jen up and down. 'Leggings and a tight tank. Damn, she's fine,' he thought to himself. He remembered being the envy of every guy in high school when he walked down the hall with her. No one ever missed a chance to watch Jen walk away. She knew it too, and secretly loved it.

"You know, she reminds me of that girl from the AT&T commercials. Kinda 'plain' cute, but pretty you know?"

"Yes," Craig said, as if agreeing with her was a sort of habit. "She's pretty. I like her. Her name is Abby."

"Well good for you. I'm glad you met someone." She squeezed Craig's arm. "How's life without football?"

"It's fine. The guys are still giving me crap."

"How's your dad?"

"He's still pissed. I don't know."

"You'll be ok."

"Thanks, Jen." Craig frowned and gazed off towards the north end of campus.

"So, I gotta go. See you later." Jen ran off up Prince Street, and Craig went to his dorm, hoping his roommate would be there. As he went into the room, he found Brent half asleep on his bed.

"Hey, Craig. What's up?" Brent said with a yawn.

"Nothing. What about you?" Craig asked, taking his phone out of his pocket and glancing at it for a moment before putting is on his desk.

"Not much. Just resting up for practice. Hey, why don't you stop by?"

Craig ignored the question. He had no interest in being around the team. He put his bag down on the futon. They had both put their beds up at waist height so they could store stuff under them. Craig had ceded to Brent for decoration, as he intended to spend most of his time in the library to study and stay out of Brent's way if he brought his girl back to the room. There were football posters all over, and Brent's desk was mostly filled with snacks and protein powders. Craig doubted Brent would be doing a lot of studying.

"Yeah, we had morning lift, and then I had two classes. This is going to kill me, man." Brent said all this without raising his head. "How was your day? Easier than mine, I expect."

Craig had grown used to the not-too-subtle way that Brent refused to let his quitting the team go. Brent was better than most though. He at least tried to be nice. Most of the other guys on the team weren't that understanding. "I met someone in biology. A girl. She's really great."

Brent opened his eyes and turned his head slowly. "You met a girl in biology class? What are you talking about?"

"Yeah. We had lunch together. She's cool. She's from up north."

Brent sat up and draped his legs off the side of his bed, his hands gripping the frame. “Let me get this straight, you met a girl in biology class and took her to lunch? Who is this girl? What does she look like?”

Craig sat down on the folded futon and kicked his feet up over the arm. “Jen thinks she looks like the AT&T girl…I guess I could see it. She has really dark, long hair and these really amazing eyes. I couldn’t stop looking at her.”

“Wait, Jen was there?”

“No, I just saw Jen when I was walking out. I’m going to meet Abby for dinner at Esker around five. If you’re done with practice, stop by and meet her.” He regretted asking the question almost as soon as it left his lips.

“Oh, will do. Who is she?” Brent rubbed his forehead.

“Her name is Abby. Wait, did I already say that?” Craig asked. “I think I like her. I don’t know, there’s something about this girl.” Craig smiled to himself, holding the picture of Abby in his head.

“Oh man. This is going to be a fun semester.” Brent laid down and went back to his nap.

Craig opened his biology text and then closed it. He had learned all of this last year, so there was no need to go over it. He had opted out of the test because he wanted to review when he got to college. Instead, his mind wandered back to Abby. Brent was right, the prospects for the semester had just brightened.

Abby had a class at three and another later in the evening at six thirty, so she went back to her room. ‘Who was that girl?’ she thought over and over as she walked across campus.

She had been at college for almost a week for orientation and, for the most part, knew where her classes were. It was a beautiful day. There were lots of trees on campus which Abby liked, but they were planned out and evenly spaced. Many had bark chips around them, and the attempt at artificial nature unnerved her. Abby missed her forest. She missed the lake surrounded by trees that never seemed to end. The allure of home captured her in moments like this. There was some thought of going to Stevens Point for school, but she finally decided to get away and go where she knew no one. Her mother had encouraged her. "Go where you can meet new people," she had said repeatedly. So far, she wasn't too impressed, save for Craig. Also, there was almost no hint of the leaves changing. She knew the color was already starting at home. If she was there, she could tour around the lake on her boat and take pictures. But she had work to do here before going home. Her dad would never give her the resort unless she got her degree. Five years to get a MBA. She could do it. It just seemed so far away.

Kate, Abby's roommate, was from Wausau, which was about eighty miles from Eagle River but still "up north." So, theoretically, they had some things in common. When Abby got to her room, she hoped Kate would be there. Kate was a studious person, but they'd talked often over the last week, and she had proven to be a good ear. Abby hoped to return the favor.

"Hi, Abby, how was your first class?" Kate looked up from her books. She was a small girl and had a short haircut because she always got it cut for charity as soon as it got long enough. Her glasses seemed as though she slept in them.

"Good, I guess."

"Ok great." Kate was half-listening and went back to her studying. She had three classes Monday, Wednesday, and Friday mornings, so Abby had assumed she would be at her desk.

They had arranged their room with Abby's bed on the floor, and Kate's bed lofted. Both of their desks were under Kate's bed, and the extra room was taken up with a small couch. Abby put down her pack and sat down on the couch.

"Hey, Kate?"

"Yeah?" She didn't look up.

"I met a guy."

"What?" Kate swung around in her chair and put her head on her hands, leaning forward. "What are you talking about?"

"This guy came and just sat down next to me after biology while I was eating at the Union. I was sitting at one of the desks on the left side of class, and he was sitting a few rows back, and he kept staring at me." Abby heard herself and was self-conscious. The whole interaction with Craig had thrown her off a bit. She couldn't decide if it was exciting or unsettling.

"What did he do?"

"He didn't say anything during class, and then he asked if he could sit down when I got to the Union for a snack."

"And you said yes?" Kate leaned back in her chair and gripped the arms.

"He said he didn't know anyone. I felt bad." Abby fished her biology book out of her bag and turned back to Kate. "He was lying. A couple of guys came up to him to say hi, and he walked out with this other girl."

"What was his deal?" Kate said with a spin of her chair. She was a whimsical girl, and Abby was beginning to love it. She was always going on about living for the now. Abby was living for the future.

"I don't know. It kind of felt like a first date," Abby said with a shrug.

Kate's eyes were stuck on Abby. "What? That's weird. What was he like?"

"Kinda cocky. Super cute, though. Not the kind of guy I'm really into." Although, in reality, Craig seemed like a guy who would never talk to a girl like her, but he did. He talked to her. He had singled her out of the crowd and talked to her. Just thinking about it made her feel a bit overwhelmed. She had always felt like she wasn't the kind of girl guys would just come up to.

"And he left with another girl?"

"Yeah." Abby said, trying to ignore the question. "We talked a bit. And turns out he's from around here. Quit the football team…"

"Wait, what? He quit the football team?"

"Yeah. Not really sure why. But the weird thing was he wanted to see me later. I mean, even though he talked to and left with that other girl, he still looked back and smiled at me."

"Well, are you going to go?"

"I guess..." She paused and shook her head. "He's really nice, but a bit weird. Can you come with me?"

"On your date?"

"Well, it's not really a date," Abby said. "At least I don't think it is?"

"Ok, when?" Kate's eyes were wide with excitement.

"Five, I guess."

"Alright, I'm in." And with that, Kate turned to get back to her work.

"Thanks." Abby put her feet up on the couch and opened her biology book.

Chapter 3

Abby and Kate walked over to Esker around four forty-five. Dinner service hours didn't start until five, but with a six-thirty class, Abby wanted to find a seat and get food right when it opened. She hoped to read her article for English 101, her three o'clock class, before math class that night. Abby was organized. Not anywhere close to being like Kate, but she liked to get things done right away. Life at the resort had taught her that things can't be put off. There's a schedule and things to get done. "Either you do it now OR..." as her dad always said, smiling because he knew what came next. "There is no OR. Get it done now." This advice had served Abby well. She didn't quite know what to expect at dinner, but she was hungry, and Kate was with her, so how bad could it be?

"Let's sit here." Kate chose a table by the window. They put their bags on the table and sat down. "So, tell me again, what's this guy like?"

They hadn't talked about it much more in their room. After reading for a while, Abby had fallen asleep and woke up just in time to get to her English class. "He's cute. Super healthy-looking and strong. Blond hair and really narrow brown eyes. Like I said, he quit the football team a few weeks into practice. He said he just didn't like it. I don't know the story behind that.

He seems smart; he said he took a lot of AP classes in high school. I don't know...he's really nice. I think he might be a player, though."

Kate pulled her glasses down her nose. "Do you think he's meeting you on a dare, or that this is some kind of a joke?"

"Why would you think that?" Abby said with her nose all scrunched up like she smelled something unpleasant. "No, he seemed nice." She hadn't thought that until Kate brought it up. He did say he met someone to the football players. Maybe there was a thing on the football team about getting a girl. "No, I can't believe that," Abby thought out loud.

Just then, Craig walked in, breathing heavily. He had the same shorts on that he was wearing that morning, but his shirt was changed. It was a Hartland Arrowhead football shirt, tight enough that you could see his shape, and his curly, blond hair bounced as he strode in.

"He's cute!" Kate said quietly. Abby turned to see who Kate was talking about. Craig looked around, lost for a bit, and then spotted Abby. She couldn't help but smile and raise her hand towards him, which she pulled down almost immediately. Craig saw her and waved back, heading right over.

"That's him," Abby said, feeling flush all over again.

"Wow." Kate kept staring in Craig's direction, unaware that Abby was scowling at her.

He reached their table, still trying to catch his breath. "Hey."

"Hey. This is my roommate Kate. She and I have the same math class tonight, so I thought she could come too."

"Nice to meet you, Kate. Where are you from?" Craig reached out his hand.

"Wausau."

"Is that up north too?" He winked at Abby, pulling his hand back.

Laughing, Abby replied, "Almost."

Kate responded, "North of here, yes. I'm going to get some food." She got up and skipped off, leaving them alone.

"Do you want to get food?" Craig asked.

"Well, that's what we're here for," Abby replied, putting her hand out to allow Craig to go first.

Craig got chicken and mashed potatoes while Abby got a salad. She found that the salad was the best deal because they just counted it as a salad, and she could still get meat with it. She wanted to stretch her food budget as far as she could.

"That looks good," Craig said. "I should eat more salads." He patted his stomach.

"I think you're doing fine," Kate said, smiling. Abby shot her a look. "Just saying," Kate continued.

"Thank you," Craig replied. "I'll need to start working out again. We should work out together." He didn't really know what to say and was feeling a little lost in the conversation.

"I need to get used to my schedule first." Abby didn't know how to take his comment. She had played volleyball her freshman year of high school and worked out by hiking around the lake. There were always things to keep her active, but she didn't do anything organized. There was never time.

"Yeah. Me too. That's why it's been two weeks since I've worked out...How was your class this afternoon? Did you get your biology reading done?"

Abby could see that Craig was fidgeting with his food, and he kept glancing at her, then Kate, then her again. Kate just looked down and ate her salad. Abby finished chewing, took a drink, and then responded, "Class was fine. I finished my reading. How about you?"

"I tried, but I fell asleep. I'll probably just review it before class on Wednesday."

"Sure." Abby was sick of the small talk and blurted out, "So, what's up?" Kate nudged Abby with her leg and looked sternly at her. "Why did you ask me to dinner?" This question made Craig look up and pay attention. Kate did too.

Craig froze for a second. "Well…I just thought…it'd be cool to get to know you. I mean…you said you didn't know anyone."

Kate got up and excused herself to throw out her food and get soda for class. She squeezed Abby's shoulder.

"Yeah…but don't you think it's a little weird?" Abby leaned in.

"Well…I guess, but…I mean…how else are you supposed to meet someone you don't know?" Craig shifted in his seat and leaned in as well. His gaze was intense as his eyes fixated on her. He couldn't believe this girl was challenging him straight out. He kinda liked it.

"I don't know, it just struck me as weird…I mean…I don't even know…I don't know. I'm confused," Abby confessed quietly.

Craig reached his hand out, but Abby pulled hers back, gripping the edge of the table. She looked down at the scraps of her salad, then reached for a napkin and patted down her face. "Why me? I mean, who was that girl you walked out with today?"

"What?" Craig pulled his extended hand back to run his fingers through his hair. "You mean Jen?"

"I don't know, that pretty blonde girl. She seemed to know you really well." Her eyes burned angrily.

Craig was transfixed by Abby's eyes for a moment. "Yeah. Jen…She's my ex-girlfriend from high school." He could tell from looking at Abby that this answer didn't help.

Abby started to pack her tray and turned slightly. Craig extended his hand towards her then watched it fall to the table, shocked. "She broke up with…I mean, we aren't together… Hey." He looked at Abby, and she saw him eye to eye as if for the first time. It was disarming.

His jaw tightened. "I think you're pretty. That's why I came over this morning. I want to know you, Abby. I want to find out who you are. Jen is a friend. It didn't work. It was never going to work. I just want to know you. That's all. Nothing more. I mean…we're going to see each other all over. Can't we," Craig hesitated, "try to be friends?"

Abby watched him closely, searching for sincerity in his eyes. This guy was so kind and intense. His gaze never wavered. She looked down and said, "I suppose." Reaching for her tray, she touched his hand. He smiled.

Suddenly, the whole offensive line came into the hall. They filled the space. Abby remembered the two guys from the Union. 'I met someone,' she thought to herself. She found herself gripping Craig's hand. She didn't let go. The cafeteria was almost full, but the team found an open table and one member, whom Abby didn't recognize, walked towards them. He was tall and wide through the shoulders. He had a little belly, but not as big as the guys from the morning.

Running his hand through his long hair, he said, "Hey Craig…is this the girl?" Abby pulled her hand back and looked at Craig. Kate had just returned and started to gather her things.

Craig looked up. "Yes. This is Abby."

"Cool! Hey," he said, nodding at Abby.

From the other side of the room, someone called, "Hey, Brent, don't hang with the quitter!"

Brent seemed to ignore the comment and said, "I'm starving. Catch you later." He passed right by.

Craig returned his gaze to Abby. "That's my roommate, Brent." He squeezed at a hand that was no longer there. Craig didn't know whether to be annoyed with Brent or just angry at the whole situation. He decided to be neither. He had asked him to stop by. Brent was a loveable dumbass. They lived only ten minutes apart when they were in high school, and although Brent had played for a rival school, they had been at the same camps and played on some select baseball and basketball teams together. Craig knew Brent was harmless. The rest of the team he wasn't so sure about.

"Oh. Hey, Kate," Abby said as she noticed she had come back to the table. She and Kate were getting up to go. Abby turned. "We have to go to class. I want to get some reading done beforehand."

"Oh. Ok…Can we meet up later?" Craig tried to get up and got caught on the table.

"I'll see you in class, if not before." She smiled and gently shook her head. "I want to get to know you too, Craig. See you Wednesday." She walked away. He watched her all the way out the door.

Abby: E-mail to Meghan, 1:30 AM

Hey Meghan,

I am writing you because it's late, and I can't sleep. I didn't want to wake you. That guy. You know, the one who was looking at me. He talked to me. He just came up to me after class in the Union while I was eating lunch. He sat down and just started talking to me. It was so weird. He said he didn't know anyone, so I felt bad. Turns out, he knows everyone. A couple of guys came up to him, and I guess he was on the football team and comes from some place outside Milwaukee and knows the campus super well. I'm not sure why I didn't get up right then, but he was just so cute and nice. Tall, blond, chiseled. I've never met anyone like him. We met for dinner too. I made Kate come along, but she left us alone for a while. He told me he wanted to be friends. I just can't figure him out, Meg. It was just so weird, and I think I like him. I just hope he's not joking with me. He said I was pretty. Me, pretty? No one has ever told me that before, except my dad. I just don't know what to do! He's really cute and not like other boys. He's smart too. Sorry. It's late, and I'm not making any sense. If you get this, call me. I am really confused. Kate doesn't know what to say. Help Meghan!!!

Abby

Chapter 4

They didn't see each other until Wednesday morning. When Craig came into class, he waved and gave Abby a side smile. He sat down with a seat in between them, took out his Chromebook, which was more than he did on day one, and waited for the professor to begin. He took good notes from what Abby could see, and even raised his hand to answer questions. This elicited a smile from the professor and a clarifying of his name. When class ended, Abby turned to him to ask a question.

"Hey, Craig?"

He was already packed to go but turned. "Yeah?"

"Can you help me with this?" Abby showed him the diagram she had tried to copy from the notes but was scribbled due to the speed of the professor's lecture.

"Sure. It's in the book, on page forty-seven. He wrote the book, so he just lectures from it. That's how lots of professors make extra money. They write the books, and we have to buy them."

The classroom had cleared, and people were starting to come in for the next class.

"Could you show me the diagram? How did you know the page?" Abby was impressed by Craig's ability to recall all of this information. She wanted to know his tricks.

"Sure, let's go find another place to sit." Craig seized the opportunity, simply disregarding the question.

They went outside and found a bench just up from the Student Union. It was away from the main path up on a circle-shaped platform which could only be reached by a set of stairs located on the right. They could sit there and be alone with each other in the midst of the chaos. The best part of fall in Wisconsin is that the temperature is cool in the morning but still warms during the day. This was a good day for sitting outside.

Craig showed her the diagram in her book. He explained that he preread the chapters and made an outline so all he had to do was take notes on the professor's information. Mostly, he just wanted to impress Abby. He heard that the professor liked to write half of his exam questions from class notes to make sure kids attended. They talked about class, and he showed her what he wrote down. She had tried to write everything. He showed her how the outline of what the professor said came straight from the subheadings of the book, and that all she needed to do was fill in information on the edges.

Abby took his computer and scrolled through the file. "Could you share this with me?" she asked with a smile. This would make her life much easier since biology was going to be her hardest class. They talked for a while longer. Craig seemed like a good friend, and Abby turned to face him as he talked. She liked how animated he got; his arms were always moving, and his face lit up. Students were constantly walking past down below the platform, but few went by them. There was a warm breeze coming from the south, and everything seemed to fade into a bubble.

Craig asked how she liked her classes, now that she had been to all of them, and she said that they were ok. Biology would be her most difficult, but she also had a Western Civilization class that sounded interesting. All of her classes were general requirements at this point. Craig told her he had the same class second semester. He still had one class to attend because he had dropped his English 103 and had taken 105: Honors class. He figured that he had already taken classes where writing was needed, so he wanted to take a challenging class that was outside his norm since he had the time now. Pre-med didn't afford much time for exploration, so he wanted to take advantage when he could.

Abby laughed at that because she had everything planned out. There was no room in her schedule, and she was hoping to get out in five years with her MBA and go home to run the resort. The day was brilliant, and their conversation continued until Craig realized he was going to be late for his new class.

Over the next few days, Craig and Abby met on the bench after classes. Sometimes it was right after biology, other times it was circumstance, usually meeting on the main path near the Union. Abby suspected that Craig knew her class schedule and was meeting her by "accident" on purpose. She didn't mind though. She was happy to see him. When he emerged from the crowd with his chiseled smile, he would jog a step or two just to get over to her. Sometimes he had to move on and would just say hi. But, more often, he had time to talk or get a bite to eat. They would talk about how classes were going or trade stories about Kate and Brent and how difficult it was to adjust to living with someone else. Although, Craig mentioned that Brent was often gone at his girlfriend's since her roommate was often gone with her boyfriend. It was a whole round-robin thing Craig couldn't really keep up with and didn't care that much about. The problem was that he never really knew when Brent would come back.

The basic biographies were shared and goofy stories told about parents and siblings. Abby told Craig how annoying is was to have a sister who was five years younger and Craig talked about the advantages of being the baby of the family and the only boy. However, Craig never shared too much about his home beyond his sisters. Abby, on the other hand, loved talking about her home, and Craig always seemed interested in her stories. He never took his eyes off her. One day, he even reached over and pulled her hair over her shoulder and let it fall through his hand. At first Abby tensed, but then turned her head to the side and brushed it back behind her shoulders, reaching down to grab the ends of his fingers before pulling her hand away. He looked down at their hands and then back at her face. She smiled softly and felt her cheeks blush. Craig laughed.

"Hey," he said playfully, leaning forward to get her focus.

"What?" Abby replied coyly.

"You know how everyone goes home on the weekends?"

"Yes." She was unsure about what Craig was getting at. She held her books up to her chest.

"So...I'm not going home this weekend..." Abby let her books drop to her lap. Craig continued, "Do you want to do something?" He caught her straight in the eye, and she could feel his intensity. It made her feel good. She was no longer uncomfortable with his unwavering stares. In fact, she found it attractive.

"Sure, what do you have in mind?" Abby asked.

"I don't know. We could go for a walk out by the lake. Maybe get a bite to eat downtown?"

"That sounds nice. What are you doing tonight?"

"I thought I'd study and work out. I don't want to have to do stuff on Sunday."

"That's cool." She had hoped to hang out but didn't push it. "Are you going to the library or studying in your room?"

"I'll be at the library. No one else will be there, so I can get a lot done." Craig could sense Abby wanted to join him.

She took a deep breath. "Mind if I join you? I have some more biology questions."

"Sure. I'll be there around six." Craig got up to go. "I've gotta get to class." He winked at her before walking away. Abby felt her blood rise again. Craig was just so cute with his bow-legged walk. She watched him until he reached the corner.

Abby was sitting at a table with her book already open when Craig got to the library. He sat down next to her before she noticed he was there. She looked up, took her earbuds out, and smiled at him. As he put his book bag on the table, reaching to open it, a hand grazed against his forearm. He looked at Abby. She squeezed his arm and then picked up her pencil. He wanted her to touch him again. Craig got out his biology book and his computer, opening the chapters he had outlined for the next week so he could be prepared to help Abby. They had created a shared document for notes, and he noticed she was already on it. He showed her how he outlined the notes and then filled in with lecture notes.

She jotted things down, then said, "I think I'll try a chapter."

"Sure thing," Craig agreed and let her be for a bit while he pulled out his literature text, opening to a poem by W.H. Auden called "The Unknown Citizen." For this assignment, he had to determine the author's initial intent. He already figured out that the guy in the poem had lived a normal life, but there was no way to determine if that life was happy. There was nothing that showed if he was satisfied with his life, and no one seemed to care.

(To JS/07 M 378
This Marble Monument
Is Erected by the State)

He was found by the Bureau of Statistics to be
One against whom there was no official complaint,
And all the reports on his conduct agree
That, in the modern sense of an old-fashioned word, he was a saint,
For in everything he did he served the Greater Community.

Craig got up and walked around the table. He was suddenly concerned that he was reading a poem about how he might end up.

"What's up?" Abby asked.

"Nothing. I just needed to stretch." He went back to the poem. The man did satisfactory work, and that was all that mattered. This struck Craig given his "job" growing up. "Satisfactory" and "fine" were words he never wanted to hear. This poem, and many of the others he was reading in this honors class, got him thinking. The guy in the poem was just a collection of statistics, something that Craig could identify with because, while playing sports, he felt that he was much the same. "Was he happy?" No one had ever bothered to ask the man in the poem. No one had ever really asked him either. It was always "How was the game?" or "How are you feeling?" But Craig knew they weren't asking about how he was, really. Rather, they were interested in his ability to play in the next game. He felt like he had been hurt for the better part of the last five years. That was one of the many reasons he had quit football. He was just sick of always being hurt.

"What are you reading?" Abby asked. Craig turned and saw her sitting with her head in her hand, looking at him. With her dark hair, the blue-green and white of Abby's eyes captured his full attention. He snapped out of it.

"Oh…just some poem for class. I'm supposed to write about it." Craig tried to be relaxed about the exchange, but he really wanted to share the poem with her. He wanted to share everything. His hopes and his doubts. His whole life. He just wanted to download everything about himself into her so she could just know.

"What's it about?" Abby pulled his book towards her and looked down.

"Some guy who the government measured in every way, but they didn't really care if he was happy." Craig tugged his chair close to hers so he could put his arm across the back of it.

"This is weird. It rhymes, and then it doesn't. What's with that?" Abby looked up quickly and didn't seem to notice that Craig was looking at her and not the book. His hand had found its way through her hair and was resting on her shoulder.

"I'm not sure about that yet. The thing that gets me is the idea that the point of life is to be happy. It's not about what we buy or what we have; it's about what we do and who we do it with." His eyes had returned to the book. "At least, that's what I think."

"That's like this line from a song I like. I think it goes like 'Are you living the life you chose, or are you living the life that chose you?' It's by Jason Isbell, you know that singer I told you about?"

They were both looking at the book. Abby put down her pencil and put her hand on Craig's knee. He gently grazed his fingers across the top of her back. She had talked with him about the music she listened to and how she always listened to Pandora to find new artists. Craig had begun to listen to some of the artists.

"I listened to that guy on Pandora. I've never heard music like that." He paused to take a deep breath. "So, which are you doing?"

"What?"

"Are you living the life you chose or the life that chose you?" Craig reached over and closed the book.

"I don't know. Maybe a bit of both." Her hand squeezed his knee, and she shifted to face him more easily. His hand moved to her right arm, and he ran his fingers up and down her shoulder. "How about you?"

"Well…I mean…I have a plan I guess. But it seems so long. I mean like…seven or eight more years of school and then residency. I'm not sure I'll even be happy. You know what I'm saying?"

"I do. I know what has made me happy for years. I want nothing more from life than to go back home and stay there."

Craig turned in his chair. His hand followed down Abby's

arm and found her hand on his leg. "I love that you have a sense of place. I've never felt that way about my home. Or anything really I guess."

"Yeah…I don't know. There's just nothing like being in the woods or out on the water. It's so peaceful. I like the routine of the resort. I know what each day holds for me, you know? Not like this place. Sometimes it's all so confusing."

"It's cool you're trying something different though, right?"

"I guess so. You're doing that too, aren't you?"

"What do you mean?" Craig was confused.

"With quitting football? When is the last time you didn't play sports?"

"I really can't remember. I think I've always played something."

"Yeah," Abby seemed to agree. "All my memories are about the resort."

"Haven't you ever gone anywhere else?"

"Not really. It's a lifestyle. You can't really leave it alone." Abby turned her head away for a moment, staring off at the books.

Craig didn't want to let go of the moment but said, "So how's that chapter coming?"

"I think it's ok." She turned her computer and pushed it towards him. "What do you think?"

He picked it up and looked at what she had written. "All seems good." He noticed that her subheadings were all abbreviated. There was enough to know what she was saying, but nothing more. She was about getting things done. Craig liked that about her.

"Great, I'm going to try to finish the chapter," she said.

"That's a good idea." They both turned back to their books for an hour or so, bathed in the fluorescence and white walls. Abby had an ability to lean in and focus, an ability that Craig didn't think he had in the area of school. He never really needed to. Things always seemed to come easily to him. He tried a few different subjects, but kept looking at Abby. She would look up from time to time to meet his gaze, but really, she got more done than he did.

At eight thirty, he gave up and packed his bag. He went to the bathroom and returned to find Abby waiting for him with her bag packed too.

"I'm done," she said. "You?"

"Yep. Want to walk back to the dorms?" Craig was out of breath. He was antsy and had jogged back from the bathroom, wanting to get back to Abby as quickly as he could.

"Sure."

"I'll walk you back to yours."

"Great," Abby said as she laughed to herself. She was having trouble with how well everything was going. Craig was great, and her head was spinning. She wasn't sure she deserved to be this happy with a boy.

They moved down the stairs through a library devoid of people and out the door. It was still warm, but nightfall was winning its daily battle with the sun. Craig walked close to Abby, not knowing if he should reach for her hand. In the end, he just grabbed the straps on his backpack.

"We still on for tomorrow?" Craig asked with a faraway voice.

"I think so. You asked me," Abby responded playfully.

"Oh, yeah. Meet at ten thirty or so at the bench?"

"Sure. Are we going out to eat or just going down by the lake?" Abby had stopped to face him. He went a step or two further.

"Well, I thought we could walk down by the lake and see what happens…We can find some place to eat if you want, nothing fancy."

"I'll just leave it up to you." She turned to go to her dorm.

"Hey…is Kate around tonight?" Craig didn't want the moment to end.

"I think she is. She never goes home," Abby replied as she stepped towards Craig and brushed her hand down his arm. "I'll see you tomorrow, Craig."

He smiled softly. "Ok."

Craig: 18, On a date with Jen in high school

I wish she would talk about something real. All we ever do is talk about what is going on with other people. She's just like my mother. It's all about the gossip. I know all the stories from school, the hospital, and in the subdivision. The comings and goings. Who is with who, and who is on the outs. It's always the same.

"So, Ben is going to break up with Annie, and she knows, but she isn't going to tell him she knows until he does it. She's sure he won't have the guts. At least not before prom," Jen said as she worked her gum like a piece of beef jerky.

"Why would she stay with him if she knows he doesn't like her?" As soon as I said it, I regretted it. *Jen launched into a rant about how embarrassing it would be to go to senior prom without a date, and how Annie would just die and on and on and on. God! It's always the same. I wish we would just break up. But, I can't do that before prom. I guess I'm no better than Ben.*

"Are you listening to me, Craig?" Jen asked, tapping her finger on the table.

"Oh, yeah. Sorry."

Chapter 5

Craig woke up late and barely had time to get ready. He wanted to get a picnic together, but now had no time to run to the store. He threw a few juice boxes, half a loaf of bread, some peanut butter and jelly, a pack of cookies, a spoon, and two bananas into his pack. Finally, he tucked a blanket from his bed inside as well. This day had to be perfect. He had spent half the night thinking about Abby. What life would he lead? One where he chose to be happy or one where the choices were made for him by circumstance? He marveled again at Abby's sense of place, her love for her home. Craig didn't really care where he ended up, but he assumed he would move to a place much like the house where he grew up. Carefully kept lawns, a pool in the back, and an interior that reflected wealth over personality. Just the thought of that made him cringe.

After getting dressed, throwing some water on his face, and running his hands through his hair, he put his backpack on and was off. He got to the bench before Abby, so he sat down, trying to look casual. Craig prided himself on always being on time. Often, he was early.

Abby saw him as she rounded the corner. She laughed to herself as she saw him sitting there, looking off in the other direction. Why had he brought a backpack? She wondered if she was dressed for what he had planned. She was happy he was there before her. Being on time was a habit of Craig's. One she appreciated.

Craig turned his head to see her coming up the path. She was wearing nice shorts and a button-down tank top. It may have been the first time he had seen her in anything other than leggings and a T-shirt. She had a figure. He admired her summer-tanned legs looking longer than normal, and how her waist curved in and out. Fit as she was, Jen was almost straight down from all angles. Abby was shapely. She was a woman. Craig sat motionless as she moved closer. Abby seemed to be in no hurry to get to him. There was a sway and gracefulness to her walk, not like the quick gate of the women in his life, always in a rush to get nowhere. Then, he noticed her hair. It was braided and up off her neck and shoulders, not falling down to her waist as usual. She was beautiful.

Abby was sure by the way that Craig was staring that he had noticed her attempt to look different. She smiled widely and sat on the bench. "What's up?"

Craig turned away a bit and replied, "Ah nothing." He felt an urge to touch her neck and run his fingers across the top of her back from shoulder to shoulder for the first time since they met. He imagined how soft her skin was. She was so pretty, and he knew that just being with her was enough. 'Know you're enough to use me for good.' The Isbell line from one of Abby's favorite songs played in his head. Why would anyone ever want more? Craig wondered what he had done to get a girl like Abby. He felt so lucky. "Thought we'd go by the lake and have a little picnic."

Abby lit up. He wasn't going to try too hard. It was exactly what she had hoped to do. Restaurants made her a little nauseous. "Sweet, let's go." She popped up. Craig rose and put his backpack on. She grabbed his hand in both of hers, leaned in against his arm briefly, and then let go and skipped ahead of him. He caught up, laughing, and reached to grab her hand. Abby interlocked their fingers as they walked up the hill to the south entrance of campus.

The day was filled with potential. Sunlight shone everywhere, and a few trees had given way to fall colors. The yellows and reds mixed with the greens. Abby loved this time of the year. Up north, the trees changed earlier, and she could take the boat out to give vacationers tours of the lake. Although the beautiful colors on the hills surrounding their resort brought weekend guests, there wasn't so much activity this time of year, and life seemed to calm down after another summer season. Abby looked around campus and noticed the planned nature that had been created. Again, she missed the forest. People couldn't organize beauty to match the natural world.

Craig said little during the walk; he was content to just be with Abby. He noticed she was looking around as they walked with linked hands. They made their way along Main Street for a couple of blocks and then turned down to the lake. There was a pavilion and a green off to the right. They went to the green and followed the path along the lakeshore for a while. Abby stopped from time to time to look out at the water or point out a plant or tree.

Suddenly, she stopped to pick up a leaf. "My dad and I used to play this game..." She paused and chuckled to herself.

"What?" Craig asked.

"No, it's stupid."

"What?"

"So, we used to play this game where we would try to find the first leaf that fell in the fall. My dad always thought it was fun, but when you live in the forest, there are leaves on the ground every day."

"It's not stupid."

"I just started trying to find the perfect leaf. You know, one with the perfect color and no frayed edges."

"That sounds impossible."

"I guess it is. But, that never stopped me from trying." She dropped the leaf and let the memory fade.

Craig stopped briefly to swoop it up, putting it in his pack, and then caught up to her. They reached a private backyard with a fence cutting the shore off from continued exploration.

"Wow, I could walk my whole lake back home if I wanted," Abby said. "It would take all day, but no one cuts off access. Besides, I know everyone, so it's not a big deal."

"Have you ever done it?" Craig asked.

"What?" She turned to him, puzzled.

"Made it all the way around the lake?"

"Sure, lots of times, why?"

"Just wondering," Craig said. "Sounds fun." Craig barely knew anyone in his neighborhood aside from the people from school. However, he knew all about their lives, thanks to his mother's gossip. He certainly had never walked all the way around it.

They turned around and walked back towards the pavilion. Soon, they found an open space under a tree about twenty feet from the shore. Craig laid out the blanket from his bed, and they sat down under the tree.

"This place is kinda nice," Craig said, satisfied with his plan thus far.

"Yeah…it's neat," Abby replied, looking towards the water. A boat went by with men dressed to fish, lures hanging from their vests. Abby liked to fish with her father. It was one of the activities she loved most. She didn't really want to tell Craig because she felt he might think it was weird. "Craig?" She turned back to him. "Tell me about where you grew up. I feel like I'm always talking about my home. What was growing up like for you?"

Craig shifted to face her. "Well, it's not that interesting. Typical suburbs, you know. Loopy streets. All the houses look the same. Nothing exciting." Abby was staring at him, her eyes disarming him. Looking closely, he could see flecks of brown. Craig thought they must've looked like the earth from space. He shook his head slightly. "I grew up like everyone else. I played sports: football, baseball, basketball, whatever my dad signed me up for. It was fun, you know? I mean, it was fun for a while. I kinda got sick of it…so I quit."

Craig's explanation seemed like a cop-out. She pressed, "Why did you quit playing football again? I mean I know you told me sort of, but tell me again." Abby sat up cross-legged between Craig's open legs as he leaned against the tree. She grabbed his hands in hers and leaned forward.

Craig felt calm and took a deep breath. He could tell her anything. "I guess I just didn't love the game enough. Imagine running into your garage door. It gives a little, right?" She tilted her head, and Craig could see she didn't understand. He got up and stood back from the tree. He started taking slow steps forward. "It's like this." He moved towards the tree and collided with it in super slow motion. His head hit first and then slid off the tree until his shoulder made contact. "See," he said, looking at Abby as she looked up at him. "Every time I get the play call, that's how it ends...That, or getting killed from behind." He came back over to Abby and sat down. He leaned against the tree, his head back and eyes closed. "Some people get really jacked about that. I used to too. It's not that I can't take a hit. I've gotten dinged up pretty good and stayed in for so many games. I just don't want to get hit like that anymore, Abby. I don't love the game enough anymore to take the punishment." He was looking at her now, his lips pressed tightly. She moved in closer, brought her thumb to Craig's eye, and wiped the tear that was about to fall. Her hand slid down to his jawline, and she pulled him in and kissed him softly. She felt Craig lean in, and then she pulled back slightly and gave him two soft pecks. When she opened her eyes, Craig was sitting forward and a few tears were still threatening to spill from his eyes. She wiped them away. She wasn't sure why he was getting so emotional.

"Do you want to eat? I got up early to work out this morning, so I'm starving," Abby said.

Craig took a deep breath in through his nose and replied, "Yeah." He grabbed his bag with a knowing smile and half-laughed. "Now, I didn't have much in my room, so I just threw some stuff together. I wanted to surprise you, but I woke up kinda late." He pulled the contents out of the bag onto the blanket.

Abby laughed and asked, "Juice boxes?" Craig blushed. "No really...it's great, so sweet." Abby grabbed the bread and opened the peanut butter. She spread a thin layer of on each piece of bread.

"What's with that?" Craig asked, looking on.

"Oh, just a habit. If you put jelly or honey on the sandwich, then it soaks through."

Craig had never seen a sandwich made that way. His sandwiches were always soggy if he didn't eat them right away. They ate their sandwiches and cookies. Abby laughed as Craig told jokes and made silly faces. He tried a few times to ask her about the other people who worked at the resort besides her family, but she would just stroke his leg and make a comment about how beautiful the lake was or change the subject back to him. He was a bit confused, but she was smiling, and they were having a good time, so he didn't press to return to an uncomfortable subject.

After lunch, Craig excused himself to go to the bathroom over at the pavilion. Even though he left for the moment, Abby didn't feel alone. She never felt alone with Craig. Instead, she felt a different kind of full. He was so nice and so smart. She had never met anyone like him in her life. Boys like him didn't exist. No one like him ever gave her the time of day, save for the occasional vacation boy up at the resort who thought he could get with the help. After getting up to stretch a bit, she took off her sandals and went carefully down by the lake to dip her toes in the water. The lake, although very different, reminded her of home. She had not been able to talk to Craig as much about home, because being by the lake just made her miss home even more. Despite her comfort with him, especially on this day, the setting had rattled her. She wasn't sure she would be able to fully explain it, even if she tried. How do you explain something you just know and feel more than anything else? How do you pour out a lifetime in a conversation or two?

Craig came back with two bottles of Mellow Yellow. Abby had told him that they were a weakness of hers, and it was getting hot. He was happy they had them in the vending machine. She wasn't at the blanket, but he saw her down at the lake wading in up to her ankles, her hair out of the braid. It kept falling forward, and she pushed it behind her ear. He sat down, opened his soda, and just watched her. She didn't kick at the water. Instead, she just looked down as though she was watching fish or something. Abby didn't seem to notice that he was back. Craig realized that he loved watching her. Everything she did caught his attention. He loved watching her take too copious notes. He loved watching her walk towards him. He even loved watching her walk away. Her movements always seemed so controlled and fluid, like there was a purpose in everything that she did. When she was lost in anything, he was lost in her. His eyes went out of focus for a moment. Then, he opened his soda and took another drink. When he looked back up, she was walking towards him, shaking off the water from her feet.

"Hey, did you get me one?" Abby questioned.

Craig dug in his bag and pulled out a soda. "You bet."

"My favorite. You're too good to me." She smiled softly.

Abby sat down, opened the soda, and took a drink. When she put it down, her hair fell across her face. Craig reached up to push it back, and she quickly moved into his chest. She snuggled up and held him around the waist, then looked up at him and kissed him quickly on the lips. "Thanks," she said. They just sat there, Craig holding Abby against him.

After a bit, Craig heard Abby take a few labored breaths and thought she was crying.

"What's wrong?" Craig said, worried, and pulled his head back to try to see her face. She nuzzled in and held him a big tighter.

"I want to go home. I miss home." She didn't cry easily. She just felt a sense of peace with Craig, down by this lake that reminded her of home.

"Oh." Craig moved his arms around her and ran his hand from the top of her head down her hair. He didn't know what to say. He just held her for a time.

Finally, Abby spoke. "It's just…" She paused and then loosened her grip and looked up at Craig. Her face was red. "I don't mind school. And, I really like you. It's just…I just want to go home to my lake. To my boat. To my room. To knowing what I have to do every day." She moved in and kissed him again, gently on the lips, and then nuzzled back into his chest as he held her close under the tree. "Can't I just go home?'

"Yes," Craig said, puzzled. He moved to adjust his position.

"No. I mean…not now, let's stay here a while longer. I just, I need to go home."

"What is it that you love so much?"

"Everything. I love the lake. I love my family. I love Frank. I love the routine."

"Who's Frank again?"

"Frank is the guy who runs the kitchen. He and Rita were on the place before my father bought it. He's like an uncle and grandpa all wrapped into one."

"He's married?" Craig asked.

"Rita passed away when I was nine."

"Really? I'm sorry." Craig gave Abby a tighter hug.

She pulled away a bit. "No. It's ok. Rita was great. She ran the cleaning service and worked the front desk. It's amazing she and Frank didn't end up owning the place. 'No interest in that,' he always said. Rita's parents ran a resort before there were many in the area. Being on a resort was kinda in her blood. She just let me run around and sometimes let me help her too. I guess she helped me learn the place before my father had me working."

Craig listened intently. Abby was letting him in in a way no one else ever had.

"When I was eight, she got sick, and she died right after my ninth birthday. Almost ten years already. She and Frank never had kids. They always said they were lucky to have Taylor and me. Frank still says that. They were married over twenty years. He kinda lost a step when she died." Abby took a deep breath. Craig didn't know what to say. She continued, "He's a really good man. He does so much for my family, my father especially. But, I've never seen him truly happy since she passed. Truth be told, I can only remember bits and pieces of when she was alive."

Even though Craig had listened through the whole story, he had nothing to offer, so he pulled her head to his chest. He had never lost anyone close to him.

Craig walked Abby to her dorm late that afternoon. They had a pleasant talk and took their time on the way back. She swung his arm playfully as they walked. Abby didn't really want to go back, although she said she did. She asked Craig if he would mind if she just went up to her room, and he agreed that would be best. He said he might meet a friend to watch the seven o'clock game. She kissed him slowly and gave him a hug. He watched her go into the front door of the dorm.

Craig texted Abby later. *Hey. I had fun today. You good?*

Yeah. I'm fine.

Cool.

I had a really good time too.

Great. Night.

Good night.

He played with the leaf he had picked up that morning after Abby had discarded it. There was meaning in Abby's story, but Craig hadn't figured it out just yet. He put the date on the leaf and put it in his sock drawer.

Chapter 6

The next morning, they met and worked out. Craig lifted while Abby went on the step machine. He was impressed with how strong she was. She wasn't ripped, but she could keep a good pace, and her legs were well-defined. Looking at her in the mirror, he caught her eye from time to time and winked or smiled at her. She smiled back. Afterwards, they went back to Abby's room since Kate was at church and would usually stay after and go out for lunch with a group of people.

Abby decided to go and take a quick shower. She grabbed some clothes, gave Craig the TV remote, and went to the bathroom. He turned on SportsCenter out of habit and looked around her room. There were a few posters of inspirational phrases and a Buddha on Kate's dresser, but he was drawn to Abby's desk. Above it was a name tag from orientation reading: *Abigail Whitworth, Eagle River, Wisconsin*. He also saw a diary. More interestingly, there was a collage of pictures from home: her parents and sister and some friends, but most of the pictures were from around the lake. There were pictures of trees and fall leaves, the lake itself, her boat, trails, and from what he could tell, pictures from the top of a hill looking down onto large forested scenes and the lake. She was attached to her home. Craig couldn't even put a finger on what it was or what it would feel like. He laid back on her bed and propped up to watch TV.

It must've been a while because Craig had drifted off. He heard the door open and saw Abby walk in with her hair up in a towel.

"Forgot my hair dryer." She was dressed in sweats and a tank top. She had not put on a bra, and Craig could see her chest bounce under the soft shirt. "Do you mind?" she asked, holding up her hair dryer. He shook his head and watched her as she threw her head back and forth getting all the moisture out. Halfway through, she stopped to look at him. "What?"

"You're just so pretty," Craig said.

"You think so?" Her eyes opened wide, and her face began to blush. She grabbed the wet ends of her hair and flicked them at him, spraying him in the face.

He covered his face with her covers. "Hey!" he said. She turned the hair dryer back on.

When she was done, she turned off the TV, walked over to her computer, and sat down by her desk. Craig closed his eyes as he lay back, figuring she was checking her emails. Calm music came on the speakers. "This is Eastmountainsouth. I love this band," Abby said. "They broke up, but they're still cool."

Craig listened with his eyes still closed. Abby crawled into bed next to him. He opened his eyes and turned to the side, shifting to give her space. She reached over him and pulled her blanket from behind him, throwing it on the floor to give him more room. She looked him in the eyes and reached her arm back over him, pulling herself close. He put his left arm under her head and pulled her even closer. He could feel her chest against his. She draped a leg over one of his and they intertwined. She kissed him first, calmly, with a few pecks and then a soft bite of his lower lip. He reached his right arm over her waist and pulled her as tight as he could. He kissed her hard, open-mouthed, and she returned the effort. They stayed like this, interchanging passionate kisses as well as softer ones. Her shirt rode up slightly, revealing the skin of the small of her back. Craig touched it with his fingertips. He stroked her gently back and forth and in circles. He was sure he had never felt anything so soft in his life.

After a while, Abby pushed him onto his back and snuggled up onto his chest. She ran her fingers up and down his chest and stomach, squeezing him from time to time. He rubbed her shoulder and played with her hair until they both fell asleep.

The next thing they heard was Kate at the door. Craig was surprised and tried to get up, but Abby pushed him down. She laid her head back on his shoulder. She didn't want to let go and responded only with, "Hey Kate." Kate just went with the flow, showing no agitation. Abby really didn't care. She was happy.

Chapter 7

There were almost no cars parked on the street Craig and Abby were walking up late one evening. They had walked a ways off campus, but Abby had heard that most of the houses on this block were occupied by students. Craig had convinced her to go to a party to meet some of his friends. She didn't really want to go, but Craig was going, and it was a bye week, so most of his buddies would be there. It was a nice night for walking, and Abby thought she would rather keep strolling around town and talking with Craig. She was not sure she wanted to meet his friends, but they were part of who he was, and it was important to him. It was just that these guys he called friends had not been that nice to him in the first few weeks, and he had spent considerable time complaining about it.

Craig wasn't sure he wanted to go either. The guys had not stopped giving him grief about quitting, but Brent, who seemed to have forgiven him, urged him to come. He was a bit scared of what might happen. When he quit a few weeks ago, he told the coach first. He tried to explain how he had lost the love for the game, but that didn't seem to resonate. The coach finally accepted his explanation, but the players had not been as kind. After practice the first day, a few guys came to his room and sat him down. They tried to start in about Craig being a "pussy" for not wanting to take a hit, but he explained that it wasn't that day's practice he didn't want to come to, it was all of the practices. He just didn't have the desire to play and thought it was unfair for him to show up if he didn't have the passion. The reasons he gave did not satisfy them. Most of them, friends included, now treated him with a casual disregard. Some were still openly hostile, totally ignoring him when he tried to wave and occasionally, bumping into him without a word.

When they got into the house, in the basement, there were posters of rap artists and girls all over. The air was damp and a bit rank. There were a few dated couches and odd chairs, but most people were standing and talking. It occurred to Abby that most of these people knew each other. It seemed, more and more, that Whitewater was just an extension of high school for many of the suburban kids around Milwaukee. Craig introduced her to a few people, but she didn't say much. Meeting people and small talk were not things she liked. She was more of a one-on-one girl. Crowds made her uncomfortable. As she glanced around the room, she saw a guy named Will from home. He played football and was a year older than her. He waved, and she nodded her head.

Craig went to get drinks, and Abby sat down on a couch where she could see the room and observe. High school had not been like this for her. She had mostly avoided parties and sleepovers. She always had work to do at the resort, and if she went out with friends, it was often out to eat or to go out on the boat or snowmobiling. While she was taking the room in, Jen sat down next to her. She more bounced down than sat. Abby instantly didn't like her. She was cute as could be and so small. Craig was standing with friends on the other side of the room.

"Hi. I'm Jen." Abby didn't like the sound of her voice. It was too high and squeaky. Jen turned to look at Craig. "Craig's great, isn't he?"

Abby turned her head slowly. "What?" she asked, looking through her.

"Craig is great, don't you think?" Jen looked back at Abby. She was just so damn pretty.

"Oh, yes. I think so," Abby responded coldly.

"He really likes you, Abby. I've never seen him like this."

'How does she know what Craig thinks of me?' Abby thought. "He does?" she asked meekly.

"Yeah. He told me. He's over his head for you." Jen was looking in Craig's direction again. "He's a great guy. It didn't work out between us. It never would." She turned back to Abby and touched her arm. "I'm glad he met you. He deserves someone good like you." Before Abby could answer, she was up and gone.

Abby was left confused as Jen walked away. 'He still talks to her?' she thought to herself. She didn't know whether to be angry or flattered. When Craig came over to sit next to her, she decided not to bring up what Jen had said. They looked at the crowd and drank their beers. Craig introduced her to a few more people, but mostly, he listed the biographies of the many in attendance. A lot of the information was statistical, but he also knew their personalities and tendencies on the field. He knew how to praise and frustrate every aspect of their being. She could barely believe how well Craig knew people. It was as though he studied them for a living. There was Brent of course, the roommate. He was from Menomonee Falls. There was Beck from Hamilton. He played defensive back, and Craig had burned him a few times. There was Doug, a lineman, who had played for Craig's team in high school, and Abby could tell by the smile on Craig's face that he had been a friend of his for a long time. It was weird. Abby wondered what he knew about her already. They sat in silence for a while, and Craig nodded or waved at a few more people, but no one came to talk to him.

"Can we go home soon?" Abby asked, finally.

Craig wheeled around. "Sure. Do you want to go now? This place is pretty boring."

She was surprised at how quickly he agreed. "Sure. It's a nice night for walking."

"Great. Let's go now." He got up and held his hand out to help Abby up. "I don't think many people want me here."

They said goodbye to a few people, and Jen waved at Abby before they went up the steps. Abby smiled and waved back. 'God, I hate her,' she thought. She didn't really have a reason, but she just got a bad feeling from her.

When they got outside, Craig reached out and grabbed her hand. It was a warm evening. Abby thought that the bite of night might have set in up north, but here it was still nice. They made their way back to campus. As the lights of the university began to surround them, Craig said, "You've been quiet."

Abby didn't know how to ask her question so she just blurted out, "Do you still talk with your ex? Jen?"

Craig stopped walking suddenly. "Yes. Sometimes." He turned to Abby and held her other hand as well. "We're just friends. I've known Jen for years. I don't seek her out or anything. We just see each other walking around campus. We chat and go our separate ways. I told her about you. I couldn't wait to tell her actually. Other than you and Brent, she's the only friend I have left."

Abby looked at him closely and squeezed his hands. “She told me that I make you happy.” She looked down for a moment and then back up to him and smiled. Craig’s eyes were locked on her, and she felt a rush that made her shiver.

“You do, Abby,” he said, and then pulled her in to kiss her.

Chapter 8

Over the next two weeks, Abby and Craig were almost never apart. They worked out together, disregarding the football team at their morning lifts. They ate every meal together and studied each night in the library at their table. Even on nights when the library was crowded, they existed in their own world. They discussed their school work, and Craig continued to help Abby with her biology. When they had time, or between classes, they sat on their bench. Craig informed Abby that he had told his parents about her, and that they would be visiting campus that weekend for a football game. He said his mother, Linda, was excited to meet her, although Linda had seemed more concerned than excited. His mom asked him a lot of questions about her family. Abby had yet to tell her parents, but she didn't want to tell Craig that, so she kept changing the subject.

They made it to the day of the game. Neither of them slept well the night before. It was the sixth weekend of school, and after two away games, the Warhawks were finally coming home. Mike and Linda, Craig's parents, had purchased tickets for every home game with the expectation that Craig would be playing. The phone call that he was quitting the team several weeks before was one of the hardest of Craig's life. His father threatened to come to campus, but his mother backed him down.

Mike was a big man. He played football for the Badgers in the mid to late 80's and ran a successful insurance business. Craig was their third child and only son. His oldest sister, Sarah, played volleyball for the Badgers, and the middle sister, Claire, the lost one, went to the University of Chicago on an art scholarship. She was a "damn liberal" and had "forgotten her upbringing." Despite his father's words, Claire and Craig had always gotten along best. Craig saw his father as a complete bullshit artist. He had "inherited" an old guy's book, expanded it a little, and lived pretty much off of three guys who hustled most of the new business. Mike shot the shit with people about the Badgers, Brewers, and Packers, but mostly talked about his playing days. He was a tight end, mostly a blocker. Craig had to play football; he had no choice. He was never going to be as big as his father, but he was quick. Where his father was a thrower in track, Craig had made state twice in both the 200 and 400 meter dashes.

Despite his emotional shortcomings, Mike had given his kids a good life, and they wanted for nothing. The house was big, the cars were nice, and whatever they needed was provided. Linda could work part-time as a nurse and attend to her social activities. Craig had nothing to worry about except their approval. However, that was something he fought for constantly.

Today would be no different.

The day itself was perfect. Bright sunlight cascaded down on the morning. It was sixty degrees, not too hot, though it promised to get warmer. After winning a national championship in recent years, even the casual fans were stoked and the campus was alive. There was a sea of people storming towards the stadium, and Craig had told his parents he would meet them there. He had bought two tickets for himself and Abby. She was excited to get some Warhawk gear and and try something new. High school football was big in her town, as it was in most small towns up north. Road trips to watch games often stretched into morning hours of the next day and provided ample adventure. She would allow herself this one night with friends, although it usually set up an early morning, since Saturdays were always busy at the resort.

For Craig, football was pain. As a receiver, despite his speed, he got hit a lot. He couldn't remember a Saturday morning in the fall where breakfast didn't include four Advil along with his meal. He was not looking forward to this day.

Abby and Craig walked hand in hand towards the stadium. He loved holding her hand. They had only known each other for only a few weeks, but there was nothing he didn't like. They had shared their stories, and it just made him like her more. Her life had been so unlike his. It was attractive to be as relaxed as she was. She gripped his hand tightly and pulled him along.

"Come on, babe. I want a good seat."

"My parents are already there. They'll save seats," Craig responded with a twist of his face.

"What's wrong? They know about me, right?" Abby asked as she pulled him to a stop.

"Yes, of course." He smiled reassuringly and put his arm around her. "I told my mom right away. You're the best." Secretly, he was nervous. Jen had been a cheerleader, she lived in his neighborhood, and his parents were good friends with hers. The only people who didn't think it would end happily ever after was them. Jen was actually the one who broke it off. She knew they didn't really have anything left to talk about. From the outside, they were perfect, but ultimately, it didn't work when they were together.

Abby was growing more confident in Craig's assurance that it was over for good. He rarely talked about Jen, and since they spent most of their time together, she was sure he wasn't talking with her anymore either. In fact, he had started to introduce Abby to everyone he knew when they met people in the Union or in passing. The way he gripped her hand and shot her a look or a wink let her know that he was proud to show her off. She was proud to be with him too.

Craig assumed that his parents would sit by Jen's parents. His dad would be talking about his playing days or the fact that he was missing the Badger game to come to this game where his son wasn't even playing.

Craig and Abby stopped to cross Schwager Drive. Abby was so completely undaunted by the prospect of meeting his parents, she bounced right along. It surprised Craig. She was just happy to be alive. It was one of the things he liked about her most. She was always smiling, happy to wake up every morning. She approached life with a positive attitude, and for her, college was starting to be like a vacation. She soaked all of it in, moment by moment. He was always thinking ahead and worried about the past. Abby seemed to not care; she enjoyed the time they spent together, and Craig was learning to enjoy every moment with her.

They got to the stadium, and it was packed. Craig texted his parents to find them, and they worked their way to the seats waiting for them. When they got to his parents, Linda motioned to Abby and said, "Sit here, next to me. We have a lot to talk about." She also insisted that Craig sit next to his father. So, they found themselves sandwiched between Mike and Linda. Mike was indeed a bigger man, Abby noticed, but Linda was tiny. She looked as though she had just come from the gym.

As Craig suspected, Jen's parents were sitting with his, and Jen was down at the end. She lightheartedly smiled at Craig and waved saying, "Hey, Abby."

Abby turned, startled, and waved back. "Hi, Jen." Abby turned to Craig, raised her eyebrows up and whispered, "I guess she made it."

Before Craig could answer, Linda grabbed her hand. "So, tell me a bit more about yourself. You're from up north, right? We used to have a cabin near the Dells."

That kind of small talk dominated the rest of the game. When Mike wasn't talking business with Jen's father, he was going on about his playing days or reminding Craig that he could have made this or that play.

Craig and Abby barely got a word together as Linda peppered her with questions about her parents, her home, and what she wanted to study. The afternoon actually went by quite quickly, and the game ended with a resounding Warhawk victory.

As they walked out of the stadium, Linda asked where they were going to eat. Mike seemed annoyed. The Badgers were playing the night game, and he wanted to get home. The neighborhood always seemed to huddle together at someone's house on a Saturday night. The game was a good excuse to get together, and he said he wanted to get some beer and snacks in case the party came to his house, as it usually did.

"Mrs. McLean, I think that you should catch up with Craig a little bit. I'm going to get some studying done before the Badger game tonight. I'll see you later, Craig." Abby squeezed his hand tightly and looked up at him, wide-eyed, and shook her head a tiny bit. He realized she had had enough for the day. "Thanks for the game. It was fun."

Linda replied, "Oh...yes. You need to get your studying done. It was nice to finally meet you. Right, Mike?"

"Oh yes, nice to meet you." He gave Abby the two-handed shake that he used on new clients.

As she walked away, Craig watched her hair, up in a ponytail, bounce back and forth. She didn't turn back.

"Should we walk?" Linda turned to Craig and Mike, excited to see her son alone. She moved close to him and gave him a half hug.

"No, Mother," Craig responded. "The closest place is on the other side of campus."

They went to the car, and Mike drove them to The Black Sheep. The old owner had been a client of his. As they walked in, Mike chatted with the new owner while Craig and Linda sat at a table that was saved for them. They were expected, and there was no other choice. Mike had planned it just like he planned everything. While Craig wanted desperately to break free from this preprogrammed life, his mother embraced it. She lived in her bubble and loved it. His older sister came back to the same bubble after college; she was engaged to her high school sweetheart with a plan of a family already. Sarah embraced the life set out for her. Craig wanted more.

"So." There was a pregnant pause filled with expectations of the coming criticism. "Abby is nice. She's not like other girls you've dated though." Linda reached across the table, taking the menu from Craig and grasping both of his hands. She rubbed the backs of his hands as she always did when she wanted attention.

"Exactly." The curt response was intended to move the conversation along.

"She certainly has a plan for her life. She seems very set," Linda persisted.

"That's a bad thing?"

"Well, the life she has planned is actually very different from the life you've always talked about."

"Yes, it is." Craig stared at his mother now with the same intensity she was trying to hold over him.

"Her parents seem like very unique people." Unique. One of Linda's loaded words. She had a lot of them. The waiter brought water and asked if they needed a few more minutes. Linda said yes and continued, "They're not our kind of people."

"What is that supposed to mean?"

"Well, you know."

Mike finally came to sit down. Linda was forced to release her grasp on Craig as he slid in. He always sat with one leg out in the path of other people. In a small place like this, his size would not go unnoticed.

"Abe's doing great. Business is good with the new guy." He looked at Craig.

"Good, I'm glad," Linda said, trying to seize the attention back. "We were talking about Craig and Abby." She looked for encouragement from her husband.

"Seems like a nice, but serious, girl. She's not like Jen, if you know what I mean."

Craig often thought his father's comments bordered on inappropriate, but everyone always dismissed them as 'just Mike.' That was how he lived his whole life. Being excused for being 'just Mike.' His size and ability to obliterate any defensive lineman catered to a life free of worries. Sometimes, Craig was envious of him, but mostly, he just hated him.

"She's from up north, Mike. Eagle River," Linda said.

"I know where that is. Went deer hunting around there once. Remember, Craig?"

"We hunted around Hayward. Uncle Tony's cabin. That's like two hours from Eagle River." Craig spoke plainly and deliberately. He looked at his mother.

"Up north is up north. Go north of 29, and it's all the same."

Unwilling to take the bait, Craig let it go.

"Her father was an engineer, and her mother teaches kindergarten." Linda seemed desperate. Her eyes were firmly set on Mike. Craig assumed she was looking for support.

"That's a weird combo, engineer and a teacher. Hate to be at that table the last few years."

"Craig and I were talking about..."

"How about that game? Hope the Badgers can kick some ass tonight."

They ordered food. Linda tried a few more times to bring the conversation around to Abby, but the owner stopped by to ask about the food, and the moment was lost. When they were done, Mike left a tip that was too large and went to the bathroom while Linda and Craig waited outside.

"Want a ride?" Linda asked.

"No, I'll walk." Craig sensed she wanted to return to the earlier conversation, and he did not.

"Are you sure?"

"Yes."

"Don't think we don't like Abby. But you've changed so much these last few months. Just be careful."

"Yes, Mother." He reached out to kiss Linda's forehead and hugged her. Mike emerged, reached for his hand, and gave him a big hug.

"Take care, son." Mike said distantly.

As they drove away, Craig realized he liked watching them go. He walked back to campus leisurely, taking in the moment. As he walked along a wall in front of a house, he picked up a leaf, yellow and red in color, and held it up to the sun. He kept it and placed it in his sock drawer with the other one.

Abby: 16, Having Fun at the Resort

The water was finally warm enough to swim, and with my new boat, I couldn't wait. Meghan, Christina, and Sydney were coming, and we were going to try water skiing. Sydney had actually never been before. I got up early and gassed up the boat to go fishing for some perch for Frank. He said he wanted it for dinner, and I knew the spot to go. He had actually shown me all the good fishing spots, and sometimes, if I got out early enough, I still saw him, sleeping in his own boat with an almost tipped cup of coffee in one hand and a drooped fishing rod in the other. I thought that one of these days I might just find him there for good. It's a morbid thought, but for as much joy as Frank has brought to our family, he never fully recovered from losing Rita. I know he thought of Taylor and me as his own children, but he had his own life too, and it was taken from him.

This morning, Frank had already gone to the kitchen, and I had breakfast with him before going to fish. It was a cool summer morning, and the lake shimmered with the rising sun. I got to my spot and dropped a line. It wasn't three casts before I got a bite. 'Today is going to be a good day,' I thought to myself. This was the first time I was going to 'play,' as Meghan would call it, with my new boat. I got it for my birthday and for doing a good job working for my father. It was my 'pay' for last summer. I loved having the freedom of going out on the lake whenever I wanted. I could take pictures and fish and today, play with my friends. School was out, the weather was perfect, and it was truly a fantastic day.

Chapter 9

Over the next few weeks, things continued as they had been. Abby sensed that the dinner Craig had with his parents had not gone well, but he never talked about it, and she never asked. Craig met Abby whenever he could. They walked to the lake a few times and spent most of the time talking about their hopes for the future. Craig talked about the struggles of becoming a doctor while Abby talked about home. She didn't want to change anything. Aside from their roommates, they were each other's only friend.

She told Craig all about the resort. They had a lodge with twenty rooms, a large lounge with a bar, a huge fireplace, and TVs for sports. There was a restaurant and game room. The game room was modeled after old resorts and camps, like the ones in upstate New York and Maine, with places for board games, ping pong, and pool. Abby's father had relented and installed Golden Tee and a driving game. They also had fifteen cabins that were spaced over the lakeshore and spread out further back. The five lakeshore cabins had kitchens and private docks. The other cabins were sleeping cabins with bathrooms, so the guests there generally came to the lodge to eat. They had their regulars but still got enough new people to make a good living. They had enough. Craig always loved hearing about

Abby's home. She lit up. Her eyes were alive, and everything about her was animated. He questioned her about everything. What was a typical day like? What did she do in her free time? How big was the lake? He wanted to know everything, and she was happy to tell him.

As the weeks went on, Abby started staying at Craig's a few times a week. They would study at the library and then head over to see if Brent was home. If he wasn't, she would crawl in bed with Craig, and they would make out and fool around a bit.

She always seemed to lead him a little further, and he would always ask "Are you sure?", waiting for her permission. They had discussed waiting and agreed that sex was not something they wanted yet. Most of the time, Abby would fall asleep on his chest, and he would look up at the ceiling while continuing to rub the small of her back or run his fingers through her hair. They hoped it wouldn't change, and even if it was going to, they didn't care.

Late in October, Abby asked Craig if he wanted to go to Madison to visit her best friend, Meghan. He agreed, adding that he could get his dad's season tickets, and they could go to the football game if they liked. They could even bring Meghan. Mike had good seats, and he could get in to sit on the sidelines if he really wanted to go. Abby was excited and arranged for them to meet up with Meghan for lunch.

The day of the game was cooler, but not yet cold. The Badgers were playing Iowa, so Craig wore his "Fuck Iowa" shirt under his sweatshirt, and Abby wore jeans with a Badger sweatshirt.

They headed out around nine thirty for the two-thirty

game, planning on getting lunch before heading to Camp Randall. Arriving in Madison around ten thirty, they parked and went out into the crowd. Craig drove and knew exactly where to go. The guy at the lot greeted him by name and asked how his dad was. Abby noticed that Craig seemed very familiar and at home. She had been to the Chicago suburbs a few times and to the Twin Cities, but this was different. There were more people in one place than she had ever seen, all dressed in red, and there was an incredible energy.

Craig held her hand tightly and led her through the craziness. Abby was happy to have him there. The whole place was a bit overwhelming. Parties sprouted up on every corner and outside bars. Everyone was drinking, parents and students alike. Around every corner, someone seemed to know Craig. They were people from high school or from the various camps and club teams he had been on throughout his youth. Most just waved, some yelled out, and a few even tried to talk for a bit. Craig was dismissive to most and wanted to keep moving. They got up to State Street, and Abby could see the capitol peeking through. She had been there on a school field trip, and all the kids had heard of State Street, but they weren't allowed to go there. It was always labeled as dangerous and not a place for kids to go. Today, it seemed like no big deal. The street was closed to traffic and packed with people. Bars spilled out onto the street, and everyone had a drink in their hand. And this was before the game. Before noon.

Craig found Which Wich, the place they were going to meet Meghan and her roommate. Meghan said she loved the place and that she would probably blow through her whole food budget by the end of first semester. "Any place Meghan loves that much has to be good," Abby had said on the way up. When they got inside, Meghan was waiting with her roommate, Mya. Abby made the introductions, and Meghan showed them how to order with the bags and markers. They filled out their orders on the bag, handed them in, and paid for them. They got their sandwiches and sat down.

Meghan was pretty. She had long, blonde hair up in a bun on the top of her head. She was skinnier than Abby, and a bit taller, with a narrow face. Craig felt as though he had seen girls like her before. A tall, slender blonde held no mystery for him. He returned his attention to Abby.

Meghan and Abby sat across from each other, and Craig was across from Mya. They drank their sodas, and Meghan went on and on about how good Abby looked, and how she liked what Abby was doing with her hair even though there was no real change other than braiding it.

Craig laughed quietly when he recognized Mya. Turned out, Mya was a track runner in high school from one of the northern suburbs, Mequon or Whitefish Bay. She was never more than third or fourth runner on the 4x800, but she remembered Craig from their sectional meet and how incredibly fast he was. Craig blushed a bit, but they continued to talk and eat while Meghan and Abby didn't even touch their food. Instead, they talked about their classes and stories of what other friends were up to.

After a while, Craig got up to refill his soda. He brushed Abby's shoulders and leaned in to whisper something to her but forgot and just kissed her on the ear instead.

Once he left, Meghan said, "Holy shit, Abby, he's hot. I know you said he was good-looking but…"

"He's pretty good-looking," Mya added. "I remember him.

He was so fast, it's kinda hard to forget. He crushed everyone in the 200 at our sectional."

"Seriously, guys…" Abby was blushing. "He's a great guy. I just love being with him, so be nice."

Craig came back and sat down. All three looked at him.

"So…whatcha talkin about?" He smiled at Abby, then looked around the table.

Mya broke the silence. "I was telling them about how I know you. You were so fast. Where'd you end up at state?"

"I was sixth. Got on the podium." Craig seemed embarrassed talking about it. He really didn't want to talk about sports at all. "Those days are over." He turned to Abby and reached his hand over to her leg, and she grabbed his hand and nuzzled to his shoulder briefly. He took his hand back and bit into the other half of his sandwich. While still chewing, he said, "You guys have hardly touched your food." Abby and Meghan looked down at their untouched sandwiches and laughed. They always got lost in conversation. The table got quiet while everyone finished eating.

When they got to the game, the seats Craig's dad had were great, tenth row, on the fifty-yard line. Everyone in the surrounding seats greeted Craig and asked him how his parents and sisters were. He introduced Abby to "Uncle" Jim in the row in front of them. He was a neighbor and was going to be his sister Sarah's father-in-law. Abby stayed busy talking with Meghan and asking Mya about herself.

As the game went on, Craig started yelling. The Badgers were losing, and he kept saying, "They're killing us on the shallow crossing route," or "Cave, it's A-gap." He swore and yelled at the refs. Some of the regulars around him acted like his dad, saying that he could've made that catch, or with his speed he could have made the corner. He thanked them, but always said he couldn't, and now, he really couldn't. Strong as he was, Abby knew Craig had not taken one fast step since he quit football. But on days like this, she could tell he missed it.

The Badgers dominated the second half and won by seventeen points. Craig said goodbye to a few people, and they headed out. When they got to the gate, Craig stopped Abby. "So, what are we doing next?"

"I thought we'd go up to Meghan and Mya's room and talk a bit."

Craig looked at his phone; it was blowing up. "Do you mind if I go meet a few of my friends? They're in town from Eau Claire and La Crosse, and I haven't seen them since July."

"No problem. Where do you want to meet up later?" Abby asked.

"I can come to you, or we can meet at this pizza place two blocks down from Which Wich, and we can grab a slice before heading back?"

"That works, around nine?"

"Sure." He turned to Meghan. "Hey Meghan, do you know where that pizza place is on State? Just down from Which Wich…They sell by the slice, always a line?"

"Yeah sure…I know where it is," Meghan said.

"Great, I'll meet you there then," Craig said to Abby. "Sure you don't mind?

"No." Abby kissed him. "Go have fun with your friends. I'll see you at nine."

"Thanks, babe." And with that, Craig was off in a sea of red. Abby turned to explain the situation and then went to Meghan's.

Mya had gone off to hang with friends, so Meghan and Abby could really talk.

When they got to Meghan's room, Abby could see that it was much smaller than hers. Everything seemed so much more cramped in Madison. It was probably because there were so many people. Abby looked around and saw a picture of their friend Sydney. It was a picture from last year when they all went out on the lake to go swimming. She pointed at the picture and said, "Did you see the latest post Sydney put on Instagram?"

"Yes. What's up with the hair and makeup?" Meghan replied.

"I know. She dyed it black and went all Goth," Abby said, scrolling through photos on her phone.

"It's weird. I bet if she was around us, she wouldn't have done that."

"Yeah. I bet." Abby got up and wandered around the room looking at some of Mya's pictures.

"So…what's really up with you and Craig?" Meghan asked as she sat down on her bed.

"I think I love him, Meg," Abby said plainly, almost surprising herself.

"I know you love him. I told you that on the phone the other day."

"He's so great. I can't wait to see him every day." Abby sat down on the bed and pushed her hands through her hair, taking out her braid.

"He seems pretty great. Has he met John and Vicky yet?"

"No, I thought he could come up for Thanksgiving." Abby had been waiting to ask. She wasn't sure why. She just didn't want to ruin things.

"Aw, I love Thanksgiving at the resort. But that's big. Are you sure you're ready for that?"

"I think it'll be fine, and once my dad sees how special he is to me...it'll just be great."

"I'm so happy for you, this is so weird. Usually, this is me."

Abby laughed, "I know. So, who's the new boy you've been talking about?"

Meghan went on and on about the new boy she had met at the rec center, and he was just the 'cutest thing.' They had been on a few dates, but Meghan felt he was trying to focus on studying and starting off right. Abby understood that more than anyone. That's exactly how she felt the first time she 'went out' with Craig. But Meghan was getting frustrated with waiting, and she just wanted to be with him. Meghan had always been more experienced than Abby. She had boyfriends all through high school and was never afraid of talking to anyone. When they were little, Abby and Meghan had planned to move to Chicago someday. They were going to open a little store downtown and live like the *Sex and the City* women, girls about town. However, Abby had found a new love in high school, the resort. Meghan had never held it against her. She had gone to Madison to pursue marketing and was still planning on moving to Chicago after college.

Eventually, topics shifted to their busy schedules and how Meghan was looking for a job and how this horrible girl from school back home was apparently pregnant. They shook their heads in disbelief at what other people's lives were turning into. Abby felt perfectly at home with Meghan, and the night carried on just how it would've if they were back in the forest.

It was nine fifteen, and Craig hadn't arrived yet. Meghan and Abby managed to find a small booth, and Meghan had already eaten her slice. Abby had her phone on the table and was checking it every thirty seconds.

"Why don't you just text him?" Meghan asked.

"He's never late. I've never once had to wait for him. He's always at our bench."

"He probably just lost track of time."

"I know, but it isn't like him. He always blows off stuff to be on time. It's so annoying." Abby opened her phone again.

"Text him then. You know you want to."

The line to get inside went all the way around the pizza place, and they were crammed in their booth. Craig would have to come inside to see them.

"Maybe he can't see us."

"Text him." Meghan was being forceful now.

"Okay." Abby typed, asking Craig where he was.

It was nine twenty.

"What the hell?" Abby finally said at nine thirty after spending ten minutes trying to distract herself looking at Facebook and Instagram. She was getting a little pissed. "Where the hell is he?" Abby reached her hand up to scratch her head. She heard the door open for the umpteenth time and got up to look.

"Relax, girl." Meghan reached for her arm. "He'll be here. How much trouble could he get in?"

"That's not the point," Abby said, sitting back down. "He could have texted and said he'd be late."

"I know, but he didn't. Don't be too pissed at him. It's Madison. He's having fun. No offense, but if you weren't here,

I'd be at a house party or sneaking into a bar or something."

"Shit…you're probably right…but I'll probably have to drive home and this whole situation is ridiculous." Abby got up again. This time she saw him. She waved.

Craig came over and slid into the booth right next to Abby. He left one leg dangling in the aisle and swayed in his seat. He was drunk.

"Did you meet up with your friends?" Abby asked, trying to be sweet.

"Yeah. Some of my boys from high school on the team you know. It was fun." Craig squinted his eyes to try to adjust to the light. He knew he wouldn't be able to drive. He was having trouble sitting up with the world spinning around.

"Where'd you go?" Abby looked at Meghan who shook her head and mouthed the words 'Don't do it.' Abby continued, "Were you drinking?" Meghan closed her eyes and shook her head again.

Craig finally responded, "A little bit."

"Well, can you drive?"

Craig scooted his leg all the way under the table and laid his head down. He murmured, "Probably not."

"I think we should get going," Abby said, trying to get up to leave. Meghan got up with her, but Craig sat motionless.

"Craig," Abby shook him a bit.

"What?"

"Let's go."

"Ok." He got up and let Abby out of the booth, then followed her and Meghan out. Abby gave Meghan a hug.

Meghan whispered in Abby's ear, "Be nice to him." She hugged Abby tight and turned to leave.

"I'll call you tomorrow," Abby said. Meghan's hand shot up and disappeared.

Turning to Craig, Abby asked, "Do you even know where we're parked?"

"Yes!" Craig barked. "Of course, I do." He reached for Abby's hand, but she pulled it away. However, as they started to move deeper into the crowd, Abby put her hand on Craig's shoulder so she wouldn't lose him. As soon as they broke into the open, she let go. They didn't talk. It took longer to get back to the car than it did to get there that morning. Abby was sure they were lost.

After a few turns, she began to recognize where they were. However, Craig suddenly ran off a few steps to a tree in someone's lawn and doubled over. He vomited heavily, heaving three or four times. Abby took her time getting to him, not wanting to get too close. Her annoyance turned to anger. "Shit!" she yelled and then took a breath. More quietly, but no less forceful, she continued, "How much did you drink?"

"Too much I guess," Craig replied. "I feel better now."

"Great," Abby said with as much sarcasm as she could muster. "Let's find the damn car."

When they finally found the lot, their car was the last one left.

"Give me the damn keys, Craig." Abby looked at him. Her eyes shined brightly in the street lights. He dug in his pocket and came to her side to let her in before getting in on the passenger side. "Why were you so late?"

"I told you, I was with my friends." Craig was breathing heavily.

"Did it come into that shit brain of yours to text me? You're a smart boy, Craig." Abby reached down to find the lever to adjust the seat.

"You need to turn the car on to adjust the seat." Craig was slow with his words. It was an Acura, and everything was automatic. Abby turned the key, and Craig unbuckled his seatbelt and leaned over Abby.

"What the hell do you think you're doing?" Abby said as she pulled at the neck of Craig's sweatshirt.

Half-choking, he replied, "I'm trying to adjust your seat." The seat started moving up, and his head almost got stuck under the steering wheel.

"Fine," Abby replied, pushing him back to his side of the car. "I don't know where the hell I'm going." She was almost yelling.

"Take Monroe south, past Edgewood College, and there'll be signs to get you to the Beltline."

"You're speaking Greek to me, bud. I don't know where I am, and what's more, I don't know where I'm going. You better stay awake." Abby put the car in drive. "Which way? And stay awake. Can you handle that?"

"Turn left out of the parking lot. That's Monroe." Craig held his head up with his hand. "Keep going past the stadium."

"Fine." Abby started out of the lot.

They made it to the Beltline, and Craig told Abby that Highway 18 turned into 12 and would take them all the way back to Whitewater. Abby recognized the highway and relaxed as much as she could while driving a car that she wasn't used to. There weren't many cars on the highway, which helped.

"So...where were you?" Abby tried to be calm.

"I met some buddies from school, and we found this house

party. I was only going to have one or two drinks, but time got away from me."

"And you got shitfaced…lost track of time?" All sense of calm seemed lost.

"What…I mean, yes…you never drink? You're from up north." Craig's voice was higher than normal.

"What the hell is that supposed to mean?"

"I don't know." Craig rolled the window down to get some air, but Abby rolled the window back up and locked it. He felt like he was going to be sick again and started to focus on his breathing, so Abby turned up the air.

"What don't you know?" Abby said.

"Well, don't you guys drink up north?"

"What do you think? Of course, but we're not dumbasses about it."

"How am I a dumbass?" Craig asked as he slid down in his seat.

"You figure it out." Craig turned to answer back, but Abby held a finger to his lips and said, "Stop. You figure out what I'm pissed about. I'll give you a clue; it's not the drinking."

Craig sat silently for a good while, trying not to fall asleep. He plugged in his phone and played Jason Isbell's *Southeastern*, hoping that one of her favorite albums would soften her. Abby looked at him with narrowed eyes. "Nice try."

After ten minutes, Craig asked, "Was it because I was late?"

"That's part of it! Keep going."

Craig thought more. He came up with nothing.

Abby pulled off the highway and drove towards a gas station.

"We don't need gas," Craig said.

"No shit. Really?" Abby replied.

Craig took a breath. "Listen, I'm sorry."

"For what?"

"I don't know, for getting drunk?"

"And?"

"Coming late."

"And?" Abby pulled into a space and turned off the car. She turned to look right at Craig.

He sat up straight and threw his arms up. "I don't know what I did, ok? What the fuck did I do wrong?" He was yelling. "What is your fucking problem?" Enraged, he leaned in.

"You want to know what my fucking problem is, Craig?" Abby yelled an inch from his face.

"Yes!" he yelled back.

"My problem is..." She paused and shook her head. "What the hell," she almost said to herself. She turned back to him and yelled, "I love you. That's my fucking problem. There! I love you, and I could use something to keep me from fucking falling asleep."

She got out and went in the store. Craig watched her go in. She loved him. His head was spinning, and he wasn't sure if he was still drunk or just shocked. He just stared at the door, waiting to see Abby come out. When she did, she was holding two cups. He reached over to open the door for her.

"I got you a coffee." She reached a cup into the car before getting in herself. The hot cup felt nice in Craig's hand. She put hers in the center console and sat down, closing the door.

As she was sticking the key in the ignition, Craig put his hand on her shoulder.

She sat back. "What?" she said softly.

"I love you too." Craig breathed in through his nose slowly and held it.

Abby looked at him with sad eyes. "I know…" She patted his leg. "Drink your coffee." She started the car and drove them home.

Abby and Craig returned to the habits of love. As fall advanced, their rhythm returned, and they didn't talk about Madison. They didn't say I love you again, content with showing each other instead.

By the end of the week, Abby called her mother and asked if Craig could come up for Thanksgiving.

"Hey, Mom," Abby said.

"Hi, Abby," her mom responded enthusiastically. "How are things?"

"Great. Everything is great."

"Well that's good, honey. How are your classes?"

"They're good," Abby responded. "Can I ask you something?"

"Sure, honey. What's up?"

"I was wondering if I could bring a friend home for Thanksgiving?"

"A friend?"

"So, you remember that boy I met a few weeks ago? Craig? I told you about him."

"Yes?" Her mother's voice suddenly became very serious.

"I would like to bring him to Thanksgiving. Would that be ok?"

"Where is this boy from?"

"He's from a suburb of Milwaukee. Hartland, I think?"

"Does he come from a nice family?"

Abby thought about Craig's silence after the dinner on the day of the football game. She didn't know how she'd been received.

"Yeah. They're nice."

"Well, I'll have to check with your father, but I think it will be fine. Abby?"

"Yes?"

"What are your intentions with this boy?"

"I don't know. I guess...I think I might love him." Abby couldn't believe she had just said that to her mother, but it was done. Her mom had always wanted her to meet someone.

After a long pause, her mother responded, "Well there you go then. That's a big step. I am not sure what you want me to say here. "

"Don't say anything then. Say you'll think about it?"

"About what?"

"About Craig coming to Thanksgiving."

"I will talk with your dad and text you later. I'm sure it will be fine."

"Thanks, Mom."

"Ok. Abby?"

"Yes?"

"Be careful. I wanted you to meet people down there but..."

Abby cut her off. "I will. Bye."

"Love you. Bye."

He mother hung up, and Abby let out a long breath.

That Friday, Brent was going out of town for an away game, so Craig and Abby hung out all day. They ate with Kate and her friend and then went to the library, as they normally did on Fridays. At about nine, they went back to his room.

Craig turned on the TV and lay down on his bed. Abby, who was changing into her 'comfy clothes,' turned and switched it off. She didn't have her top on yet and turned back towards Craig while putting her shirt on. He forgot about the TV.

He leaned back against his pillows, half-sitting, half-lying. Getting up on the bed and straddling him, Abby leaned over and kissed him quickly. He sat up and grabbed her around the waist and buried his head into her chest, but she pushed him back, gently.

"I have a question for you." Abby rested her hands on his shoulders and straightened her arms so he would look her in the eyes.

"What?" Craig looked up, caught by her stare.

"Do you want to come up to my place for Thanksgiving? Do you want to come to Wood Lake?" Abby couldn't help but smile. Craig could see she was so happy.

"Yes." He nodded and took a deep breath. He repeated, "Yes."

"Will your parents be alright with it?" Abby asked.

"Sure…we don't really do anything. Head down the block to make drinks and watch football. Even if they aren't, fuck them. I'm in."

Abby leaned forward and kissed Craig hungrily. He ran his hands up her back and pulled her in.

Abby: 18, Poem for College English Class

Ode to Wood Lake

The leaves are falling
At my home in the woods
But the needles hold on
To the tops of their tapered canopy

The air will frost and mist
As I go out to do my rounds
My feet move on the paths
Extensions of my very being

In the place that made me
I will find myself again
I will leave the busy world
To find a new list of tasks

Those that are familiar
A place that I can master
And call my own
I will be going home.

Chapter 10

A week before Thanksgiving, Craig knew it was time to call and tell his mother that he would be going to Abby's for the week. They had made arrangements to be gone for classes and complete their work online. With deer hunting and the holiday, many students would be going home early, and the professors knew the week was not going to be serious. Craig knew his mom would be pissed about him not being home, but he was determined to get it done. He had already cleaned his room, top to bottom, and he had done all of his studying. It's not like they did anything for Thanksgiving anyway. It was like any other weekend during football season; there was a buffet-style meal set out for friends and a few relatives, and his father held court. When Craig was younger, he remembered the day being fun because he could play with his friends and cousins. They would go out in the yard and try to be like the guys they saw on TV. Craig enjoyed the friendly competition. Lately, it was all talk about his season just past or seasons long ago at Camp Randall. Craig was looking forward to a change of scenery. He wanted to see the place that Abby loved so much. He wanted to see what made her her.

Craig was sitting on his bed when Brent came in.

"What's up, dude?" Brent said, looking around. "The place

looks great."

"I gotta call my mother. Tell her I'm going to Abby's for Thanksgiving," Craig said, admiring his work around the room. "I guess I've been trying to avoid it."

"What's the big deal?" Brent was looking for a fresh set of clothes, since he just came from practice, but was having trouble because they weren't on the floor where they were usually kept.

"I don't know...I mean...she's going to be pissed," Craig said. "I don't think they really like Abby."

"Why?" Brent asked as he walked to the dresser.

"They don't think she's 'our kind of people.'"

"Do you?" Brent said, looking up at Craig from the now-open bottom drawer.

"Do I what?" Craig asked, confused.

"Do you like Abby?"

"Yeah, of course. I love her." Craig realized what he had said right after he said it.

Brent stood up and looked directly at him. "Well, shit."

"No. I mean…" Craig couldn't find the words.

"I know what you meant, dude," Brent said with a big, shit-eating grin on his face. "I heard you. You love this girl. That's cool, man. She's a great girl. I mean that too. She's a great girl."

Nodding his head slowly, Craig said, "She is."

Brent left to take a shower. Craig dialed his mother's number. It rang twice.

"Hi, honey. What's up?" His mother never answered the phone calling him by name.

"Hi, Mom. How are you?" Craig said plainly, by rote.

"I'm fine. What's going on? How's school? Do you need anything?"

"No. I'm fine. School's fine," Craig responded.

"Do you want to talk with your father?"

"No. I want to talk to you."

"What's going on?" She was still cheerful.

"I'm thinking about going to Abby's for Thanksgiving. Her parents are fine with it, and I want to go there for the week."

"Oh...well...our whole family is going to be together for the first time in a bit. And don't you have classes?" The cheer was gone, and Craig could feel guilt starting to seep through.

"Come on, Mom. We never really do anything anyway. We just watch football. It's like every other weekend in the fall. And classes? Are you really worried about that?"

"Well no, but Sarah and Brad are coming, and Claire is actually going to be here."

"Are they going to be there over the weekend?"

"They will actually be here the whole week." Craig's mom said, sounding despondent.

"Well...then I can see them over the weekend. I won't be leaving until Tuesday, and I'll be back the following Saturday, with Abby."

"You really like this girl?" The question was delivered with a flat tone.

"Yes...of course." This time, he stopped himself.

"Well, I guess I could put a dinner together for Saturday evening to celebrate everyone being home." Craig could tell by the shrill tone of her voice that she was really annoyed. "Your father and I are concerned about all of this."

"Concerned about what?"

"Oh nothing. We'll talk to you when you get home."

Craig knew not to push things with his mother on the phone.

She continued, "See you in a week." She hung up.

He texted Abby, *I'm in for Thanksgiving!!!*

Abby texted back a heart.

Kate's parents didn't want to drive down to pick up Abby and Kate for Thanksgiving until Saturday. Kate's dad had to work and was planning to get to Whitewater around eleven that morning. Then, Abby's mom would pick her up in Wausau and drive back to Eagle River from there. Abby heard there was just enough snow to go snowmobiling, and ice was starting to cover the lake. It would only get thicker as the nights grew colder. Seeing her family and house and the resort was all she could talk about the entire week before leaving. She told Craig that they could go skiing at Whitecap, and that Thanksgiving was always a gathering of friends, hunting buddies, and family. It was the best holiday of the year, and she couldn't wait to share it with him.

"What don't you have planned about the week?" Craig asked with a laugh while setting down his tray for Friday dinner.

Kate laughed too. "I don't think you will have a minute's peace, Craig. Abby has been planning this for weeks."

They were the only three in the cafeteria. Craig and Abby were eating as quickly as they could because they wanted to get to the library for their normal Friday date. Kate wanted to go back to her room, where she always studied alone. All three were determined to clear their workload before going home. Both Craig and Abby were sure they could do it, until Craig's English professor assigned an essay based on a piece of creative nonfiction. They were supposed to read a book over break and begin working on an essay about a place or event that held meaning in their lives. Craig was having a hard time thinking of something genuine. The book he chose to base his essay on was *This House of Sky* by Ivan Doig. He chose it because he liked the title, and it was one of the books on a list of suggestions from his teacher. The book was also on hold at the library, so he wouldn't need to look for one on his own. After opening it, the first few lines certainly pulled him in. "Soon before daybreak on my sixth birthday, my mother's breathing wheezed more raggedly than ever, then quieted. And then stopped. The remembering begins out of that new silence." He showed it to Abby, and after reading those lines, a few tears rolled down her cheeks. She knew what it was like to have someone you were afraid to lose. She told Craig that it reminded her of what she had told him about Frank and Rita. The cancer had taken several months to bring about her end. There was nothing the doctors could do. For a time, the air at the resort was heavy. She told Craig, "The summer brought joy back to the resort, but I knew things had changed for good."

"Wow," Craig said. "You are really attached to that place."

"Yeah. I guess I've never really thought that much about it. I've never really had to explain it to anyone, you know. It just is what it is."

"That's so cool. I guess I never really felt like that about anything."

"Really? Not about your sisters or football? Nothing?

"No. Nothing. Especially not football. I've never felt connected to much. I just go with the flow. Whatever comes, comes."

"See, that's just something that I couldn't really do."

"Well maybe you'll get used to it," Craig said with a wry smile.

Grinning with a little shake of her head, Abby responded, "Maybe."

Craig had never had a connection to anything that deep, until he met her. Abby had known suffering. He knew nothing like it.

Up in the library, Abby got up and did a few laps of the floor and even began to rub Craig's back and read over his shoulder. She was finished with all her work by seven and asked Craig twice if he was ready to leave. By eight, he finally gave in and began to pack his things. As they walked to Craig's room, Abby, holding Craig's hand, swung his arm playfully as she always did and walked slowly. It had started to snow lightly, but she was pulling him in the direction of their bench. When they reached it, she brushed off the few flakes and sat down.

"It's a little cold, isn't it?" Craig asked as he sat down next to her. He wanted to get to his room where it was warm, and if he was honest with himself, he really just wanted to fool around with Abby all night because he wouldn't be seeing her for a few days.

Abby wasn't stupid, and she wanted to get up to Craig's room just as much, but she felt like sitting for a while first. Friday nights had been the times she felt most at home on campus. There was a rhythm to the evenings and they almost always, eventually, ended up in Craig's bed. She didn't mind. They would fool around for a bit, laugh and talk about what they wanted to do, or tell silly stories about their past. Sometimes, they just lay there and said nothing. Everything faded away in the moment. This night, with the exception of the attempt to study, Abby wanted to extend the moments. On the bench, with the light snow, Abby was reminded of one of her favorite spots back home. She had spent hours sitting on a bench at the end of the permanent dock, watching the snowfall in the moonlight.

"I can't wait for you to meet my parents and Frank. I think you'll like Frank." Abby said, looking up at the snow in the lamplight.

Craig slid closer to her. "What about Taylor?"

"She'll be really excited to meet you. She probably won't let you alone. Actually, she will probably ask if we're getting married or something." Abby was laughing.

"Ok," Craig said sarcastically. He put his arm around her shoulders, and she nuzzled in closer. "How many people are going to be there?"

"Close to fifty or sixty, maybe more. A lot of friends of my parents from Chicago and family. There are friends of friends and such. The group has grown considerably over the years. People help out to get the place ready. It's a great time."

"I'm not intruding or anything?" Craig asked.

"No," Abby said confidently. "To tell you the truth, you'll hardly be noticed." Craig didn't know how to feel about that, but then Abby added, "I'll know you're there." She gave him a squeeze.

"I'm staying with you guys then?"

"No. I'm sure my dad will give you a room in the lodge or maybe a cabin if one is open." Abby smiled and continued, "Depends on how far away he wants you."

"Really?" Craig said, grabbing his backpack. "I'm getting cold. Want to get going?"

"Sure."

Craig took her hand, and they skipped off towards the dorms.

They tried to watch a movie, but ended up making out throughout and snuggling all the way under the blankets. Craig turned on some music, and they tried to fall asleep, but Abby kept running her hand up and down his chest. He rubbed her back under her shirt, and then they would kiss, and Abby would invite Craig to touch her wherever he wanted. Things would progress and then quickly calm down. They had decided they were going to wait, but the freedom of college was making it difficult.

When they finally fell asleep, it was around two o'clock. They woke up at nine, and Abby rushed to get her things together. She kissed Craig while he was still in bed and said, "I'll see you Tuesday?"

"Yes." He sat up a bit. "I'll try not to get lost."

Abby smiled. "Text you tonight when I get home. Have a nice weekend."

"You too."

"For sure." She was off.

Craig realized that Abby was the only friend he needed. With all of his other friends, mostly athletes, fading away, he had begun to spend all of his time with her. He didn't mind though. She never judged him. With her, he felt content.

Craig: 18, Thanksgiving at his house senior year.

"You want to go upstairs for a bit?" I asked Jen at halftime of the first game. We had already eaten, and with the buffet my mom laid out every Thanksgiving, there was sure to be enough food for later, and even later. People had been at our house since ten in the morning, and no one was going to leave anytime soon. It was always this way, and I needed to get away from all of it.

"Ok," she said pensively. "Is something wrong?"

"No. Not really. I just want to get out of here for a bit."

"Could you grab me a beer, dear? Thanks!" My dad yelled out.

"Sure, Mr. McLean!" Jen called back. Turning to me, she said, "Let me get your dad's beer and go the bathroom. I'll meet you in your room. You sure you're ok?" Jen smiled. She was so beautiful. Her face just lit up every room. It was like having a fitness model who only looked at you. I wasn't sure why I deserved her.

"Yeah. Sure." I turned and went upstairs.

The women usually spent Thanksgiving at the kitchen table or in the living room watching anything but football and gabbing about the news of the neighborhood. My mom was the queen bee, just as, I assume, she'd always been. Jen was a lot like her. I wasn't so sure I was comfortable with that. Today, Sarah was the center of attention. She and Brad just announced their engagement and were getting married in eighteen months. Brad's ok. His parents and mine have been friends for years, and he's like a dorky older brother to me. Jen's parents were over too, and other neighbors. By the end of the day, it would be a full-on party. That's the way my parents liked it. Drove me a bit crazy.

I made my way up to my room and laid down on the bed. I turned on my side to get comfortable. Our football season just ended at Level 2 of the playoffs, not as far as we wanted, but my back still hurt, and it cramped if I lay flat. I was almost asleep when Jen came in and lay down next to me.

"Sorry. I got caught up with your mom. She's so excited about Sarah."

"Yeah. It's cool. We all knew it was coming."

"It's still exciting, Craig." She kissed me and moved in closer. We made out for a while, but it all seemed so rote. I used to be excited to kiss Jen. She's like the hottest girl in the school, but now it's just routine, and I think she does it more because she doesn't know what to say.

After a while, I rolled back onto my back and said, "I just hate days like this."

"Why's that?"

"Do you ever get sick of being the center of everything? We have people over all the time. It's always the same thing."

"I don't know. It's kinda nice to have friends around."

"Sure, but by tonight..." I paused to think. "Tonight, my house will be so full there won't be room to move."

"I guess," Jen said as she rolled onto her back as well.

I sat up. "I guess I'm just tired, you know? It's always a performance. People are always looking at you and me and waiting for what's next."

"I don't mind so much. It's better than no one taking an interest, you know."

"I guess."

"You're just bummed cause football's over."

"You think?"

"Yeah. You always get down after the season, Craig. It's normal. And you're not playing basketball this year, so there's nothing to look forward to until August."

"I guess."

"Let's get back to the party...oops, I mean dinner, or whatever." Jen rolled off the bed.

"I'll be there in a minute."

"Ok. Don't fall asleep on me." She came and kissed me on the forehead. "I don't want to be left alone with everyone."

It wasn't the end of the season. It wasn't the normal blues. I was glad not to be playing basketball, and I wasn't sure I really wanted to play college football either. My back was starting to hurt so I got up and went downstairs. Jen was at the table with the other women, sitting next to my mom. My mom loved Jen. Jen was the perfect girlfriend in her eyes. I got a plate of food and went back to the basement for more football. Nothing out of the ordinary.

Part Two: *Craig's Story*

Chapter 11

I drove home soon after Abby left. I figured I had clothes there, so all I brought was my laundry and a few pairs of shoes. The snow of the night before had not amounted to much, only clinging to the grassy areas that had not given way to direct sunlight. The drive was so uneventful, I had a lot of time to think. I had done this drive so many times for games and camps, it felt like my entire childhood had taken place on the fields and diamonds of the southwestern suburbs and small towns of Greater Milwaukee and Waukesha. Every memory of my childhood involved a game of some sort. I tried to remember something different, but nothing came to mind besides Abby. Thinking of her made me smile. Was I really in love with her? Is this the feeling of love? I know I told her I loved her, but I said it because she did. Did I actually mean it? I wasn't quite sure I was there yet.

All of this was rolling around in my head when I got to my neighborhood. I was struck, as if for the first time, by how many of the houses looked almost exactly like mine. The same styles and colors kept turning up around every corner and loopy street. Each one was the same shade of gray or brown. There were uniform light posts in every yard and the same number of trees, all at the same height. This was a young subdivision.

I was older than all of the homes. The only history this neighborhood contained were a few bumps and bruises from trampoline accidents and the occasional epic game of Marco Polo in one of the many inground pools. We didn't have a pool. My dad had been unwilling to cover the expense, although, I always suspected that he just didn't want to do the extra work that always seemed to accompany the fall leaves or a broken filter. Besides, Uncle Jim had a pool, and he lived only three houses down. It still makes me laugh to see Jim hovering over the pool all the time, trying to fix a filter or get some foreign object or another out with a net. Maybe my dad had a point.

I drove into my driveway, off to the side of the garage where my parking spot was and sat in the car for a while. I wasn't sure anyone saw me, and I didn't care. I really didn't want to go in, but, after a few deliberate breaths, blowing out hard, I opened the door and headed in through the garage. There was activity in the kitchen, so I moved quietly through the hall and tried to get upstairs unnoticed. However, my mom poked her head around the corner and caught me just as I reached the first stair.

"Well hello there. Trying to sneak past without saying hi to your mother?"

"Sort of," I said with a smirk. Reluctantly, I dropped my things and went over to give my mom a hug.

"Uncle Jim and Aunt Barb and Brad are coming for dinner. Sarah's helping me right now, and Claire said she would decorate cookies later. You get your things together and go ask your father if he needs help with anything." She went back into the kitchen, and I went upstairs.

When I got to my room, I threw my bag on the desk and

sat down on my bed. Nothing had changed about my room. I guess I hadn't expected it to. I mean, my video games had been straightened and my bed was made, which it never was when I was home, but, everything else was just as I had left it. Exhaling, I sat back and reached for the remote, but then thought better of it. Since I met Abby, I realized I watched a lot less TV save for the few movies we actually made it through. 'Why watch TV when I could watch her?' I thought, chuckling to myself. God, I wanted to see her. I reached for my phone and looked at her picture on the home screen. I could call her, but she was probably in the car with Kate's dad. That would be weird. As I looked around, I noticed there were no books, not even on my desk. I dug in my bag for my book for English class and leaned back to start reading it. Instead of reading, I found myself peering around the room, searching for anything that showed me a sense of who I might have been. I was never really a poster guy, so the white walls were populated with pictures of my teams or pictures Claire had taken while I was playing. Claire had an eye for capturing just the right moment. Despite the personal pictures, the room seemed to be missing life. Or at least life as I was now beginning to see it. It was not really a home, but rather, an ode to my parent's version of who they thought I should be. I didn't want to be that guy anymore.

I opened *This House of Sky* and reread the devastating first lines. I wish I could open a story with a line like that. The ramblings in my journal never amounted to much, certainly nothing like that. Don't get me wrong, I never wanted a tragedy of that magnitude to hit me, but the language was beautiful, and the opening pages of the book revealed something I had never felt, a profound sense of place. I just wanted to belong to a somewhere. From what I had already learned, Doig was a Western writer, and the land seemed to not only inform and inspire, but render itself on the page. The mountains were as much a character as his hardscrabble father. Doig seemed to be as much a part of the setting as he was part of the story he was telling. Nothing seemed to matter to him as much as every blade of grass meant to the younger narrator he had created. Right now, the only thing that mattered to me was Abby. Abby had a sense of place. She was from somewhere. I was from nowhere. I pulled out my phone and texted her that I was home, and that I was not excited about dinner with my family. She replied, *Sorry...I can't wait to get home. I can't wait for you to come see it with me.* I texted a smiley face.

I went back to the book. Just as I started to drift off, there was a knock on my door, and it opened.

"Hey kid." It was Claire. She had her hair tied back and was, surprisingly, wearing a full zip Badger hoodie. "Heard you're the reason we're having this dinner tonight. Thanks." She sat down in my desk chair and put her feet up on my bed. "So...you met a girl, huh?" she asked, now right at the edge of my bed, tapping her fingers on the frame. She knew it annoyed me. I didn't take the bait. She continued, "And Mom doesn't like her. Imagine that. You didn't even think to send me a text?" She shook her head.

"Wait, Mom doesn't like her?" I asked.

"Mom doesn't like anyone unless they're from the neighborhood," Claire delivered with more than a hint of sarcasm, which was her preferred mode of communication.

Agreeing, I said, "I know. But shit, they only met once." I took out my phone and showed her a picture of Abby.

"She's pretty, Craig. Definitely not Jen."

"That's for sure. She's really cool. Her family owns a resort on the lake in Eagle River. That's where I'm going for Thanksgiving." I could feel myself buzzing with energy again.

"That's great. I'm stuck here," Claire said, smiling pensively.

"How's school?"

"School's school. You know. I'll be having an art show in the spring. You and Abby should come down. God knows no one else will."

"Just tell me when." I got off my bed.

"You better go help Dad. Mom wants a fire, and he's trying to find wood in the backyard."

"This dinner is going to be a pain in the ass," I sighed, knowing what was coming.

"You got that right," Claire said. "Just do what you want to do, Craig. Screw Mom and Dad."

"Thanks, Claire."

I finally changed and went downstairs to find my dad. I looked in the basement family room and then in the backyard. When I found him, he was looking through a stack of wood that was probably as old as the house. I walked out and yelled, "Hey, Dad!"

My father turned from the pile and walked towards me, still holding a piece of wood. We met in the middle of the yard, and he gave me a half hug. So annoying. "Welcome home. Come have a look at this pile with me." We walked towards the wood that was up against the back fence. Beyond the fence was the fifth hole of the Wooded Hills Country Club. The golf course setting, much like the wood pile, went largely unused by my family. "All this stuff is old and wet," he said as he tossed the piece he was holding back on the pile. "I'd burn it in the fire pit, but not inside the house. Tried to talk your mother out of a fire," he said, turning to me, "but you know how she is."

"I do," I replied. "Do you just want me to go to the gas station and get some fresh stuff?"

"That would be great," he said, reaching in his pocket. "Get a couple of packs. Never know when your mom will get the itch." He gave me forty dollars.

I took the money. "Can I take the truck?"

"Sure." He reached back in his pocket and threw the keys. "I'm going to see if the damper is open."

I hated when my dad tried to sound like he knew what he was talking about. The problem was that this was standard operating procedure for him. I went to the garage to go get the truck.

Sarah was in the garage checking the beer and soda supply. Happy to see her, I walked up and said, "Hey, Spike." She turned from the fridge and immediately gave me a big hug. Sarah had always taken the time to listen to me. She had played with me as a kid, kicking the ball and pitching when I wanted to hit. As we got older, she, most of all, understood the pressure I was under from our dad. I always felt like she had paved the way.

"Hi, yourself. How are you? How is school?" She had a tendency to stack up the questions like our mother.

"I'm fine. School is fine. You know school's never been that hard for me."

"Yeah. You suck." She pushed me away. "So, we're having this family dinner because of you I heard." She smiled.

"Claire said that too. Is that what Mom's been saying?" I was annoyed. Was this all my mother had been talking about?

"Well, you're going to this girl's house for Thanksgiving. What's her name? Abby?"

I showed her the same picture I showed Claire. "Wow. She's pretty, Craig. She's really pretty. Not the kind of girl you usually go for."

"No. She's special."

"So you really like her then?"

"Yeah," I said, starting to blush. "She's great."

"Well then don't worry about Mom. She's nuts. You know that."

"Yeah." I opened the door to the truck. "Dad needs me to go get some wood for the fireplace."

"What? We haven't had a fire in like ten years."

"Well...Mom wants a fire, so Mom gets a fire."

"Figures...Special day for the special boy."

I smirked and got in the truck.

"I'll go with you. We need more beer. Brad only drinks Miller Lite, and we're out." She got in the passenger seat. Before we went out of the garage, I had already started in about Abby. Sarah just let me talk. I was happy to have the ear.

About four in the afternoon, Uncle Jim showed up at the house with Aunt Barb and Brad. These people were family. They would officially be family in the spring, but as far as the McLean's were concerned, there was never a doubt. Our families had built homes in the neighborhood around the same time and hit it off right away. My mom and Barb belonged to the same gym, and various combinations of both families had been going to Badger games for as long as I could remember.

My dad was entertaining loudly in the basement family room with Sarah, Brad, and Jim. He was fixing drinks and watching football like he did every Saturday. I just got a soda and went to see if I could help my mother in the kitchen.

"Why don't you hang out with your father?" my mom asked.

Claire was in the corner decorating cookies with Barb hovering over her and marveling at her work. My mom was trying to do too many things at once in one of her attempts to be the perfect hostess.

"I can help, Mom," I said, surveying what needed to be done.

"Well, I guess you could cut the cheese and sausage to take downstairs. That would help a lot." She directed me to the drawer where the knives were kept as if I were in the home for the first time. Over the course of the day, I felt like she might be right.

"Fine." I knew my mother would continue to orchestrate ways to get me downstairs to hang with my dad, but I really didn't want to get caught in the same pattern of telling stories about the past and analyzing plays. That banter held no interest for me anymore. I took out the knife and cut my way through the sausage and two blocks of cheese, eating several pieces as I arranged them on a large platter. I passed through the dining room, where the table was set like it was Christmas. We normally didn't have Thanksgiving dinner at the table. I was surprised my mom hadn't gone to buy new dishes for this one. As I went downstairs with the platter, I was aware of how much of a showpiece this house was. It didn't feel like a home. It was more like the houses you see on HGTV. I had often questioned who lived in houses like those. The answer, me. Moreover, Sarah and Brad were moving into a huge house a few loopy streets away. A wedding gift from the parents. Why would anyone want to live here?

In the basement, I dropped off the platter without announcement. I rolled my eyes at Brad, and then escaped back upstairs. Back in the kitchen, my mother seemed surprised by my return. "What's next?" I asked, holding my hands out trying to look ready to help. Claire laughed softly from the table as if she knew exactly what was going on. She probably did. Claire always knew.

Mom said, "The potatoes need to be whipped." She pointed to a huge pot on the stove. "Just season them to taste." I got right to it. I retrieved the mixer, butter, and garlic salt and took my time trying to get it right. Mashed potatoes and ham were among my favorite foods. The ham that Mom made, and really the whole meal, was clearly a play for my affection, as most of the foods were not favorites of the rest of the families. I guess I appreciated the effort.

After the potatoes were done, I covered them in foil and asked if there was anything else. I suspected we would be eating around five because there was no way they would be at the table at the beginning of the seven o'clock game. There was no doubt in my mind that other neighbors would be showing up as the evening progressed. This was the way of the McLean household.

The food was out, drinks were made, and people were seated. After the initial passing of food was done, the conversation naturally went to the wedding plans and how school was going.

Sarah and Brad were having their wedding in Madison, at The Terrace. It was over spring break because everyone could be home, and Brad was finishing his last semester of his MBA program this fall. Claire and I were expected to stand up, and we had already begun to bitch about this privately.

The clinking of utensils and glasses continued as both Claire and I shared our stories of school, and Claire mentioned her senior art show. Mom said that she would need to put it on the calendar.

Claire beat me to asking if she could clear the table and get dessert ready. Mom agreed because dessert was largely Claire's project. She had tried to show pride in her daughter's artistic abilities, but it never sounded genuine to me. Claire actually kept most of her work private.

In the lull, Jim asked me, "So where's Abby?" It was an innocent remark, but I knew the shit storm was coming. I really didn't want to hash over my relationship with my parents.

"She's home," I responded in a curt way, trying to get out of the conversation. "Actually, she is probably just getting home now."

"Well...she seems likes a nice girl. Really pretty."

I knew that Jim meant well, but he was born with his foot firmly planted in his own mouth. I just didn't feel like justifying my trip to Abby's house to my mother, at least not at the table.

"Where's she from again?" Jim continued.

"Eagle River. And thanks. I like her." I smiled, trying to play nice.

"It would be nice to have her here," Mom said.

"We'll stop on Saturday night on the way back to school." I looked straight at her, trying to will her to end the conversation.

"That will be nice." Her face could not hide the annoyance I was reading into it. She looked down at her plate.

Claire came with dessert. I could breathe again.

After dessert, I helped get the dishes clean. Once again, I was just trying not to go downstairs. I was more than content to hand wash the nice plates with Claire drying. After a while, my mom took over for Claire. I kinda felt abandoned.

She started right in, "So how serious are you with this Abby girl?'

"Pretty serious, Mother." I was very conscious of adding a hard edge to the last word of the sentence.

"I suppose you ARE going up there for the week."

"Four days."

"Five."

"Ok five."

"Your father and I are are worried about you." She reached for a dish, and I handed her one to dry.

In a consciously sarcastic tone, I said, "Really. That's nice."

"You've just been making so many changes in your life, and she's just another one of your puzzling decisions." There was genuine worry in her voice, but I couldn't tell why.

"She makes me happy," I replied and looked up. "Isn't that what really matters?"

"I suppose, but you were happy before. You were happy playing football. You were happy with…"

I cut her off. "You know, Mom..." I held out the last dish and turned off the faucet. "I wasn't really happy. I was just good at it. No one really stopped to ask me if I was happy." 'The question was absurd,' I thought to myself. "Abby makes me happy."

Mom took the dish gently. "Well, ok then."

I dropped the cloth and left the kitchen to go up to my room.

When I got to there, I checked my phone, and there was a text from Abby. It was a picture of a partially frozen lake framed by frosty pines. There was snow on ground, and half of Abby's face was beaming. It was captioned *HOME!* I felt a little rush.

Looks nice. Glad to hear, I wrote back.

How are things by you? I read it and was excited that Abby was by her phone. I wanted to talk to her about my mother. I wanted to tell her everything. About my sisters, the tension, everything. Instead, I wrote, *Fine. No big deal. Just finished dinner.*

Cool. We are just about to eat so I gotta go.

Ok. Send another pic.

Of what?

Of you.

Abby sent a picture with her hair down. She looked alive and happy. Her eyes were all I needed to make me feel better. Another picture came through but with her sister. Taylor was looking over her shoulder with her mouth all scrunched up. *Tay said I had to send this. Talk tomorrow?*

Yeah. I'll call you tomorrow. I was a little bummed. I wanted to talk with her more now.

I better call you. Lots to do around here.

Ok. Good night.

Night.

I tried to stay up in my room, but Sarah came up and told me to get my ass downstairs. She was tired of deflecting all the shit our parents were dishing out and said she needed backup. It was time I took my share. She must have retrieved Claire from her room as well because she was in the hall. We all looked at each other and headed down together.

"Once more into the breach, dear friends," Claire said, smiling at me. Sarah didn't seem to get it.

As I had suspected, other neighbors had made their way over, and the small dinner became a party. The beer and booze flowed, and my parents, running around to provide for everyone, were in their element. This was their home. I was losing faith that it was mine. I put on my mask and jumped in, answering a dozen questions about why I quit football. It was clear there was a sense of community in these gatherings, but the topics of conversation were always the same. No one ever challenged anyone or anything. It was like high school thirty years later. I had to escape.

Craig: 12, Leaving for Little League Tryouts

"I don't want to go. I hate baseball."

"That doesn't matter much to me, son. I asked you before we signed up, and you said yes."

"But I don't want to. I just said that so you wouldn't be mad at me," I said, looking over at Claire for support. She stared back at me and went back to her sketchbook. She didn't know what to say.

"Doesn't much matter now. Tryouts are today, and we're going." My dad began to get up and walk towards the kitchen.

"Why do I even need to tryout? You're one of the coaches. I'll make the team." I was hoping to put it off for one more day.

"Everyone tries out, Craig. Most of the boys spent the offseason at NX Level training. You never know."

"Whatever, Dad. Baseball's a drag. You're not going to make me pitch, are you?"

"Of course you're going to pitch," he said, shaking his head.

I kicked my bag across the floor. "I hate pitching. You know that." I was yelling and trying not to cry. I tried to run out of the room, but my dad, still quick for his age, caught me from behind. He sat me down.

"Listen. You're going to play, and you're going to pitch. You won ten games last year. That's all there is to say. We have a chance to win the league championship."

"I don't care," I said, waving my arms. "Who cares if we win? We won last year, and no one cared. The trophy just sits in Justin's basement."

"But we won. That's the point."

"What's the point?"

"Winning. There are winners and losers in the world, and McLeans are winners. You hear?"

"But it's just baseball."

"No. This is life, Craig. I'm preparing you for life. That's what sports are for. Winning is the point of life."

"I don't care if I win!" I yelled.

"You will. We win in this house. I'll see you in the truck." He got up and walked out of the room.

I turned back to Claire. "I hate him."

"I know, Craig. I know."

Chapter 12

When my mom woke me up at nine the next morning, I was confused. I threw on a shirt and shorts and checked my phone. It read, *Good Morning. Off to work.* The time signature said six thirty. 'No freaking way,' I thought to myself, then made my way downstairs. Claire was already sitting at the kitchen island eating a bowl of Frosted Flakes.

"Why are we up so early?" I asked, hoping someone could answer in a way that would clear my head.

Claire looked up from her bowl and snorted, "We're going to church." She then stuffed another spoonful in her mouth and began to chew deliberately.

"What?" I screeched loudly, now fully awake.

Claire repeated, louder this time, "We're going to church. It's Mom's new thing. We get to be her showpieces."

A little panicked, I asked, "Where's Dad? Where's Sarah?"

Still deadpan as ever, Claire explained, "Apparently, Dad is too hungover to get out of bed, and Sarah and Brad have an apartment together while they are waiting for their house to be finished." She began to speak even louder and more angrily. "Because it seems shacking up before getting married is a thing we do now in this family." Claire was almost at the point of yelling.

This was too much for me to take in at the moment. "So, we're going to church?" I asked slowly, not yet coming to grips with the whole situation.

"Yes, dumbass. And then Mom wants to us to go with her to the outlet mall. I think it's an elaborate bribe to get me to stop complaining."

"That's not true," Linda said as she came into the kitchen. "I just thought it would be nice to get you two some winter clothes to take back to school. Especially you, Claire, since you're taking the class over winter break this year."

"Mom, I told you I need to get ready for my show."

"I know, honey. I'm not saying anything." This was a familiar phrase in the McLean household. Claire and I looked at each other, rolling our eyes. It clearly meant she disapproved of the situation. With me and Claire, our mother disapproved of almost all of the situations all the time.

Both Claire and I went upstairs to get changed after breakfast, and I drove us to church. This was not our normal Sunday morning, but my mother got what she wanted; her two college-aged children were props in a play where every mother is the star. Others were made to do the same. The smile our mother made, even when introducing Claire, displayed clearly that she simply wanted to prove her children were successful. Whether her pride was true or false, she was determined to make everyone around us believe it.

We escaped after donuts, a bonus in my mind, and made our way to Johnson Creek Outlets. Mom insisted that we move as one unit since she was buying. This meant I would get to stand near the front entrances of stores I had no business being in. However, I conceived a plan. "Hey, Mom. I'd like to get home to watch the game with Dad. It's at three, so can we make sure we get home for that?"

I hoped this orchestrated time limit would work. We had parked at the Nike store side of the lot, intending to hit it last. Mom had a dozen stores on her list, and I doubted we would make it, but I didn't really care. It was worth a try. Actually, I was hoping that Abby would call so I could excuse myself, but all I got was a text. *Really busy here. Turnover Day. Call you later!* I couldn't fully visualize what she was talking about, but I could tell she was in her element because she had talked about it so often. I turned my attention to the next store, American Eagle. It always surprised me that Claire was really into shopping with Mom. It just didn't seem like something she would like. But what girl didn't like new clothes?

Mom approached me while I was engrossed in my fantasy football stats. She was holding a flannel shirt that she described as "rustic." "Do you think Abby would like this?" She was wide-eyed and smiling. I tried to appreciate the effort. I mean, the shirt was lined and looked very warm.

"Yes," I said with tight smile. "She'd love it. Looks comfy."

"What size? Small?"

"You should probably go with a medium."

She looked puzzled.

"Shirts like that are supposed to be oversized, Mom," Claire said, carrying a bigger size of the same shirt. She exchanged it for the one that Mom was holding. "I'll take this one back." She winked at me.

We actually made it through the rest of the shopping trip without incident. I got a few sweatshirts and a new pair of hiking boots, which I soaked my generous mother for to the tune of $175. Take advantage while you can.

When we got home around four, Dad had DVR'd the game so we could watch it from the beginning and speed through the commercials. He had an entire bag of chips poured into a bowl and a large Bloody Mary with all the fixings on the table between the two theater-style recliners that faced the seventy-inch TV in the family room. I had spent so many Sundays here. I couldn't tell you when it started, but some of my earliest memories were of sitting on my father's lap watching the Packers. We rarely talked, other than to review a play. Dad had shown little interest in my school stuff, I assumed because I had been a good student, but we could always talk football. Actually, I was like him in most social situations. That much I realized when people compared the two of us. I had been brought up with the expectation that I would handle my own problems by talking to those I needed to to talk with when the time came. There were no bailouts in my upbringing. McLean children were trained to be forthright and honest, even if that honesty meant saying the hard truth. I guess it was a blessing in a way, but it could be a burden.

When I sat down, I thought about how my dad told me never to be intimidated by anyone. "Always stand up for yourself no matter what," he would say all the time. Despite that statement ringing in my ears, Abby intimidated me a little. Challenged me was more accurate. She saw through my bullshit. That was one of the things I loved about her. Even her anger, like the fight in Madison, was something I found attractive, in a weird sort if way. I didn't want to live life being excused for all my misdeeds. I had to earn Abby's respect daily, and I kinda liked the process. I knew my dad was seen as a good guy and treated clients well, but I always felt the respect came from his past and not his present.

We watched almost the entire first half before Dad "woke up" and started to yell at the TV about the officiating. He was fastforwarding through the commercials so quickly that we were going to catch up to the live broadcast by halftime. He paused it and went to refresh his drink, asking if I wanted anything. Both my parents had never been shy about allowing us to have a glass of wine with dinner or a drink on special occasions, but this was different. This was a football game on any old Sunday. "No thanks, Dad. I'll just get myself a soda later."

"Suit yourself." He poured more vodka into his glass and came to sit down. Without turning the game back on, he said, "So, Craig...your mother isn't too happy about you going up to this Abby girl's house or resort or whatever it is for the whole week."

"Really? Why's that?" I asked sarcastically as I leaned forward and faced my father, who wasn't even looking at me. My dad tapped the remote a few times and picked up his drink to take a huge swig.

"I mean...we don't even know these people. What kinda guy leaves a career in engineering to open a resort on some lake up north? And what does her mom do?" He still didn't look at me. This was not really that odd. He was not one to start a confrontation. That was more my mom's thing.

"She teaches kindergarten," I growled under my breath.

"Well that figures."

"How's that?"

"They're a bunch of liberals then."

"Why would you say that?"

"Put it together, son. She's a teacher, and he's some kinda wannabe hippie who couldn't make it in the real world, so he went and bought some rundown resort to escape."

"You don't know anything about them. Why would you assume?"

"I know people, Craig. That's my business. I know people."

"Well he seems to be the type who started his own business and has been running it successfully for over fifteen years. What's wrong with that?" I rarely challenged my father because it did no good, but this time, I went all in.

"He's living off his wife's income and benefits, which my taxes are paying for, and he gets to play camp counselor for the rest of his life." My dad had a way of leveling an insult so quickly that no one had time to think of a response. It was his gift.

"You're full of shit, Dad." I got up to leave the room.

"But I'm right. You'll see."

I went to my room and opened my book. But truthfully, I couldn't concentrate, so I laid it open on my chest and stared at the ceiling. I was just hoping Abby would call soon.

It wasn't until after dinner that Abby called. I took leftovers to my room and watched the second half of the Packer game alone. They lost, despite Rodgers throwing for almost 400 yards. I had to roll off my bed to reach the phone on my desk where it was charging.

"Hi."

"Hi, Craig. What's up?"

I wasn't sure if I wanted to tell Abby about the fights with my parents. I didn't want it to become a thing.

"Craig. Are you ok?"

"Yeah. Just a bit tired. How was your day?"

"Great." I could hear in her voice that she was excited. She had a crispness and clarity that only came when she talked about her home. "I had a fantastic day. I fell right back into the rhythm of the place. Sunday's a big day cause lots of people left this morning after a two-night stay, and the whole Thanksgiving hunting crew is moving in for the week. We only have two cabins left open and five rooms. I had to turn over several rooms today and get the cabins stocked. The same group comes every Thanksgiving. Mostly friends and family, but you want to get the place looking nice for them." Abby took a deep breath and continued, "We still have a few left to check in. It's going to be a busy week. Lots of old friends of my parents and a few family members who haven't been here for a while." She was repeating herself, but I didn't mind.

She went on to detail her entire day. She talked about Frank, her mother flying around doing this and that, and Taylor, her fourteen-year-old sister, following her around and asking all sorts of questions about him.

"That sounds like a lot," I said. I was just happy to hear her voice. She was alive in a way that was perceptively different. She was excitedly calm, and the work didn't seem to tire her out. Instead, it brought her to life. "How's your father?"

"He's conducting his orchestra like he always does. I swear, there seems to be three of him during weeks like this."

"That's cool." I said, partially engaged, but at the same time I felt the overwhelming desire to see her. I wanted to touch her and hold her. I wanted to smell her hair and run my fingers through it. Finally, I blurted out, "Can I come up tomorrow?"

"Tomorrow? Why? Is something wrong?" Abby's voice was sharper.

"No. I just want to see you. This place is...I don't know. I just don't want to be here anymore. Can you see if..."

She cut me off. "I'll check. Give me a minute."

I could hear Abby in the background talking, and then she came back and said, "My mom says it's fine if your parents are ok with it."

"They'll be alright. We've got nothing going on."

"Great. I'll see you tomorrow then."

"Yes." Suddenly, I felt very excited. I stood up and paced around my room. "Can you send me directions?"

"Sure. I'm going to send you a surprise too, so it might take a while."

"Ok. Bye."

"Bye. Lov...Bye!" She hung up.

I continued to pace around, wondering how I would tell my parents. I mean, I figured I'd fulfilled my obligations to family, and no one would mind. After several minutes, two text messages came. The first one had directions. They didn't seem too hard. The second was a list of songs followed by *Driving mix. Download and make a playlist. See you.*

I got to work on the playlist. For the first time since I came home, I was happy.

Chapter 13

The next morning, when my parents had left for work, I told Claire I was going to Abby's house. "I don't blame you," she said, chuckling a little.

"What?"

"Nothing. They're just going to be pissed."

"Probably. Run interference for me?"

"Don't I always?"

I left a note on the kitchen counter.

The drive was rather uneventful to start. It was pleasant to be on the road with a goal in mind. The playlist kept my mind on Abby, and I could hear her speaking through the music. "Now I've traded those lessons for faith in a girl." I sang along with some. They were all her favorites: Eastmountainsouth, Peter Bradley Adams, The Weepies, Jason Isbell. She had timed it out to take just about the length of the ride. After a gas stop in Stevens Point, I was almost 'up north' as Abby would say. The snowline hit in the hills north of Wausau, and a forest of pine and birch took hold of my view. The forest seemed to get deeper and press closer to the road as I went further north past Woodruff and Rhinelander. I could feel my fingers getting sweaty on the wheel and kept wiping my hands on my jeans.

When I got to Eagle River, I turned off the mix Abby made

so I could focus. The town looked like a combination of what I assumed a northern Wisconsin town might look like and a quaint tourist town. All the amenities one would need were next to cute little local shops and service stations. With the snow, the town was really lovely. There was water everywhere, lakes and rivers. I took a right out of town onto County CC. Five miles and two turns later, I was there. I pulled into a small lot, two-thirds full, and took the driveway to the left out of the lot, past the main lodge. About a hundred yards through the forest and waist-high snow banks, I saw a large A-frame house with two snowmobiles in the driveway. To the right of the house was a wood pile, and through the woods, towards the front of the house, was an expansive white plain with open water in the middle of it. There was Abby's lake.

As I stood outside the car, I could hear Abby running down the hall, and she barely managed to get to the door without falling. A smile washed over her face. My heart was racing. I had only a duffle and my jacket slung over my shoulder. Abby skipped out into the mild wintery air to greet me. I felt an overwhelming smile and waited until she was almost to me to open my arms and hug her, lifting her from the ground. She felt weightless in my embrace for a moment, and then I felt the gravity of her mother's gaze, who had reached the door and was now watching us. Abby disengaged and took me by the hand, leading me to the entrance.

"How was the drive?" Abby asked.

"It was fine...made good time I think," I replied, looking around the forest. I had never seen so many trees all in one place.

"You found it fine," she said affirmatively.

"Yes. Your directions were spot on," I responded.

We reached the stairs leading to the back door, and Abby made introductions. "This is Vickie, my mother."

I reached out my hand, and Vickie took it. She motioned me through the door, allowing me to pass in front so she could place herself between Abby and me. "It's nice to meet you, Craig. Abby has told us a lot about you. You can leave your bag in the laundry room. John has you in Cabin #2, so you'll be moving."

I took off my boots, and then we moved to the main room where I made my way to the window. There was a deck extending twenty-five feet further towards the lake, and the great expanse was framed by frosty pines. All of what Abby had told me over the past two months suddenly made sense. The home was warm and inviting. The lake was exactly as she had described it. Everything was beautiful, alive, and welcoming.

"Can I interest you in a snack before Abby shows you around? John and Taylor are out right now, so we'll be eating a little later tonight," Vickie called out.

I turned around. The kitchen was tucked under a lofted area with stairs on the opposite side from the hall. I walked to the kitchen island and said, "I would love a snack." I turned to Abby. "It's beautiful. Just like you said." I pointed up towards the lofted area with a confused look.

"That's my parent's room. Mine and Taylor's are down the hall. We passed them as we came in." She grabbed a warm cookie and handed it to me. "Let me show you around." Abby let me walk first down the hall. I could feel her looking at me, I assumed to see how I was reacting to her home. I chose the right room and walked over by her desk. There was a bulletin board with pictures just like the one she had at school.

"Is that Meghan?" I asked, pointing.

"Yes...and some of my other friends."

I looked around the room. There was a string of Christmas lights just like in Claire's room. Abby moved closer to me and scratched my back. She put her arms around my waist and squeezed me gently. "Did you take those pictures?" I asked as I pointed to a set of framed photographs of various lake and wooded scenes.

"Yes. Those are from around the lake, and that one," Abby pointed towards a picture that was on the wall at the foot of her bed, "is my favorite spot."

I looked at the picture for the moment and then turned to face her. I put my arms around her and pulled her in tight. Just feeling her pressed against me made all my worries of home fade away. We kissed each other, but I could tell she was holding back. I stayed content in the embrace for a minute. Abby's mother called from the kitchen, "Are you going to show the boy around before supper? It's going to be dark soon."

Startled by her mother's intrusion, Abby gave me one more peck and said, "Let's go. Grab your coat."

I went down the hall to grab my boots and coat, then called, "Should I bring my bag?"

"No. We can get that later," Abby emerged from her room. "Come on." She waved me down the stairs.

We went into a family room/library area. There were college textbooks up on a bookshelf, as well as children's books of all sorts. A huge fireplace and a woodpile stood next to a sliding glass door. "What's with that?" I asked, pointing to the pile, which seemed unusually large for an indoor fireplace.

"Oh." Abby stopped at the glass door. "We heat with wood. That's the furnace. We have a regular one that kicks in if it gets too cold, but that never happens."

"Ok." I said confused.

"Don't worry. There's going to be a lot you don't know."

"Is that right?"

She shook her head. "Lace up your boots. We've got some hiking to do." She opened the door and moved out into the cold. We walked down to the lake and onto a permanent dock. Abby watched as I took in the whole lake. Long sweeps of shoreline were punctuated by sections hidden from view where land jutted out. I tried to comprehend how someone could live here. I had visited plenty of resorts, but never thought much about who owned or ran them. I zipped up my coat and fished a hat from my pocket.

"Let's walk along the shoreline a while. We'll go see the cabins and grounds, then work our way back to the lodge. I want you to meet Frank before dinner." Abby reached for my hand and led me down the footpath towards the water.

We walked past the lodge, and Abby pointed out the main boat launch. All the other docks had been taken out and placed beside the cabins.

"What was the big building I passed on the way down the driveway to your house?" I asked, turning back towards Abby's house.

"That's the storage building. We keep the paddle boats and canoes in there. I guess it's just where everything goes really."

We came up from the shore, and the lodge was now behind us. There was a road that led between the cabins. "What's the difference between all the cabins?" I asked, as I looked to the left and right. “Why are they all different sizes?”

“There are one-, two-, and three-bedroom cabins. The three-bedroom ones are along the shore. They’re four-day minimums.”

“How’s that?”

“We only allow the big ones to be rented for a minimum of four days. It wouldn’t be worth the time to clean them if we didn’t get at least that much. This week, we will be hosting people from tomorrow through Saturday or Sunday. Everything is full.”

We sauntered down the road leisurely. I was aware that all of this belonged to Abby’s family, but it was a great deal to take in. When we came to the end of the road, I noticed a small cabin, through the woods, set apart from the rest. “What’s that? Over there.”

“That’s Frank’s place. It looks like the ours from the outside, but a lot smaller. He and Rita lived there for their whole marriage.” Abby turned away, staring back down the road. “Let’s head back to the lodge.”

I took her hand in both of mine and rubbed it gently. “Sure thing.”

The deck of the lodge stretched out thirty feet or more, and when we went in, my eye was pulled upward into the expanse of the room. Two stairways went up to long hallways with a lofted area in between. I walked over to a floor-to-ceiling fireplace to warm my hands, then turned to warm my butt a little. Abby had made her way to the bar area on the other side of the room. I saw what could only be described at a sports bar area with TVs and a long counter. I walked to her, still looking up towards the second floor. “What’s up there?”

“The hallways lead to a few rooms, mostly suites. Bigger

than the ones on the first floor. In between is the game room."

"Cool. What do you have up there?"

"Not much. Just pool and ping pong and a few card tables." Abby walked towards me.

"Is that the kitchen?" I asked, looking under the loft to a large window with a counter below it.

An old, bearded man called out from the counter in front of the kitchen. "Hey girl!" The voice was low and thick. "Is this the special guy?"

Abby grabbed my hand and pulled me towards the kitchen. "That's Frank. I think you're going to love him." She had a skip to her step, and I could barely keep up. We followed Frank into the kitchen as he went to put something down on the make table. Abby watched me look around the space. I could feel her eyes on my back. What was she thinking? She never lost her gaze, and every time I caught a glance, she snickered and smiled at me.

Frank walked over and gave Abby a hug and then reached out his hand to me, giving me a firm, two-handed shake. I returned the gesture. "You got yourself a great girl here, young man."

"Yes...thank you...I think so," I stammered out, trying to look him directly in the eyes.

"I think he's a little overwhelmed," Abby said, walking over to me and squeezing my arm. She nuzzled into my neck and gave me a quick kiss. "What's for dinner tonight?"

"Well, darling," Frank said, shuffling back to his make table, "We have some venison steaks and the last of the lake perch you caught this summer. You and Taylor need to get out and catch me some fish this winter when the ice gets thick enough."

"She fishes?" I looked at Abby and then back to Frank. I was aware my voice just cracked.

"Oh yes. She's the only one who knows all the spots on the lake. She catches most of the fish we serve in the summer," Frank said with a sense of pride. "Of course, she had a pretty good teacher."

"The best, " Abby said, winking at Frank.

"Well, I heard you guys are eating at your place tonight," Frank said. "What's Vickie cooking?" He laughed at the last bit and began to work again at his table.

"Probably pizza," Abby replied. "That's her go-to right?" They smiled at each other knowingly. I realized Abby was right. There were a lot of things I didn't understand.

"We better get going, Frank." Abby walked over and gave him another hug.

"Hey, Craig," Frank called as we were almost out.

I turned, holding the door open. "Yes, sir."

"Come by later. After dinner. We can talk football and I can check you out. See if you're a good guy."

"Frank!" Abby yelled from the front room.

"I will, sir," I said and went out the door.

By the time dinner was ready, Abby's father and sister had returned from town. They had been in to get some deer meat that they had processed for a friend and purchased other supplies for the week. Abby made introductions, and both John and Taylor went to get changed.

Abby and I helped Vickie get the table ready and poured drinks for everyone. A fire crackled in the large fireplace in the corner of the room, and through the window, moonlight started to creep over the lake. I was surprised that I didn't feel nervous. When we sat down, Abby sat next to me, Taylor across from us, and John and Vickie at the ends. We had a simple meal of salad, homemade pizza, and garlic bread. It was cool that they weren't trying to show off. About halfway through dinner, John got up, went to the kitchen, and returned with a bottle of red wine and four glasses. "Who wants some wine?" He began to pour, and I looked at Abby. She nodded and gestured for a glass.

"So, Craig, Abby says you're pre-med?" John asked. "That must be busy."

I shifted to look at John. "Well not just yet, Mr. Whitworth, but I believe it will be soon." Abby ran her fingers zigzag down my back. I looked at her and smiled.

Leaning back from the table, John asked, "So, you'll be transferring to Madison?"

"That's the plan for now, sir." I patted Abby's thigh and then drew my hand back to the table quickly. "Plans can change though."

"It seems like a good plan. I'd stick with it," John responded. He moved forward and poured the rest of the bottle into his glass. "Shall we sit by the fire and get to know this young man, Vickie?"

"Yes. I think so." Vickie said. "The girls can do the dishes."

Abby got up immediately. Taylor lodged a brief protest and then relented. While cleaning up, I saw Abby watching me and her dad talk. Her father asked probing questions, and I could tell that he was good at getting to know people, kinda like my dad. I told stories Abby had heard before, and she finally focused on what she was doing. I felt free from her attention for a moment.

When Taylor and Abby finished, Taylor went off to her room while Abby joined the conversation. She smiled at her mother, who nodded her head. Vickie opened another bottle of wine for her and John. She came to sit by Abby and whispered loud enough for me to hear, "He's a very nice boy."

This made Abby smile. "I know," she responded.

That made me feel pretty good.

The night went on like this until John announced that he was going to go help Frank shut down the kitchen and tend the bar for a while. His normal evenings were shared with his extended family, the guests of the resort, but this evening had been a rare treat according to Abby. The holidays were never for their immediate family alone.

I asked if I might help, and John said yes. He told Abby and me to meet him in the lodge in fifteen minutes and instructed Abby to show me to Cabin #2.

"Why do we have him staying in a cabin?" Vickie asked as she began to put away the dried dishes.

"I thought the kid would be more comfortable with a little privacy," John replied. "He doesn't need us watching over him all week."

"True," Vickie said. "Better make sure he has what he needs, Abby."

"I turned the cabin over myself this morning," Abby responded. "I didn't know he was staying there, but I fully stocked it."

"Great," John said. "Get him situated, and I'll meet you at the lodge." He went to say goodnight to Taylor before heading out.

When Abby and I got outside, the air was cool and damp, and there were more stars than I had ever seen. I found myself just staring up. Abby waited for me at the entrance to the woods. I had only been here a few hours, but I was already beginning to love it.

I finally refocused and looked around for Abby. She had almost disappeared into the darkness of the trees. "Come on. Follow me," a voice said. I tried to follow her down the path, but I could barely see her ahead of me. She seemed to move by stealth while I stumbled and hit every root. Just like our walk in the afternoon, Abby was sure-footed and calm. She walked slowly and purposefully, only looking back to see if I was ok.

We went behind the lodge and over to the cabin. Abby grabbed a few pieces of wood from the pile on the side wall and got out her keys to open the front door. "It'll be a little cool in here. We have electric heaters, but they only kick in when the inside temp gets down to fifty degrees. We'll get a fire going and head to the lodge so it'll be all warm and cozy when you get back." Abby flipped on the light switch and put the wood in the fireplace. She went over to the bedroom and opened the door and turned on the light. "Put your stuff in here."

I was looking around again. I noticed that the main room had a log cabin style while the bedroom and bathroom had drywall. A small kitchenette with a sink, mini fridge, and microwave made up the wall to the left. The TV was on the wall next to the fireplace. The cabin had a cozy feel, certainly meant for one or two. The pictures hanging on the walls were familiar, and as I moved closer, I noticed that they were the same as some of the ones at Abby's house. "Are these your pictures too?" I asked.

"Yes," Abby said. "My dad has my photographs hung in all the cabins. I like taking pictures when I'm home."

"Why don't you take pictures at school?" I asked cheerfully.

Abby smiled and walked back into the bedroom. "Because it's not home."

I followed her and set my things down. She stood in front of me, and I reached for her to pull her closer. It was the first time we had really been alone. We kissed slowly, but I wanted to push it further. She gently pushed my hand away and said, "We should probably get to the lodge."

"I missed you,"

"I missed you too. Let's start a fire." Abby moved to the main room. "There are towels in the bathroom, and I suspect you can catch a snack in the lodge if you're still hungry." She knelt down to get the fire going.

"Are you going to come over tonight after we go to the lodge?" I asked.

"Not tonight, Craig," Abby said, not turning back toward me. "We have a full day tomorrow."

Over at the lodge, Frank had already closed down most of the kitchen, save for some pub grub items. He and John were tending the bar with some of the regular Thanksgiving crowd, who were planning the hunt for the next day. Deer season was a big deal around here.

"Hey, Craig, Abby," John called as we came in. "Come over and take a seat." Abby walked over and found an empty seat at the bar. I stood behind her. After greeting a few people and having a glass of water, Abby whispered to me, "I'm going back to the house. I'll get you up in the morning."

I was a bit startled. "Ah...ok..wait what?"

Abby patted me on the shoulder and gave me a squeeze. "I'll get you up around seven." She kissed my ear and was off. I watched her all the way out the door.

I was left with the men of the camp. There was a muted TV on with SportsCenter. Frank moved over to talk with me. "So Abby tells me you played football. I played back in the day."

We talked until late in the night. As I made my way back to the cabin, I felt tired, excited, and comfortable.

Chapter 14

At seven the next morning, I felt an ice cold set of hands crawling up my body, under my shirt. I was half awake, but this shocked me into consciousness. When I opened my eyes, I saw Abby. Her hair was pulled back, she was smiling, and her eyes were wide and alive. She bent down and kissed me gently on the lips. "Good morning, sleepy. You need to get up. We have a lot of work to do. Most of the Thanksgiving crowd comes tonight or tomorrow morning, and we need to have things ready."

I reached up and softly pulled her down onto the bed. I rolled on top of her and kissed her hard. Then, in a quick move, I rolled back over and out of bed. The air was cool as I ran off to the bathroom. Although I longed to stay in the warm bed with her and just fool around all morning, there was a part of me that wanted to get out and explore the resort more. I wanted to see what made everything go. I wanted to live what I had been hearing about every time our conversations drifted back to Abby's home.

I came out from the bathroom and jumped on top of Abby, pushing her down and pinning her. I kissed her and then popped up saying, "So, what are we going to do today?"

"First, we have to check requests for the cabins and get bedding and towels if needed. Then, we have to do final prep on the rest of the cabins. Frank might have some things for us to do as well," she responded.

"Seems like a lot." I rolled off and up. "Do I go throw a log on the fire before we go?"

"No." Abby said, getting up. "Turn on the electric for a bit. It probably won't even get that cold in here. We can start it up again tonight." Abby walked by and hit me hard on the butt. "Stick with me today. If we get going, we can have some fun later." She went out the door.

The day went as Abby had planned it, I think. She and I visited all the occupied cabins. We ran back and forth to the lodge more times than I could count, fetching things we needed or changing loads of laundry. I just followed Abby as she moved from place to place with an internal checklist I didn't follow. She seemed to know exactly what to do next without even giving herself time to think. I just did as I was told and never stopped moving.

After over two hours of following Abby around, John met us on the cabin road. "It's sure good to have you home, Abby." He gave her a half hug. "How's your little helper?"

I was carrying a load of towels so tall I could barely see around them. "He's keeping up so far," she responded.

"Mind if I borrow him for a bit?" John asked. "We're well ahead of schedule today."

"Sure." Abby took the towels from me. "What are you going to use him for?"

"I'll make use of his talents," John said with a wink.

I was a little scared of what he had in mind. I had been interrogated as the new boyfriend before, but somehow, this felt different. Instead of questioning me, John moved quickly through the wooded paths with the same proficiency as Abby. Not one step was out of place while he pointed to this or that in the same way Abby had done the afternoon before. I hung on every word as much as I could between slips and the occasional reach for a tree to catch my balance. John went on about the history of the place and how they came to buy this particular resort after visiting for a couple of years in the summer. Vickie had been reluctant he said, but she saw how relaxed it made him and how much joy Abby had running around as a toddler. She agreed it was an adventure they could never give their children if they remained in Chicago.

"Abby's a good girl," John said, turning back and laughing a little at my inability to keep my feet. "She wants to take over this place when she graduates. She's got her whole life planned. I don't know." We came out of the woods by the storage garage. "Vickie wants her to see the world and experience things." John took off his hat and wiped his forehead. "She's got a point, but what's out there that we don't have here? We make a living." He seemed to be talking to himself, but I responded anyway.

"I don't know what's out there, but this place seems more like home than anywhere I've ever lived," I said. There was a relaxed pace here. There were things to do, a rhythm to the work, but nothing that seemed to push against your life and made you feel pressured or rushed.

"Well, son," John said, picking up a large sledgehammer, "we have some chopping to do."

There was a loose pile of cut logs all between eight inches to a foot in diameter that needed to be split. "Now I could get one of those big splitters and make quick work of this, but where's the fun in that?" John placed a log up on a stump that rose a foot from the ground. He positioned a spike that looked like an oversized arrowhead in the center and tapped it in until it stayed upright on its own. He lifted the hammer over his shoulder, then above his head, and finally brought the hammer down on the spike and sunk it deep into the log. Another shot split the log completely, sending it falling in pieces to the ground around the stump. "That's how we do it. We use the wedge to make quick work of things."

I went and gathered the pieces and threw them in a trailer where I saw other split pieces stacked.

"We need to get wood for all the cabins up to the line painted on the sides. Then, we need extra wood for the lodge. We like to have a week's worth of wood set up. We turn the wood over every few months." John handed the sledge to me and turned to grab another log. "Give it a try. Just set the wedge and give her hell."

I reached down to grab the wedge. I placed it in the middle of the log John had put on the stump and tapped it into place. Then, I raised the sledge, grabbing it near the end of the handle and brought it down on the log. I hit the wedge with such force that is sunk deep into the log, sending pieces flying in all directions. I felt a rush as I saw the log explode. It felt good to do something physical.

"Lucky hit," John said, smiling. "Can you do that again?"

I set another log on the stump, set the wedge, and struck it. Again, it exploded, and I had to dance around the stump to avoid tripping. I looked at the pieces on the ground and bounced a little as I went around to pick them up.

"Good. Remember to pick up the wood in between and put it in the trailer."

I grabbed the pieces, stacked them in the trailer, then went back for another log.

"Do you think you could handle this?" John asked as he pointed at the loose pile of logs.

"Yes, sir," I responded. "You want it all done?" I was breathing heavily.

"Just fill the trailer. I'll send Abby over to show you where it goes. We'll see how much she needs." John started walking away and then turned. "Don't get cocky, kid," he said with a wink.

"No, sir."

I set to the task. I got into a rhythm of grabbing a new log, placing the wedge carefully, and driving it through. Occasionally, it would take two hits to drive the spike through, but more often, I struck it once, and the log shattered.

As I picked up the last of the logs I planned on hitting, I saw Abby. She was leaning against a tree, smiling.

"Hey you," I said. "How long have you been there?"

"For a while," she replied in a low, soft voice.

"Really?"

Grabbing my arm and running her other hand down my back, she said, "You look good. You look like you were enjoying yourself."

There was mist rising from my shirt and each breath produced its own cloud. "Yeah. It was fun. There's something about seeing your work get done, you know."

"I do."

"You know, sometimes I miss work like this."

"Chopping wood?"

"No. Work you can see."

"You mean like football?"

"Yeah. Sometimes. In a weight room, you can throw weights around or get on a machine, but you can't really see what you've done. On the field, either you go forward or back. You see what your work gets you after each play."

"You do miss it, don't you? I can tell sometimes."

"Yeah. It's hard to let go completely." I turned to the trailer. "Not bad huh?"

"Not bad," Abby agreed and squeezed me around the waist. "You're about half done. Now we have to put it away." She walked over by the four-wheeler. "You know how to drive one of these things?" Abby asked as she swung her leg over the seat.

"I drove one when my my dad and I went hunting," I said as I put on my sweatshirt and walked over.

"Get on," Abby said, smiling. "I'll drive." She turned the key.

I got on, and Abby started down the driveway. I grabbed her around the waist tightly. She felt warm in my arms.

After we got all the wood unloaded for the cabins, we went back to the pile. Abby watched as I split a dozen or so logs for the lodge. We delivered the load, this time with me driving carefully. Then, we went in to have a simple lunch in the kitchen with Frank.

"Should be a busy couple of days, huh girl?" Frank announced as we finished our lunch.

"That's fine," Abby replied. "Looking forward to seeing some old friends."

"Yeah," Frank said. "It's going to be a full house through Saturday from the sounds of it. Well, we'll get some good game today and tomorrow from the hunting. I got all the stuff we need for Thursday. Another Thanksgiving." He took in a very slow breath and released it deliberately. I could see how tired he was already. I could not yet conceive how something like this was going to get done.

"It's always fun." Abby said with enthusiasm.

"What are you young folks going to do with your afternoon?" Frank asked. "It's supposed to snow anytime."

"I thought I'd take Craig around the lake on the snowmobile, and then we might hit town to see Meghan before the day gets away from us."

"That's a good plan." Frank leaned over and squeezed Abby's shoulder and gave me a slap on the back. "You two have fun."

It was a enjoyable afternoon. I sat behind Abby as she showed me around the lake. Sometimes, we could be right up against the shore, while other times we needed to be on trails with the lake barely visible. Abby took us to a high point where we could see almost the whole lake. She took off her helmet and kissed me. I had been waiting for her to do that for most of the day. It was the best way for me to get lost in the moment with her. She had an energy being outside that was hard to describe. The change in her was addicting, and I wanted more of it. This is why I came up a day early. I wanted to be in any moment with Abby more than one more moment in my own house. I kissed her back. "This is quite a view," I said. "Is this where you took some of your pictures?" Before us, the lake was blanketed with snow, and there were two large holes of open water in the midst of the frozen lake. Pine trees were tipped with snow as far as we could see. The sky was a soft gray.

"It is," Abby said. She put her helmet back on. "It's going to snow soon. We should get back."

"Sure thing," I said, also putting on my helmet. "Let's go." I again put my arms around Abby's waist and held her tight. This was one of the most beautiful places I had ever been.

By the time we got back, it had begun to snow. Abby parked the snowmobile by the house. It was still a little warmer, so the falling snow was right for packing. I took advantage of Abby putting the helmets away to make a few snowballs. When she came out, I tagged her with one and then went to hide behind a tree.

Abby scooped up some snow and ran behind her own tree. I threw another snowball against the tree where she was hiding. She immediately tried to throw to where she thought I was, but I had moved. I hit her in the leg from a completely different direction. "Hey!" she yelped. Scooping up more snow, she made for another tree.

I came out with my arms up, making myself a target. "What?" I had a cocky smile. I had been in so many snowball fights, I knew all the tricks.

Abby hit me right in the chest and ran as I reached for more snow. Just as I came up, she hit me, shoulder to the chest, and drove me to the ground. She lay on top of me. "Gotcha."

I rolled her over, but she fought me off. As she got up, I caught her by her leg and tripped her. I scrambled to get on her, but she reversed me and pinned me hard to the ground. "Uncle!" I yelled, giving up too easily. Abby laughed as her hair fell over me. Snow melted off of her forehead as she moved to kiss me. I lay there and accepted her affection, feeling a rush of adrenaline so intense it almost hurt. After a few moments, I gently grabbed Abby's face, holding it above and away from mine. "I love you." The rush fell over me again. I thought, in that moment, that this is what love must feel like. I had never felt anything like it before.

“I love you too,” she responded and gave me a passionate kiss. Then, I pushed snow in her face and rolled to get up. She laughed and continued to lay on her back.

“Are you getting up?” I asked.

“No. I think I’ll just lay here for a while.”

In that moment, looking at Abby making a snow angel, filled with contentment, I knew I loved her, genuinely. I was finally there with her.

Part Three

Abby: 15, At Taylor's Soccer Game

I couldn't believe my mother let me sleep in just so I would miss fishing and have to go to Taylor's game. I needed to catch enough fish for Frank tonight so he could serve fresh instead of frozen. She must have come in and turned off my alarm. Shit, now I have to go to the game.

"Mom! Why did you turn off my alarm? I needed to go fishing, and I also have cabins to turn today for Sunday arrivals." I had no interest in hiding my annoyance. I walked into the kitchen.

"I thought it would be nice for you to see Taylor play. You've missed all of her other games for 'work,'" she said with her famous air quotes. Taylor was at the table eating her breakfast, so I couldn't be too mean.

"Fine. I'll get dressed. When are we leaving?"

"In about twenty minutes, dear. Don't forget to eat something," she said.

I didn't really want to fight it further, but I was pissed. There was work to do around the resort, and my mother always tried to sabotage it. I got dressed and grabbed two pancakes for the road. It was a quiet ride.

We set up our chairs on the sidelines. My mom has been trying to drag me to these games all season so I could show my support for my sister. Not sure why I would want to watch that brat, but whatever. Taylor's what my mom wishes I would have been. Sporty. Mom played soccer, volleyball, basketball, and whatever else growing up down in Chicago. I played volleyball last year, my freshman year, but I quit because there was always so much to do around the resort. Mom hates that I work all the time. "Be a kid. Hang out with your friends." Why? I want to work. It's not like Dad doesn't need the help.

"Will you get off that phone? You're burning through our data," Mom said about halfway through the first half.

"What else am I supposed to do? Besides, I'm just texting friends. I'm not on the internet. You think I'm that stupid?" I didn't look up.

"Oh. Well, you should watch your sister."

"Why?"

"Because that's the nice thing to do," she said, staring at me.

"Her team is up 2-1, and Taylor had an assist. See, I'm watching."

"Well, why do you need to be so snarky about it?"

"Because I don't want to be here, Mom. I need to be working."

"You and your work. What's so important that it can't wait? Enjoy your life. Be a kid for God's sake."

"I had to catch some fish for Frank for dinner tonight, and three families are leaving today with three more coming in tomorrow. The cabins need to be flipped."

"Your father can do that. Besides, it's way too hot to catch anything today."

"You're right about the last part. That's why I should've been out on the water already. I would be coming in now."

The whistle blew for the end of the first half. Taylor came over to get her extra water. "Did you see me Abby? Abby, I'm doing good." She was damn cute in her braided pigtails, but I wasn't fooled.

"I did see you, Tay. You're great. Now score a goal for me in the second half," I said, smiling at her ten-year-old enthusiasm for life. It was kinda catchy in the moment.

"Ok," she called as she ran off. I heard her shout at her coach, "Abby wants me to score a goal, Coach. Can I play forward again?"

I went back to my phone. Meghan and I were trying to get plans together to go out tonight with some other friends. I can't wait until I get my license next year so my parents don't need to drive me everywhere.

"Mom," I said loudly. "Can I go out for pizza tonight with Meghan and some other friends?"

She stared straight ahead, seemingly thinking about her next move, but then said, "Sure, honey. But don't you have a lot of 'work' to do?" There are those damn air quotes again. They are supposed to piss me off, but I don't let her gain an edge.

"Like you said, it'll be too hot to fish when I get home this afternoon. We'll just have to use frozen. I can go out tomorrow morning. I'll get right on the cabins when I get home."

"Ok," she said, although she seemed to be thinking. I just set up a scenario that allowed me to skip church, but she didn't figure it out. "You and your father and that damn resort. Always work, work, work!"

"I like the work, Mom."

"What fifteen-year-old girl likes the work?"

"This one," I said. "I can't see what else I would ever want to do."

"Oh, you will when you get out of here for a while."

"Not likely."

I put my phone in my pocket and sat back to watch the game.

Taylor really is good. She's got footwork and speed. I don't like skipping work to come here, but Taylor's love of life is undeniable. My mom thinks if I don't play sports, I'm going to get lazy. Not sure how she came to that conclusion given that I carry shit all around the resort all day. Besides, my dad won't let me take the motorboat out by myself yet, so I have to canoe everywhere on the lake. He said if I do a good job this summer, he'll get me my own boat. That's part of the reason I'm working so hard. I love helping out, but if I can get a boat, I can go anywhere. I wish my mom could see that.

Taylor was playing defense, but she got a good run and did a give-and-go with her friend to score her goal. I've seen them practice that play at home. My dad set up a net for the guests, but I always guessed it was for Taylor.

After the game, Taylor ran up to me screaming, "Abby! Abby! I scored a goal."

I caught her in my arms, lifted her off the ground, and put her down again. "You sure did, girl. Nice job." We gave each other a high five.

"Can I go fishing with you this afternoon?" Taylor asked.

"Sure. When I'm done with my work." I knew I was lying to her, but what could it hurt?

Chapter 15

Craig left to take a shower and change after the snowmobile adventure. Abby did the same. Almost as soon as she got out of the shower, her mother was on her. "You're going to take Taylor to the Dome so she can go skating with her friends. Be home by nine." There was no room for argument.

"But, Mom, we're going to meet Meghan and some others. I don't want to be home at nine." Abby tried even though it was a losing battle.

"You have to be up early anyway. No buts! You're taking your sister, and that's it."

Abby went in her room to get dressed. She had had such a perfect day. It was just like her mom to ruin stuff. Her mother had been at work and was just taking it out on her. There was so much to do around the resort and going into school was just another thing added to her list. At these times of the year, she was annoying, but it wasn't all bad. Abby knew that if it wasn't for her mother, she would never have gone to Whitewater, and she would not have met Craig. Her mom pissed her off, but she also had a way of being right most of the time. Abby heard Craig come in, so she hurried to finish getting ready.

"Hi, Craig," Vickie said loudly. "Come in the kitchen."

Craig walked down to the kitchen and stood, almost at

attention, waiting for Vickie to continue.

"You guys are going to town tonight?" Vickie asked.

"Yeah," Craig responded. "I guess that's the plan."

"Good! You're going to take Taylor to the Dome so she can skate with her friends and then be home by nine. We have a busy couple of days coming up."

"Sounds good to me," Craig said with a smirk, realizing how annoyed Abby was going to be with the arrangement.

Abby came up behind him and poked him in the side.

Craig jumped. "Hey!"

Vickie laughed.

The ride to town was uneventful. Taylor talked the whole time, and Abby responded just enough to act interested. Craig noticed how dark it was at six in the evening. The headlights and occasional reflective mailbox stickers were the only lights. Even out where he lived, the ambient light from the houses and streetlights was enough to see your surroundings. Here, like the silence of the night before, the darkness was striking.

After dropping Taylor off, Abby and Craig went to Butch's for pizza and to meet Meghan. There were other people there Abby knew, and she introduced Craig before finding a place to sit. They sat down and Meghan started in, "So, I see you made it back from Madison without any marks." She was looking squarely at Craig. He tried to look away, but her stare was penetrating him.

"Yeah. I guess I did." Craig returned the stare. "Looks like you made it out too."

Meghan laughed, releasing the false tension of the moment. "I suppose."

Abby and Meghan began to catch up as Craig sat back. He looked around the place and decided that it wasn't that much different than the small, family-owned pizza places around Hartland. Craig hoped the pizza was as good as Doc's Dry Dock in Pewaukee. That place was a bit of drive, but their pizza was one thing he and his father could agree on every time. The smell of it lingered in your car for days, making you want more.

Their pizza arrived, and Craig ate thoroughly. The plan was to have some left to bring home because Butch's pizza was John's favorite, but he ate more than his share, and the tray was soon empty. The work of the morning and adventure of the afternoon had made him hungry.

Craig excused himself to go to the bathroom, and Meghan seized on the moment, "So, how's Craig getting along with John and Vickie?"

"He's doing fine," Abby responded. "He's like the son my dad never had, and my mom's been nicer to him than she is to me. Frank likes him too."

"Well, that's good. Frank's the key." Meghan took her last nibble of the pizza.

"I think my mom likes him because he's not from around here." Abby looked at Meghan, waiting for an answer.

"She's a pill," Meghan replied. "But she means well, Abby. You know that."

"I guess." But this didn't satisfy her. She wanted Meghan to tell her that her mother was full of crap. She wanted her to confirm that her plan to come back and take over the resort when her parents retired was the right decision. But Abby knew Meghan was ready to fly from this place as strongly as she desired to return to it. These pinewood walls would always be enough for her. Why would she want more?

Abby saw Craig come out of the bathroom. He was beckoned by some of her friends whom she had introduced him to earlier, and she watched as he integrated into the group. He leaned on the side of the booth, using his other arm to animate what he was saying. Abby couldn't hear him, but his smile and the engaged laughter from her friends made her a bit jealous. Craig could talk with anyone about any topic. People liked him immediately. It was part of what attracted her to him initially. He could lock into her as though she was the only person in the room, but he could do that with anyone. She knew he was hers, but in instances like these, she had to share him.

"Earth to Abby," Meghan said, waving her hand in front of Abby's face. "I know he's good-looking, but you don't need to stare."

Abby turned her attention back to Meghan. "He can talk to anybody," she said out loud. "He's just like my dad."

"Whoa!" Meghan said, straightening up a bit. "Is that a good thing?"

"You know what I mean," Abby shot back, shaking her head.

"I do," Meghan reassured her. "He's good. Seems to have the gift."

Abby looked back at Craig. "He does."

Craig gave a little wave in Abby's direction and winked at her. Then, he pulled up a chair and sat down with her friends to continue talking. Abby knew he was giving her time to talk with Meghan, and she appreciated him even more for the gesture. Meghan and Abby went over their plans for break, discussed their finals schedules, and made plans to go skiing at Whitecap on Friday.

Craig came back over after about twenty minutes. "Nice people. They said they were going skiing on Friday and invited us to come along." His smile was wide and alive as he squeezed into the booth next to Abby.

"We're already planning to go," Abby responded.

"Oh, sounds good," Craig said. "Are we going to Indianhead?"

"No. We're going to Whitecap."

Meghan nodded in agreement. "Less people, more local, cooler runs. Not as big, but the skiing is better."

"Fine by me," Craig said. "When do we need to pick up Taylor?" He looked at the time on his phone.

"Eight forty-five," Abby responded.

They cleaned up their table and went out to pick up Taylor. The snow was really coming down by now. Craig paused on the way to the car to try to catch a snowflake on his tongue. Abby laughed.

Taylor talked a mile a minute from the moment she got in the car. This time, Craig listened to her and actually paid attention so that Abby could focus on driving. Craig saw how tightly Abby gripped the wheel. The darkness was alluring to Craig in its aboluteness, but the snow-covered roads were nobody's friend.

They got home just after nine. When they went inside, there was a fire burning, and Vickie was sitting in her chair with a book in one hand and a glass of wine in the other. She put the wine down on the table next to the chair, turned to the kitchen, and lowered her glasses. "How was your time, girls?"

Taylor took over the conversation while pouring herself a glass of milk and grabbing a piece of banana bread. Craig went to warm his hands by the fire, but Abby silently waved him back to the hallway.

"Let's go over to the lodge and get out of here," she said. Craig went with her down the hall, and Abby called out, "Going to the lodge, Mom. Be back later."

"Ok," Vickie responded. "Don't be out too late. Lots to do tomorrow."

"Sure thing," Abby yelled. She was already out the door and in the snow.

There wasn't much going on at the lodge. Abby went to talk with Frank while he closed down the kitchen, and Craig talked with John. John was telling some guests at the bar about Craig's ability to "blow up" logs, and Craig obliged by giving a little flex. In short order, Abby came back, and they walked to Craig's cabin.

When they got there, they lit a fire and made out for a while.

Abby enjoyed how gentle Craig was with her. He had a tender way of touching her that made her feel special.

Craig loved everything about Abby. She was soft and intense. He felt that she was always present, there with just him. She was constantly in the moment.

After a while, Abby and went into the bathroom. When she came back, Craig had moved to the bedroom and was reading his book. He had hoped to have time over break to read, but other than the first night at home, he hadn't gotten as far as he would have liked. Tomorrow promised to be busy too. He had no clue what the day held for him, but from the sounds of it, he would have no free time. Craig looked up and noticed Abby had her hair down. He loved the way she tossed it from side to side and over her head. She moved slowly and naturally.

"We have a lot to do tomorrow?" he asked.

"Yeah," Abby replied softly as she sat next to him on the bed. "Frank likes to have most of the food prep done before we go to bed, and every room is booked tomorrow through Saturday. It's going to be quite a feast. We have to get the dining area prepped and make sure all of the cabins are good to go."

"No problem," Craig said. "Just tell me how I can help."

"Thanks." Abby leaned over to kiss him. Craig grabbed a bunch of her hair and ran his fingers through it. She stood up. "Got to be up early tomorrow, so I'm going to get going. Want me to get the light?"

"No," Craig said. "I'm going to read for a while."

"Ok. I'll see you in the morning."

"You bet. Good night."

Abby left without telling Craig that she loved him. Something about being the first to say it made her freeze. She assumed Craig was way too distracted to notice, but she couldn't be sure. Maybe this afternoon was just the rush of the moment. She didn't know.

Craig tried to return to the mountains of western Montana and the sense of place that was being rendered in the book, but he soon fell asleep.

About an hour later, the door quietly opened and shut as soft footsteps hurried to get out of the cold. Abby hung her coat by the door and dusted the fresh snow from her hair, trying to be quiet. Before going into the bedroom, where she noticed the lamp was still on, she threw two logs on the fire. She went into the bedroom and undressed down to her underwear and a cotton T-shirt. Craig was lying under the covers on his back with the book resting open on his chest. She removed the book and switched the lamp off before crawling under the covers with him. Craig woke startled. "Shhh," Abby said as she reached for his face. She kissed him gently on the cheek. "It's just me." She continued to his lips. Craig turned toward her and kissed her back.

"Won't your parents know you're gone?" he asked. "What about your dad?"

"I'll worry about them, not you," Abby responded. "Craig." Her voice took on a serious tone. "Why do you think they put you in a cabin? They knew I would sneak over. They just don't want anything going on in their basement."

"Oh," Craig said cautiously. "You think?"

"Don't worry," Abby said more playfully this time. "It's fine. Trust me." She rolled to face away from him, hoping he would snuggle up and hold her.

Craig sensed exactly what she wanted and put his arm over her. "The covers in the cabins are so warm," Abby said. "I just love them."

Craig slowly moved his thumb and index finger across Abby's stomach where her shirt rode up slightly. They got comfortable, and he started to fall asleep again.

Just as he drifted off, Abby turned her head halfway toward Craig. She spoke quietly, almost a whisper. "Craig."

"Yes," he responded in a sleepy voice.

"Did you ever do anything with Jen?"

"What do you mean?" Craig replied softly, but he was now fully awake.

"Did you ever...sleep with her?"

"No...we never did that," he said quickly. He could feel that he was shaking a little, and his heart was beating hard.

“Then, I’ll be your first?”

“Yes,” he responded meekly, then kissed her ear gently.

“I love you,” Abby said confidently.

“I love you too,” Craig said.

Abby grabbed his hand with her fingers intertwined in his and pulled it to her chest. She kissed his fingers, then nuzzled her body back into his and held tightly. Within minutes, they fell asleep.

Craig: 18, Prom night with Jen

"So, are we going to the hotel with everyone, or do you have something else in mind?" I asked.

"Why would we go to the hotel, Craig?" Jen said without looking at me.

"What do you mean?" I glanced at her, keeping my eyes on the road.

"Why would we go to a hotel? I've been trying to get you to sleep with me for months, and you always come up with a reason not to."

"I guess I'm just scared, Jen."

"You can stop saying the right things all the time, you know. You're not scared. You just aren't that into me. I've known it for a while now."

I pulled off the road into a parking lot and turned off the car. She was right, but it still came as a shock. "What are you talking about?"

"Come on, Craig. We hang out and talk, but you're not interested. I do all the talking, and half the time you're not even looking at me."

"So are we breaking up?"

Jen sat quietly in the passenger seat, looking out the window. "I think that would be best. Listen, you're a good friend, but this isn't working."

Secretly, I was relieved. I had not been into us since fall, but didn't have the guts to say anything. How do you break up with the hottest girl in school? "Ok. I guess." I tried to sound casual.

"Can you just take me home?"

Chapter 16

When Abby woke up the next morning, Craig wasn't there. She was tucked in tightly and didn't want to get out, knowing how cold the cabins were in the morning. When she finally got the courage to roll over and emerge, there was a note:

Good morning, sleepy,
I got up to get to work.
Hope you slept well.
See you soon,
Love, Craig
P.S. I threw some logs on the fire
so you wouldn't be so cold.

Abby pulled back the covers, and the warmth of the room made her smile. Suddenly, she remembered she was going hunting today. She quickly got up and dressed, then ran to the lodge to grab a bite to eat. Frank and her father were standing on the deck, which had obviously been shoveled off. Then, she looked back and realized the path from the cabins to the lodge had also been cleared. About five to six inches of snow had fallen that night. The cool morning created a wonderland of snow falling from the trees and a pure, white-washed landscape.

Abby stopped. “What are you looking at?”

John spoke first. “It seems your boyfriend got up early and shoveled all the paths and front entrances to all the cabins with a shovel he found on the deck.” He pointed down the road to the cabins. “Now he’s shoveling off the road.”

Abby saw Craig at the end of the road. He had made a path down the center of it and was pushing the snow off to either side.

“Do you think we should tell him that Tim comes over later to plow, or should we let him get started with the parking lot?” Frank asked with a chuckle. John joined him in the laughter.

“Dad!” Abby said.

“Don’t worry. We’ll let him finish the road and then tell him.” John turned to his daughter. “Weren’t you going hunting this morning? It’s getting late.”

“Oh yeah.” Abby ran off towards the house. She was happy her dad didn’t say anything about her staying in the cabin last night. When she got to her house, her mother just greeted her as normal. She laughed to herself thinking about how Craig would react to her going out hunting and knew he would be surprised. She went to get dressed.

After John finally informed Craig that there was a guy coming to plow, he told him to come over to the house. Craig was nervous because he thought John and Vickie were going to ask him about Abby sleeping over the night before. He figured Abby had already been home, so the blow may have been softened. He returned the shovel to the lodge’s deck and headed to the house.

The garage door was open, and when Craig peeked in, John was there with an orange snowsuit in his hands. He had an orange coat on and a matching hat. "See if this fits." He threw the suit at him. "We're going over to the other land for a bit where some other people are hunting."

Craig started to put on the suit, and John continued, "Have you ever been hunting, Craig?"

"I went with my father a few times," Craig replied. "We never really got anything. It was more for the experience."

John climbed into the truck. "Well, it's a little late, so that's about all we'll be doing today. How's that fit?"

Craig zipped up the suit. "It works. Have you seen Abby?" He got into the passenger seat.

"No more than you," John said, giving Craig a little pat on the shoulder. He laughed to himself as he shook his head. "I think she's already out scouting." John pulled out onto the road. "We only have the morning. It's all hands on deck in the kitchen this afternoon. Frank likes to have everything ready to go for tomorrow. He runs the show for the next two days."

"Well, I'll do whatever I can to help, sir," Craig said.

"We'll find something for you to do," John replied. "No worries there."

As they drove out to the forty acres, Craig asked lots of questions about the resort. He wanted to know again why they bought it. What it really took to run the place. How much planning it took to put on big events like a holiday or wedding. On and on…

John seemed to be happy to answer any question, so Craig kept on asking. He hung on every answer, and the time went quickly. When they got to the land, they first came upon a little fenced in parking area where Vickie's truck was parked, along with a few others. Beyond the small field, the woods stretched as far as Craig could see.

"Here's the homestead. There's a small creek running through the middle of it. Vickie and I are thinking of building a cabin out here when we retire. But for now, there's just a few deer stands and a bench by the creek for fishing."

Craig got out of the truck and picked up some equipment John had begun putting on the ground, including an empty cooler. John threw a gun over his shoulder and picked up another cooler. "What are the coolers for?" Craig asked.

"I got a text telling me to bring them out," John said, looking towards the woods with a smile. "We'll see."

They went into the woods, following a path through the snow that had already been worn in. Craig could not believe that Abby had already been out. He had gotten up early, so she must have followed him soon after. They snaked their way through the woods and came upon a scene Craig did not expect. A deer, the biggest one he had ever seen in person, was hanging from a tree. A rope was around its head, and the body hung down. There was a cut down the belly, and a pile of entrails and blood below.

John put the cooler down. "Nice kill, Abby." He approached the deer and walked around it.

Craig couldn't believe it. He dropped his cooler and looked at the deer.

Abby gave her father a hug and looked at Craig, who stood motionless with his mouth open. "You shot that deer?" Craig asked her.

She walked over by him, still holding a knife. Snow fell from the surrounding treetops as the wind blew above them.

Deep in the woods, the wind didn't even reach the ground.

"Yep," Abby said. "She's a beauty." She smiled to herself.

"But..." He was having a difficult time expressing his feelings. "So you did...wait," he stammered. "You hunt?"

"Of course I hunt. I fish and hunt. Most of what we eat at the resort is locally sourced. Who do you think gets all of it?"

Craig looked at Abby and then the deer and then back at her. "But...you gutted it and everything."

She nodded her head. "Yes. It needed to be done. Now that you and Dad are here, we can get it cut up and into the coolers. We can't leave it here. Frank said he wanted some fresh game, so here it is." Abby walked back towards her kill.

John had cleared the last few things out and was wiping the insides with handfuls of snow. "We've got to skin this thing and get it chopped up. Frank's on his way. We got Vickie to handle lunch so we can get this thing out, so he should be here shortly."

Still somewhat shocked, Craig said, "Are we going to be eating this thing tomorrow?"

"We might have some for dinner tonight," Abby responded. "Most of it we'll pack away and let it age for a while. Frank might smoke some of it."

Craig had no idea. He was sure Abby had mentioned hunting, but he couldn't remember. Maybe she hadn't. He watched as she walked back to her father to help skin the deer. Craig was in awe at the ease with which she handled the knife. It almost made him sick to look at the puddle of blood and pile of body parts laying on the ground. Instead, he focused on Abby.

Frank came whistling down the path with another cooler and a sled. He caught Craig's eye and walked over to him. He put his arm around him, saying, "She's a beauty."

"She sure is," Craig said quietly.

Frank turned his head towards Craig and said, "I was talking about the deer, kid." He chuckled.

Craig looked at him cockeyed and shook his head.

"Well let's get this thing carved up and back home." He chuckled. "Vickie handling lunch? I think not. Going to be up all night at this rate." Frank took over for John, and he and Abby started carving up the deer.

"Let's go for a walk, Craig," John said, putting his gun back over his shoulder. They left Abby and Frank and walked deeper into the woods. When they got to a tree stand near the creek, they stopped. John took the gun off his shoulder. "We're not going to see much I don't think. Too late in the morning. Besides…" He took a deep breath. "...deer aren't dumb animals." He took his hat off and rubbed his forehead. "She's quite an outdoorswoman."

"Seems so," Craig responded. He sensed that John was trying to have a moment, so he did his best to stay engaged, but he couldn't get the image of Abby standing with bloody pants and a knife out of his head.

"Let's go sit on the bench over there," John said. Craig followed, and they sat down. He watched the water bubble by between the ice and snow.

"I worry sometimes," John continued. "I worry, cause I know Abby wants to take on more responsibilities at the resort when Vickie retires." He turned to look directly at Craig. "I raised Abby outside in the way I wish I had been raised, you know. Taylor is Vickie's girl through and through, but Abby's tied to this place." He paused.

"You mean to the resort, sir?" Craig asked.

"The resort, the lake, the whole thing, you know? She's so tied to the land, but you need to be a people person. To run this place, you need to know people. That's not her gift." John spoke slowly. Craig could tell he was thinking about every word.

"She's great, Mr. Whitworth."

"I know that. She's my daughter." He chuckled. "I'm glad she met you. Vickie is too. You're a good kid, and it's clear she really cares for you." He paused and looked up at the surrounding trees. "Take care of her for us, Craig. Look after her. We know she misses home, but she needs to see more of the world. You know what I mean?" John was speaking more rapidly now, and his face was getting red.

"I will. I care for her a lot too."

John reached over and patted Craig's knee. "I know you do, son. I know you do." They sat for some time watching the last of the flakes fall from the trees. "We better get going. We have lots to do."

When they got back to the resort, Craig was happy to be released from an almost silent car ride. It seemed John had said too much, and Craig sensed he was afraid to say more. He took off the snowsuit and thanked John for the morning, quickly running off to take a shower before he had to report to Frank in the kitchen. When he got out, Abby was waiting for him with a sandwich, some fruit, and a Mellow Yellow. "Thought we might have a little bite to eat alone before the crowd and work sets in. There are just so many people. You can't imagine."

Craig had only a towel around his waist, but he had lost all pretense with Abby. He simply turned his back, dropped the towel, and began to look for clothes in his bag.

Abby watched him the whole time. Craig was thin, but his body was ripped. He put on underwear and turned to walk towards her. She liked it when he came towards her. He was hers, and it made her feel special that he was so comfortable around her. He winked and walked past her into the bathroom. When he emerged, he had jeans on, but still no shirt. His abs cut into his body, and Abby always assumed from the definition of his chest that he could do push-ups until someone told him to stop. He gave her a quick smile and sat down to eat his food. "Are we helping Frank the rest of the day?" he asked between bites.

"That's the plan. He thinks he'll be up half the night getting everything done, but he says that every year. I think we'll get done by nine or ten. I just want everything to run smoothly," Abby said as she got up to walk around the room. She set her sandwich down and started to make the bed.

"I can do that," Craig said.

"No," Abby replied, pulling the covers tight on one side and walking around to the other. "You eat. This is just force of habit. I've made a few beds in my short time on earth. This won't be the last."

"When did your dad start making you help around the resort?" Craig asked.

"He never really made me. Middle school, I guess. I was always hanging around, and it just kinda happened." Abby pounded one of the pillows. "I was never forced. If I had other things to do, I did them. It just ended up that the work was what I had to do most of the time. Taylor plays sports, so she does a lot less around here than I did at her age."

"You like the routine of it though, right?"

“For the most part. Sometimes it gets boring, and other times, the big events can be nerve-wracking.” Abby finished the bed and sat down on the end of it, grinning.

“Like tomorrow?” Craig said as he got up to find a shirt.

“Yeah. There’s just so many people. It’s a really nice party, but it’s difficult to always be the ones putting it on.” She stood up and hugged him before he put on his shirt. He was always so warm. Craig hugged her back tightly. Then, she let go, saying, “We better get going.”

Craig could tell something was not quite right, but he supposed it was just the long day that was ahead, so he didn’t press. He finished getting dressed, and they were off to the kitchen.

Abby was right about Frank. He wanted everything ready. Pies baked in the ovens. Veggies needed to be washed and cut. Endless bags of potatoes had to be peeled and cut. He had several large turkeys, each prepared differently, two of which Abby had shot. There was venison to marinade. Condiment containers to fill. The list on the freezer door was down to the floor. They would be serving close to a hundred people by the end of the day, including the people from town who usually joined the guests already there. There would be fifty to sixty formally for dinner.

They worked through supper, eating only two venison steaks cut from Abby’s deer so Craig could taste them. He thought they were close to the best thing he had ever had. That made Abby happy. The work was done around ten, and Frank decided to close the kitchen for the day. Getting through the dinner rush along with prep had been a bit much for him, and Abby wondered how many more years he had left. Although he had been doing it for so long and tired easily, he didn't seem to know any other way of living.

Craig and Abby went to the bar to say goodnight to John and Vickie, whom Abby was surprised to see were still there. Vickie was drinking wine with some Chicago friends and catching up. These women had been coming for so many years, they seemed like family. Abby greeted them like aunts and introduced Craig, who looked dead on his feet, but still managed to be charming. They said goodnight again and walked off towards the cabin.

When they got there, Abby decided to take a shower. She had brought stuff over that afternoon to change into. Craig washed his hands and face. Looking in the mirror, he saw Abby's silhouette in the fogged-up shower and was intrigued, but too exhausted to pursue any flirtation. He figured going to bed was the better choice. There was no energy to find clothes, so he stripped to his underwear and got into bed. When Abby came to bed, Craig rolled over to spoon her, and she turned her head to kiss him.

"Thanks for all your help today," Abby said quietly.

"No problem, babe," Craig replied. He let out a long breath.

Abby realized he was already asleep. It didn't take her too long to join him.

Abby: 4, Earliest memory of the resort.

"This is all ours, Daddy? All ours?" I asked, looking at the woods and lake and lodge.

He knelt down and spoke calmly in his deep voice, "All ours, honey."

I took off down the path and ran towards the lake. My mother hustled after as my dad talked to the big man who met us in the lot. I think his name was Frank. I ran to the dock and stopped. Then, I ran to the end of the dock and jumped into the lake. My mom had to jump in after me to fish me out. At least that's how my dad tells the story. My mom just remembers being wet.

Chapter 17

The morning was a blur of food prep and decoration. The guests seemed to know that lunch was the primary meal so only a few came down for breakfast. Frank was in his element, and everyone simply executed his commands without question, even Taylor. Craig did simple, labor-intensive jobs, mashing potatoes and moving tables. He barely saw Abby, who seemed to drop into a routine all her own.

Abby watched Craig when she had a chance. She was proud of how he took to the work. He never once complained and always looked for more to do or someone to help. It was really remarkable. It was as though he had a vested interest in the resort. At times, she caught herself staring until Frank would call her back or her dad would send her to fetch something or other. She knew how much planning went into these days and how important it was to her father that they seemed like laid-back affairs. From her point of view, they were anything but. This was the first year in some time that Abby had not been involved in the details of the planning. Vickie had recruited Taylor to help with decorations, and a few of the Chicago friends had come to help as well. The expectations were high, as well as the tension. This was no longer the playtime it had been when Abby was younger. There were no small tasks punctuated by hanging out with cousins or distant friends. Abby felt, for the first time since publicly declaring her intention to take over the resort in a few years, that this was her dinner. She had been given the responsibility of hosting, and she felt the pressure.

Craig and Abby were food runners, which at most restaurants would not be that important of a job; however, the resort served the big meals family-style with a backup buffet. They had to be sure that everyone had enough food on their table at all times as well as mingle and chat with guests. John would be at the bar and Vickie at the head table, leading prayers and directing the courses. Taylor could still play with her friends and cousins.

Craig was impressed with the efficiency of the setup. The room was decorated beautifully in orange and brown tablecloths and colorful turkeys that Vickie's students had made out of paper. Candles adorned each table and were scattered on shelves around the room. The fire was raging. Everything was set.

Frank was a pro, and it was clear that his direction came from a sense of habit in having done this for years. The tiredness of the night before had been replaced by a man, sturdy and ready to serve. Craig had come to respect Frank immensely in the short time he had known him. Frank was the wizard behind the curtain.

Guests arrived, prayers were said, and dinner was served. The din of conversation was like Craig's basement on steroids. He had been at weddings before, but the conversations and mingling were always interrupted by toasts and dancing. This was altogether different. The place seemed a bit small for the number, but adequate for the job. It took him a while to begin to recognize what food needed replacing. Abby often tapped him on the shoulder and pointed, saying what needed to be done or what table to go to next. It was dizzying to start, but he began to pick it up.

Abby again found herself watching Craig whenever she had a moment. Having introduced him to a few relatives and old family friends, she saw that those were the tables he seemed to gravitate to and linger at a bit longer. However, he held court well. At times, she had to keep him moving. She was envious of the ease he had in talking with people. Hosting was in Craig's wheelhouse. After a while, it annoyed her that she was doing most of the running while he was doing most of the hosting. Abby caught some of the conversations. He talked about football, the weather, and what a nice place the resort was. It was as though he had lived here all his life. In the end, she was caught between annoyance and jealousy and couldn't decide which one would win.

The time of dinner service stretched over an hour. Finally, people started to go to the buffet rather than calling Craig or Abby over to get this or that. The football games came on the TVs, and the bar became the center of the room. Some people went to their rooms while others lingered, and some family members began to help with the clean up and dishes. Craig helped rearrange the tables. A large crowd gathered along the wall opposite the bar to watch the projection screen of the game, and many of the children went up to the game room. The buffet and pies would be available all afternoon and into the evening. The room began to settle down.

In the midst of the post-dinner confusion, Craig noticed that Abby seemed to be missing. After asking around and checking in the kitchen, he decided to go over to her house to see if she had gone to lie down. Craig went outside and chose a path along the lake to get to the house. The day was damp and cloudy. There was a chill in the air, but one could get used to it if need be. As he went down the shoreline, he saw someone sitting on a bench at the end of the permanent dock. It was Abby. Her hair was down, swaying in the light breeze. She was slumped down, staring out at the lake. He stayed off the dock for a minute, just looking at her. This was her home, and she looked a part of it. She knew every turn in the shore and every tree along it. There was a longing in his heart to know any place like she knew this one. The desire to be a part of somewhere he could truly call home filled him in that moment. There was a feeling of being part of the event this afternoon, but knew it wasn't his event. His love for this place was growing, but it was not his home. Maybe someday it could be, and he would be the one behind the bar.

Abby saw him. She wasn't sure she wanted to talk to him, but she reached her arm up to beckon him down to the bench. Craig waved back and skipped onto the deck, almost slipping on the ice. He walked carefully the rest of the way. Abby laughed at the sight of her nimble man being such a klutz.

"Hey there," Craig said as he sat down. "You disappeared on me." She felt his hand reach for hers and grabbed it tightly, holding it in her lap, then leaned her head on his shoulder. A gentle wind blew across the quiet lake, and the white plain stretched out before them. The open water holes were a bit smaller than the day Craig had arrived, and there were a few ice houses visible on the shoreline waiting to be taken out.

Abby let out a breath. "Glad that's over," she said.

"Yeah. That was a lot of work," Craig agreed.

"There were just too many people," she continued. She lifted her head to look right at Craig. "I've never worked the whole meal from the front before. I've always been able to escape to the kitchen if things got too busy."

Turning to meet her eye, he responded, "I didn't mind the people so much. There was just a lot to keep in your mind."

"You seemed to get along just fine," Abby said, turning her body to Craig. She had been crying. Craig took his free hand and rubbed his thumb beneath her eyes, then rubbed the back of his hand over her smooth cheek. She nuzzled into his chest. "You're so warm."

"What's wrong, Abby?" He leaned in to kiss her forehead and pushed her hair back behind her ear. "Are you tired?"

"No. That's not it. I'm just…" She paused and looked down at her lap.

Craig gently pulled her head back up to face his and met her eye to eye. "What's wrong? Tell me, please."

"It's just that you're so good...my dad and you, my mother... you're all so good."

"Good at what?" Craig asked, now concerned. He didn't like seeing Abby so sad. She was home. She was in her element. He couldn't figure out why she was so upset.

"You're good with people," she finally responded. "I'm just too shy."

"What are you talking about?" Craig said with a little laugh. "You're great." He took his hand free from her hands and put it around her shoulder. "You were talking to all kinds of people."

"I introduced you to lots of people and asked if I could get them something. I wasn't actually chatting them up. I just can't.

I mean, what do you talk about anyway?" She wasn't as upset as she was concerned.

"I don't know. I just talk about stuff. Whatever they want to talk about. It's not a big deal."

Abby could tell Craig was getting upset and confused. She looked up and kissed him. "I'm alright. Really. I'm just overwhelmed. We haven't really had any time off. I'm sorry. Some break, huh?" She kissed him again.

Craig returned her kiss and said, "No. I'm having fun. All I'd do at home is sit around and play Xbox. I'd rather be doing this. I'd rather be with you." He held her tightly for a few minutes, looking out over the lake. Getting cold, he asked, "Do you want to go back inside?"

"No," Abby replied. "Could we just go back to your cabin and lay down for a while?

Craig smiled. "That would be great."

They got up and walked hand in hand down the dock, past the lodge, and down the road to the cabins. While they were walking, big, heavy snowflakes started to fall. Craig tried again to catch one in his mouth. Abby laughed at him and then tried herself.

Abby fell asleep almost immediately. Craig built a fire, and when he went into the bedroom, she was asleep on her side, snuggling with a pillow. He decided to read his book for a while since he was going to have to write that final paper soon, but he felt like he had no events that could really work. He jotted some notes and ideas down, but after thirty minutes, he had nothing worth pursuing. Instead, he wrote a note to Abby saying that he was going to the lodge to watch football.

When Abby woke up, she saw the note but wished she had

seen Craig instead. She walked to the living room and saw that he had built a fire. Again, she was happy for the warmth. She sat down and opened his book. There was a Post-it note with the words "Essay Idea: Thanksgiving at Wood Lake." She smiled at the idea. Turning to the beginning of the book, she started to read.

When Abby finally went to the lodge, she found Craig at the bar chatting a small crowd up, again. He had made friends with the Thanksgiving regulars, and they were deep, deep as they could be, in analysis of the second football game. Abby went to check on Frank in the kitchen.

In the back, Vickie and her crew were almost done putting the dishes away, and they were onto yet another bottle of wine. Abby went upstairs to find Taylor fully engaged in one of the many tournaments that had arisen, including an overly athletic game of ping-pong and an intense game of hearts where one boy tried to shoot the moon every round. She decided to join Craig at the bar. After making reintroductions, which he did every holiday, John insisted that Abby get a place next to Craig because he was her boyfriend. Abby could tell her Dad had had a few drinks, but he could handle himself.

"Hey, babe," Craig said. "Did you have a nice nap?" It was just like school. Craig's intensity for her made the rest of the world disappear. He never broke his stare. It was as though the football game wasn't going on, and the conversations he was having never existed.

"It was nice. Thanks for the fire," Abby responded. Her father gave her a glass of red wine and got Craig a beer.

"You want anything to eat? There's still food."

"Yeah," she said as she started to get up.

Craig squeezed her shoulder. "I'll get you a plate. Just relax." He got up and skipped towards the kitchen.

Abby watched him all the way. She didn't know what she had done to get so lucky. His kindness towards her was not an an act. It seemed second nature.

"He's a good kid, Abby," her uncle Phil said. "I think you should keep him." He was laughing.

"I'll do my best," Abby responded, drinking from her wine glass. Phil patted her on the back a little too hard and went off in the direction of the buffet. Craig returned with two plates of food and set them on the end bar and went to get himself a some water.

"You guys going to Whitecap tomorrow?" John asked.

"Yes."

"Well you better check if some of my stuff fits Craig. It'll save you some money."

"We'll check in the morning, Dad. Thanks."

Craig came back, and they ate hungrily.

The evening progressed with more wine and beer and football. Craig watched the game intently but never forgot to turn his attention to Abby. He explained things to her and made sure she was a part of every conversation. It was a really nice evening. Abby felt part of both worlds, the resort and the small talk she had missed that afternoon. Craig provided a bridge between the worlds.

By the time they got back to the cabin, both Abby and Craig had consumed a bit more than they should have. They managed to get a fire going safely and got into bed. She was wearing nothing more than her underwear. This shocked Craig initially, but he was quickly swept up. With both of them shaking a bit, they began with the habits of their intimacy and pushed further into the unknown. When they reached the point where decision met principle, Craig rolled off. Abby pawed at him a few times, but she knew they had almost gone too far. They allowed themselves to cool down uncovered, and then Abby laid her head on Craig's chest while he ran his fingers up and down her moist back. They fell asleep soon after.

Chapter 18

When they woke up, Abby was in a panic. Not only was she mostly naked, she knew they were late for skiing. She checked her phone, and there was a text from Meghan. "Shit," she said, going into the bathroom to get clothes. When she opened her messages, it said, *Raining. Not going. Maybe I'll stop by later if that's ok.* She let out a long breath and wrote back, *Great. Lots to do around here. Come over for dinner. We can watch a movie.* When she hit send, she realized that watching a movie with Meghan and Craig might not be that fun, but what was done was done.

She got dressed, then crawled into bed with Craig and kissed him. She ran her hand across his face. It was rough. He opened his eyes slowly; obviously, she had woken him up. "No skiing today," Abby whispered. "It's raining."

"Oh," Craig said, rolling to face her. He kissed her softly on the lips and reached for her back. He was surprised to feel that she was dressed. He found the bare small of her back and then tapped her on her butt. "I'm going to get dressed." Craig said as he sat up.

Abby rolled onto her back and brushed her hair up and behind her. There was always so much to do at the resort, but she wanted to have some fun. She didn't just want to hang out all day.

Craig returned with a shirt and shorts on and jumped up on the bed. He fell forward onto Abby but stopped in a push-up position and kissed her on the nose. "What's up? We going to get some breakfast? What are we doing today?"

Abby took a while to respond. She was content to look at Craig's face and run her fingers through his hair, now long enough to fall over his eyes.

"What?" he asked.

"I don't know," Abby said, pushing the hair away from his eyes. "I like you. Why are you so good to me?"

"Because I love you," Craig said, startled by the question.

"But why? Isn't it weird to you? We only met a few months ago, and we love each other. Why me?"

"You're the best girl I've ever met. Who else would put up with me? You're the prettiest, smartest, most put-together girl I've ever been around." He laid his head on her chest.

"I'll bet I'm not the prettiest girl you've ever seen." She smiled and rubbed his head.

He looked up. "You are. I've never met anyone like you. You've got it all figured out. You have goals." There was a seriousness to his voice.

"I've got less figured out than you think," she said under her breath.

"How's that?"

"Nothing," Abby said. "I don't know." She turned the tables on Craig and rolled up onto his chest. She kissed him hard. He submitted until she loosened her grip.

Then, Craig pulled Abby in so he could feel her against him. He got lost in her hair and whispered, "I love you. Don't forget that."

"I know. I won't." Abby peeked her head up. "Let's go eat breakfast at my house. I should visit with my mom a bit before we leave tomorrow."

"Sounds good to me."

After breakfast and a nice visit with some of Abby's aunts and uncles, they set to the tasks of the day. A fun day was lost in the sweep of responsibility. Craig went to catch up on the wood, the rain having let up slightly, while Abby went off to the kitchen. Lunch came quickly, but there were still other chores to do. Before they knew it, it was two thirty, and Abby was frustrated that they hadn't been able to do anything fun. Meghan would be there shortly, and then all they were going to do was hang out. The weight of the resort hit Abby for the first time since she had been home. It was never all fun, but now she had something she would rather do. She set herself to the other chores and tried to forget the burden.

Craig caught up with Abby just before dinner. He was sweaty, full of wood chips, and smiling from ear to ear. "God, that was a great day. Got all the wood up to the lines on all the cabins. The lodge will have enough wood to last through Christmas."

Abby pushed the hair from in front of his eyes. "Good for you, babe," she said with an exhale. "You stink. Go take a shower."

Laughing a bit, Craig asked, "Are we eating in the lodge or with your parents?"

"Meghan is coming over, and we're going to eat at my house and hang out. Leftovers I'm sure. Nothing too special."

"That's alright," Craig said. "I've got homework that I haven't even sniffed since I got here. I might just work on that if it's ok? You guys can catch up then."

Abby smiled at Craig. He was always thinking of her. "That would be nice." She hit him on the chest. "Now go take a shower."

"Ok." Craig ran off towards his cabin.

Abby watched him go.

The early evening dinner was filled with laughter and exhaustion. There were stories of the week, a time to allow Meghan to share, and a gentle ribbing of Craig. They talked about what they still had to do at school and classes for the next semester. There was no dominant force directing the conversation; it grew organically. Craig enjoyed the equality of the exchange. Frank came by, having handed the kitchen off to the weekend cook who helped him from time to time, especially in the summer. He was home for the week, and Frank decided to take advantage.

There was a fire started, and Meghan and Abby set to doing the dishes. Craig tried to help but was shooed away. He sat with the adults by the fire, and the last wisps of sunlight shone over the lake. He said little, but listened to the conversations he believed were being had by rote, a mention of this uncle or that friend, all discussions so familiar that the laughs seemed preprogrammed. There were no questions directed his way. He assumed that this was more a product of exhaustion than any slight or sign of disrespect. He was there, and the others took no notice because he was now part of the setting, no longer a novelty.

When the dishes were done, Abby announced that they were going downstairs. Craig went along. The girls gathered a few blankets and turned on Netflix to look for a movie.

As the girls settled in, Craig stayed standing. "I'm going to go read for a while." He looked at Abby and then Meghan.

"Oh...ok," Abby replied. "Are you sure?"

"Yeah. You guys need some time, and I need to get started on that paper for my final." Craig made a move for the stairs. Abby followed him up to the landing.

"Are you ok?" she whispered, reaching to embrace him.

Craig hugged her and kissed her on the ear, whispering, "Yeah. No problem. I'll see you in the morning."

"Oh...don't you want me to come over tonight?"

"If you want. No worries. Catch up with Meghan. If you come over, great, and if not, we have plenty of nights when we get back to school." He kissed her on the lips and felt her wanting more. He went up the stairs. "Bye, Meghan."

"Bye, Craig," Meghan called after him

As Craig moved down the paths in the dark, his feet felt a little more sure. His hands reached out for trees instinctively, and he never lost his balance. Before he made his way into the cabin, he bent down to pick up a leaf. It would dry enough to put in his pack if he left it by the fire. Then, he allowed himself a look at the lake. The moon was coming up, and Craig breathed in the crisp air. This was a home. It was a place where a person could write a story with their life rather than fill in lines on a stat sheet. Abby's woods held a mystery he longed to discover. It would take time, but the resort rushed no one. Instead, it dictated the rhythms of a life you could plan for yourself. With one more deep breath, he turned towards his cabin.

Abby never came over that evening. Craig woke up with his lamp still on and his book notes laying next to him on his bed. He looked at the prompt sheet and saw the words "Chopping Wood." He had an idea. He wanted to capture what the week had meant to him. It was all summed up in that action.

Craig stripped his bedding as he had seen Abby do on the first morning. He knew where the bedding and towels had to go for washing. The larger cabins had laundry, but his was small and was treated more like a lodge room. He got out cleaning supplies and wiped the rooms down again, just as Abby had done. He packed his things, swung his pack over his shoulders, grabbed the bedding and towels, and headed for the lodge.

After dropping off his stuff, he went to the kitchen to see Frank. "Hey, Frank," Craig said loudly, almost announcing his presence. It was early, and Frank wasn't fully awake. He only grunted. "Mind if I make myself something to eat?" Craig asked, trying not to be a burden.

"Sure, kid," Frank replied. "You know where everything is by now."

"I do indeed." Craig went off into the cooler and got some eggs, cheese, leftover ham, and a green pepper. "Got any onions?" Craig called.

"Already out here," Frank called back.

Craig emerged with his supplies and set to work making an omelette. Frank watched as he found the pan and utensils with no issues and cooked himself a great breakfast. Craig ate in the kitchen, talking over the Badgers' prospects with Frank. He could tell Frank enjoyed the company. Frank laughed and told jokes. It was good to have easy conversations, and Craig felt as though he had known Frank for longer than a week. When he was done, he cleaned up his plate and put everything away. “Mind if I leave my stuff here while I bring new linens back to the cabin?”

“Not a problem. Most folks are leaving today, so there’s bound to be a lot of hauling around.”

“Great. Thanks.”

Craig went into the storeroom and found the supplies he needed—fresh sheets, a blanket, pillowcases, and towels—and brought all of it back to the cabin. It was a warmer-than-average morning, and the sun shone brightly. There were no clouds as there had been on previous days. He took his time moving down the path.

Abby met him in the living room of the cabin. She came to wake him up, but instead, finding him gone, went into cleanup mode. The problem was Craig had left nothing to do. Even the toilet was clean. “You’ve been busy this morning,” Abby announced as Craig moved to the bedroom.

“Yes. I have,” he said proudly. “All I have to do is make the bed, place the towels, and sweep up.”

“Impressive. Then we can do five or six more cabins and a few rooms before we go,” she said, smiling.

Shaking his head, Craig replied, “Is that all?” He dropped his load of linens and reached out to hug Abby. He kissed her on the top of her head and continued, “I really don’t want to go.”

“Me neither,” Abby responded. She looked up to meet his eye and waited for a kiss. He complied immediately. A moment later, she said, “But we have to. Your mother is expecting us tonight, right?” She made a pained face.

Through pressed lips, Craig said, “Yep.” He was nodding his head. “Some fun.”

They made the bed together. Craig swept as Abby arranged the towels in the bathroom. They set off to the other cabins together. They were determined to meet their goal and leave less work for everyone else.

Chapter 19

The ride was perfect. Abby was nervous about two days at Craig's house but happy to be spending it with him. The pine and birch of the northwoods gave way to increasing farmland, and the snowline had just about given up by the turn towards Madison. They listened to Abby's riding mix, laughed at the events of the week, and went over their schedules for the weeks to come. The conversation never waned. For a time, Abby forgot that they weren't going back to school, and Craig never spoke of what would be happening at his house other than supper that night and church the next morning. Besides, Abby assumed Craig also wanted to get back to school as quickly as possible.

Her nerves didn't return until they got off the highway. They drove up a hill past the frontage road mini malls and restaurants. There was a wooded county park to the left and a few condos to the right. When they turned off the main road, the condos surrendered to increasingly larger houses. There were subdivisions in Eagle River, but nothing like these. Northern subdivisions were carved out of the forests. Here, the woods had simply been cut down. All the houses were uniform.

They turned onto a side road and were immediately met by a train. "Damn it!" Craig yelled as he came to a stop. He was trying to hide his nerves, but failed.

"Really?" Abby was taken aback by the outburst. She looked at him crossly.

"I'm sorry. This happens all the time. There always seems to be a train. And a slow one at that. I'm just nervous about being home." He put the car in park and turned to Abby. "You've been quiet. How are you doing?" He forced a smile.

Abby smiled in a pensive way, looking out the side window. "I don't know." There was a distance in her voice. "I'm not sure what to expect. Your parents seem nice...I just want them to like me. And your sisters."

"Oh, Sarah and Claire will love you. They're super cool. I wouldn't worry." Craig sneaked a glance at the crawling train in front of them and then looked to Abby. She felt his hand grasp hers, looked back at him, and smiled at his energized face. She could trust him. Craig would make it all ok. Her face broke into a soft laugh. "There she is," Craig said as he leaned in to kiss her. The train ended, and he put the car back in drive.

They eventually reached a fork in the road, the street to the right leading to a golf course and the street to the left showing a gate which separated them from the subdivision. A sign next to the gate read 'Wooded Hills.' When they got into the neighborhood, Abby's head was spinning all around. The houses were all the same shade of brown or gray. The trees were mostly new and strategically placed, and the street lights and mailboxes were all uniform. All the lawns were perfect, despite the lateness of the season. She first saw a house with a four-car garage and then one with six. "Shit," Abby said out loud, not meaning to.

"What?" Craig asked, turning onto another loop.

"This is where you live?" There was a playset in every yard despite the fact that they had just passed a large park in the center of the neighborhood.

"Yeah," he replied. "Kinda boring, huh?"

"They're all so big."

"Just a bunch of people showing off." Craig shook his head. "Here's mine."

They pulled into a drive that had only a three-car garage and a space on the side. Craig pulled into the space. Abby saw a golf cart in the back, just beyond the fence. "You live next to the golf course?"

"Yep," he replied. "It seemed like a good idea to my dad. He barely ever goes." Craig got out of the car and popped the trunk. "You coming?"

Abby got out of the car and was suddenly aware that she was wearing yoga pants and hiking boots. However, she had remembered to wear the flannel Linda bought for her with Craig on their shopping trip the week before. As she put it on this morning, all she could think about was trying to score points with Craig's family.

"Let's go," Craig said as he punched in the code, and the garage door began to open slowly.

Abby grabbed her small bag and her dress out of the trunk and closed it. She was shaking slightly, and tried to take a few deep breaths before walking behind Craig.

They came in through the mudroom and went down the hall to the living room. When they got there, the first thing Abby noticed was the height of the room. It was not like the lofted A-frame they lived in. The height of these ceilings served only for show. The whole room looked straight out of a magazine. The walls were white and unadorned save for a few family pictures and a mounted sixty-inch flat screen TV on the wall next to the fireplace. All the furniture matched. The only accents were a few lamps and fake plants. The bank of windows on the back wall, facing the yard, reminded Abby of her home, but instead of woods and a lake, there was just sculpted green space. This was a showpiece. No part of it said home.

They started up the wide stairway when Mike came up from the basement. “Hey, you two. Hi, Abby.” He had two empty beer bottles. “Welcome,” he said in a voice too loud for the situation.

Abby noticed he was in sweatpants and an old Badger T-shirt, tucked into his pants. It made her feel better about what she was wearing. He seemed much larger than the last time they met.

“We’re going to put our stuff upstairs, Dad. Where’s Mom?”

“She’s shopping. Where else?” He walked towards the kitchen and then stopped suddenly. “Oh right...put Abby in Sarah’s room. She’s staying with Brad now. Claire’s with Mom.” He walked away and called out, “No funny business.”

Abby could hear him laughing from the kitchen. She shot a side-eyed look at Craig, who was shaking his head. Turning back up the stairs, Craig took a jog step, and she followed.

Sarah’s room was like a boy’s room with a girl’s touch. There was a bulletin board above her desk with pictures of her friends and a queen bed with light green sheets, but the rest of the room was covered with Badger posters. Most of them were volleyball, but some were basketball, and even a football poster from the last time the Badgers won the Rose Bowl in 2000. Abby liked it.

Craig showed her the bathroom, which adjoined with Claire's room. Then there was the closet, which seemed to be the size of Abby's bedroom at home. "Wow!" she said, walking back into the room. "Big. Where's your room?" she asked as she dropped her bag on the bed and laid her dress out.

"Down the hall." He took her by the hand and led her down to the other end of the top floor, past another bathroom. Abby guessed that his parents' room must be on the first floor, and that room had to be huge. Craig's room was as she expected it to be. It was the stereotype he had been running from since she met him. He threw his bag on the floor and pulled her in close to hug her. She looked over his shoulder and saw his senior prom picture hanging above his desk. It was Craig and Jen. "Nice picture," she said.

Craig turned to look. "Oh shit." His face was red instantly.

Abby laughed. "No big deal." It was a bit bigger deal than she was letting on. Jen had been a sore spot for her from day one. It wasn't that she worried Craig would go back to her. Jen was just so damn pretty, Abby couldn't help but feel self-conscious even at the mention of her.

Craig walked to his desk and pulled the picture down. He turned to Abby and was about to tear it when she put her hands on his. "It's fine, Craig." He dropped the picture on the floor and kissed her gently.

"It's only you. I love you."

"I know. I love you too." Abby hugged him around the waist. "I'm going to get cleaned up for dinner, ok?"

"Sure."

Abby went to take a shower and change clothes. She walked slowly down the long hall, which was filled with pictures of the kids. There were more pictures of Sarah and Craig than Claire. It struck her as a bit weird. She had never been in a house this big. Although her parents may be considered "technically" rich by owning a resort, Craig had lived a very different life than she had. She knew this, but had no idea how different it was until she came here. She appreciated how he had worked to fit into her life this past week. However, despite his efforts, Abby felt out of her element. Feeling overwhelmed, she went into Sarah's room.

When Abby came downstairs, Craig saw her first as he was reading in the living room. She had braided her hair just like she did on their first date and wore tight jeans and a tight flannel with the sleeves rolled up. There was something too about her face that was different. He couldn't quite figure it out until she was closer. Abby had put eyeliner and a hint of eyeshadow on, and it made her eyes pop even more than they already did. Craig couldn't stop looking at her. She was just so beautiful. His eyes followed her all the way as she walked towards the kitchen. 'Wow,' he thought. He had never seen her look this confident. Turning to him, she said, "Let's do this thing." He rose as if pulled and followed her into the kitchen.

Linda and Claire were busy making dinner. Linda came over to Abby and ran her hand down her arm and gave her a half hug. "Why, don't you look lovely." Abby looked past Linda's shoulder to Craig with her eyes open wide. "This is Craig's sister, Claire. Claire, this is Abby," Linda continued.

"It's very nice to meet you, finally," Claire said, looking past Abby to Craig.

Abby walked over to the counter next to Claire. "Is there anything I can help with?"

Craig tried to diffuse the tension. "Abby is a great cook. She practically grew up next to Frank in the kitchen. She hunts and fishes and...she can do anything." He realized he was talking very fast. Abby shot him a glare.

"Well, isn't she something," Linda announced.

"Mother," Claire said sharply. "I would love your help, Abby. Why don't you leave her with us, Craig?" Claire shooed him away.

Craig went to find his father in the basement. He assumed he would be in his chair watching football, and his suspicions were confirmed. Craig could tell from the empties that Mike was half in the bag.

"Craig. Get whatever you want and get me another beer," Mike called, holding up another empty bottle.

"Sure." Craig went to the bar. He found a bottle of red wine and thought Abby might like it. He opened it to let it breath and got his dad a beer. "Here, Dad. Who's playing?"

"Thanks," Mike said, not even looking up. "I don't even know who I'm watching." Craig sat by his father, and they said almost nothing for half an hour.

Finally, the silence was broken by Linda calling Mike to build a fire. He complained as he marched upstairs. Craig grabbed the wine and two glasses and followed his father. He went to the kitchen where he found Abby and Claire sitting at the kitchen table. They were talking and laughing, which made him happy. He walked behind Abby and put the wine on the table. "Want a glass?"

"Sure," she said, looking up at him. She smiled. As Craig poured a glass, he heard his father yell, "Damn fucking matches!" He went to the living room to see what the problem was, and when he got there, he saw his father kneeling down by the fireplace and striking another match. Linda was standing over him.

"Can I help?" Craig asked.

"Sure. See if you can get this shit started." Mike handed him the matches.

Craig knelt down by the fireplace and rearranged the wood.

"Don't hurt yourself, honey," Linda said.

Mike stood over him.

"You have to get oxygen to feed it, Dad. If you pack it too tightly, it'll never get going," Craig said as he put a few small pieces of wood and one piece of crumpled paper in the middle. He struck a match, and the wood took in seconds. The fire was blazing within a minute. Craig looked over at Abby, who had come in the room, and she winked at him. He smiled.

Sarah came for dinner without Brad, who wasn't feeling well. She greeted Abby warmly and made small talk about Abby sleeping in her room. Abby, Claire, and Sarah set the table together and brought out the food.

When they took their seats, Linda and Mike were at the ends. Sarah and Claire sat on one side, and Craig made sure to sit next to Abby to shield her from his mother, putting his left hand on her thigh to let her know he was there. The food was passed around, and everyone took their fill. Abby didn't talk too much, and Craig looked right at her most of the time. He seemed to fully understand what she was going through. They had eaten so well and so naturally for an entire week, and despite his mother's best effort, this was not a meal they enjoyed. The ham was dry, and the vegetables were just frozen and steamed, but not long enough. The only thing Craig liked was the potatoes, but it's hard to mess up potatoes.

Abby was careful to sit straight and eat small bites. She was cognizant of being judged since silence surrounded the table. Finally, Sarah asked, "So, what did you guys do all week?"

Abby looked at Craig, who took the hint. "Well, we fell into the routine of the resort pretty quickly. There was a lot of work to do to get ready for the holiday weekend."

Linda interrupted Craig. "So Abby, how many people do you have for Thanksgiving?"

Abby finished chewing her food. "Excuse me. We always have between fifty and sixty for dinner and more throughout the afternoon and evening. This year I think we had around a hundred." She smiled at Craig. "Craig was a big help."

"I'm sure he was," Linda responded. "A hundred people is a lot."

"Is that typical for a holiday?" Sarah interjected.

"For the most part, yes," Abby said. "The resort holds forty to fifty most weekends. More in the summer. We are at capacity from Memorial Day to Labor Day."

"You make a living with that?" Mike asked.

"We do ok," Abby said, trying to sound confident.

"Ok?" Mike seemed to think out loud.

Craig broke in, "Like I said, lots to do. But we had a little fun. I got an expert tour around the lake, and Abby shot a deer."

Abby's head swung from Mike to Craig. Her eyes burned through him.

Linda seized. "She shot a deer?"

Abby moved her hand to Craig's leg and dug her nails in. He didn't flinch.

"Yes, Mother, she shot a deer and cleaned it herself. We had venison steaks for dinner that night. It was something."

"I'm sure it was," Linda said, smirking in apparent satisfaction. Linda's sarcasm wasn't lost on the table. Claire closed her eyes and shook her head.

Unphased, Craig continued, "There was always something to do, and Frank kept us busy all day on Thanksgiving."

"Who's Frank?" Claire asked.

"He's the guy who runs the kitchen," Craig said.

All eyes turned to Abby for clarification. "Frank has been at the resort longer than my family. He runs the kitchen, as Craig said. But, he's really the soul of the place. He's lived on the resort for almost forty years. Before she died, his wife ran the cleaning service and the front desk. They're great people."

Linda responded, "Well, isn't that nice." Then, she took a large drink of wine. She continued towards Craig, "So I guess you'll be going up there over Christmas break?"

Craig took his time responding. "Perhaps." He looked at Abby, not breaking his stare. His hand was still on her leg.

"Well not for the actual holiday. I get Christmas."

"That's fine, Mother." Craig was calm and deliberate. He winked at Abby and, for the first time during the meal, he took his hand off her leg and cut his ham.

Abby offered to help clean up but was shooed away. Instead, she went downstairs with Craig. The downstairs was a different kind of showpiece. It was a sports bar. Abby's family room was small and one of only two finished rooms in the basement, but this was huge and there was no storage. The whole basement was finished, a billiards room and two extra bedrooms.

There was no conversation. Mike had the game on and

had opened another beer. Craig didn't want to sit, so he stood behind the bar, playing with the dice, and Abby sat on a stool. There wasn't much to say. The girls were up in the kitchen with Linda. After a long, uncomfortable silence, Abby finally asked, "You want to go upstairs?"

"Yes," Craig said.

They went upstairs to his room. Up on the bed, they faced each other, and Abby started to laugh, Craig following suit. She buried her head in Craig's chest and curled up her body. "Why don't your parents like me?"

"They do."

"No, Craig, they don't."

"I don't know. I like you." He rolled onto his back, pulled Abby to his chest, and rubbed her head. She calmed down quickly as he kissed the top of her head, and she squeezed him tightly. They lay quietly.

After a while, there was a knock on the door. "What?" Craig called.

"Can we come in?" his sisters asked in unison.

"Sure." Craig and Abby sat up. His sisters came in the room.

"Hey!" Sarah said. "We should play a game or something. Mom and Dad are in a foul mood."

"It's probably me," Abby said.

"Probably," Claire agreed. "But screw them."

"Yeah!" Sarah added. "Let's do something fun."

They all went to Sarah's room, dug out *Life* and *Cards Against Humanity,* and sat down on the floor to play. For the first time since being there, Abby felt like she was in a home. After playing for a while, Sarah and Claire told Craig to go. "We want to get to know this girl. And we can't do that with you here. Come on now, get out." Sarah waved him off. Craig winked at Abby and went to his room to read.

The games ended quickly as the girls questioned Abby about everything. They wanted to know how she met Craig and what her impressions of him were and asked about every aspect of her life at the resort.

"How did your family come to own a resort in Eagle River after living in Chicago?" Claire asked.

"Well, my dad went to Northwestern. He's from out East. My grandpa worked for a research lab in Boston and did very well from himself. He was able to send my dad to summer camp, and I guess my dad kinda fell in love with the idea." Abby was happy to talk about her home with them. She hadn't not really gotten into the specifics of how they came to the resort with Craig, but she felt instantly comfortable with Sarah and Claire. "My mom had gone to Eagle River as a kid. It's kind of a normal place for Chicago folks to go in the summer. She brought my dad up after they got married."

"But how did they get the money to buy a resort?" Sarah asked. Claire glared at her.

Abby didn't flinch. "My grandpa died in his early 60s, and my grandma came to live with us. I was only one or two at the time. The money from the life insurance and selling the house out East gave my dad enough money to buy the resort."

"I'm sorry to hear about your grandpa," Claire said. She reached over and touched Abby on the shoulder.

"It's fine. A few years after we moved to the resort, my grandma died too. I think she was just lonely without my grandpa."

“That’s so sad,” Sarah said.

“It is,” Abby responded. “But without it, we wouldn’t have the resort. It seems like it was a gift to my father from his father. I think that’s why my dad works so hard. He feels like he owes it to his parents.”

“Are your other grandparents alive?” Sarah asked.

“Yes. They’re pretty old, and they live in Florida so we don’t see them that much.” Abby turned to Sarah. “So, tell me about you and Brad. When are you getting married?”

Sarah seemed happy to discuss the wedding and got up to get her wedding book. Abby reached out to Claire, whose eyes rolled dramatically. They both laughed.

When Abby came to Craig’s room a few hours later, she was in pajamas. She was smiling and clearly had a good time. “Your sisters are really cool. They told me a lot about their little brother.” She walked up to the edge of his elevated bed and leaned over to kiss him. Craig tried to lightly pull her onto the bed, but she pushed him back slightly saying, “No. We can be together tomorrow.” She kissed him again, slowly and softly. “When is church?”

“Nine or ten, I think,” he replied.

“Great. I’ll see you in the morning.”

Craig watched her as she walked towards the door. Right before she left, she kicked her leg up, turned, and blew him a kiss. Then, she was out. Craig thought it was too cute. He could hear her laugh as she went down the hall.

Chapter 20

Abby didn't come down for breakfast. Claire said she heard her in the bathroom, so Craig went ahead and ate his bacon and eggs. He didn't know how to feel about Abby in his house. He knew she could handle herself, however, he worried constantly about what his mother might say. Mike had obviously chosen casual indifference, mostly, Craig assumed, to avoid conflict with Linda. They had all settled into their meals when Abby came around the corner, dressed up as Craig had never seen her. She had a black, sleeveless dress on, knee-length, and shoes that actually had heels. Her legs were bare, and she held a sweater in her hands. Her hair was curled, and she had done her makeup much like the night before, understated and highlighting her already mesmerizing eyes. Craig sat transfixed.

Abby planned on making a splash. She knew Craig would be impressed. He was easy. It was Linda she was after. She didn't want to change for anyone, but what was the hurt in pretending a little? She had fun with the initial silence and walked over by Craig. "Am I late?"

Craig stumbled over his words, "No...I don't think so."

Linda gave a sideways glance and shook her head as though she was trying to clear her thoughts.

Claire said, "Don't you look nice."

"Thanks, Claire."

"That's a nice dress," Linda said. "Going to a wedding?"

"Mother," Craig said sharply.

"Well, at least someone wants to look nice for church." Linda smiled at Abby.

They rode to church together. Craig had to sit in the third row of the Escalade, which to Abby looked like it had not seen a day of work. As they drove out of the subdivision, Abby's head was once again on a swivel. Craig pointed out a few homes of people he went to school with.

They drove only five minutes from the edge of the subdivision before pulling into a huge parking lot filled with expensive cars. The church looked more like a large theater than the small churches Abby was used to when her mom had taken her. Vickie had abandoned trying when she turned fifteen. Abby hadn't been to church since, although Kate had tried to get her to go for the first few weeks of school. She had not even been confirmed.

The inside of the church was huge. It seated around five hundred and had two large projection screens. The McLeans sat in the middle row, about halfway back. Abby saw a rock band set up with drums and guitars, and they were playing upbeat music as people started filing into their seats. The screens had pictures from a recent youth event. Abby sat between Craig and Linda. She immediately began looking for a hymnal, but Craig pointed to the screens. "Everything will be up there." She felt totally out of place.

The service began, and everything was cheerful. It was a prosperity ministry church, and it seemed to Abby that the message of the service was that wealth was a sign of God's favor.

The sermon made her uncomfortable. She always thought of religion as a challenge to live a better life, but this sermon was more of a congratulations for a life well-lived. There was a lot of nodding, a few more songs, and then time for donuts.

Linda paraded Abby around, introducing her to everyone. The meeting room for coffee and donuts was bigger than the whole dining room at the resort, with ceilings just as high. Craig had tried to keep up with his mother but got lost in the crowd, and Abby felt the pull to yet another one of Linda's friends. She heard phrases like, "Well isn't she lovely" or "So, you're from up north" and "We have a place up north" over and over. Obviously, she had been a topic of conversation over the last few weeks, which was somewhat surprising since she was fairly sure Linda didn't like her. The whole thing was overwhelming, but she played the part as best she could. There would be no giving Linda the edge she seemed so desperate to get.

When Abby finally freed herself to get to Craig, he was hanging on the outside of a group of people their age. Her arrival opened the group. "This is my girlfriend Abby," Craig announced. The members of the group looked her up and down. One girl commented on her dress, asking where she got it. Abby told her it was a shop in her town, but by the time she explained, the girl had already lost interest. Undeterred, Abby talked with some other members of the group until Craig brought her some coffee and a donut.

When they finally got in the car, Linda announced that she was taking the girls shopping. Mike rolled his eyes, and Claire shook her head. Abby looked back at Craig, panicked. She had fulfilled all her obligations and wanted to get back to the safety of their bubble at school. Craig closed his eyes and took a deep breath. He knew exactly what she was thinking. Claire leaned in and whispered, "This is what she does. I'll text Sarah to come. Just roll with it. We'll get it done quick."

Abby reached for Claire's hand and mouthed the words, "Thank you."

When they got home, Claire insisted that she needed to change, and Abby said she needed to go to the bathroom, both of them stalling to give Sarah time to get there. Abby went upstairs to Craig's room. When he came in, she sighed. "What the hell?"

"I know. I'm sorry. I'll get the car packed and be ready to go right away. Do you want a change of clothes?"

"I'll leave them out and leave the hanger for my dress."

"You bet."

"I better go," Abby said, shaking her head as she left.

Linda seemed determined to go to the outlet mall, but Sarah, who came quickly, suggested that they make a quick stop at the Hwy 83 shops and just go to Kohls. She had a 30% discount and wanted to use her Kohls Cash. Linda relented.

They went around the store, and Linda picked out shirts and a few skirts for Abby, always in sizes too big. Claire reminded her that everything would be ok as she trailed behind picking sizes that actually would fit. Abby went into the changing room, Sarah following behind her, and just sat down on the bench and put her head in her hands. Sarah sat down next to her, laying her hand on Abby's back. "This is just what my mother does," she said. Abby recognized the phrase from Craig. Linda had run her children's lives, from schedules to what they wore. "I know she can be overwhelming. Shopping for you is her way to connect. Just accept what she wants to get you."

Abby was trying not to cry. "She doesn't even like me. Why? I'm a nice person. What did I do?"

"It's ok. She means well, Abby. But she's not good when plans change. You should have seen her when Claire said she was going to art school." A tear fell down Abby's cheek. "Listen," Sarah said. "She'll come around. Now, just be you. You're the best thing that ever happened to Craig. He adores you, and that's all that matters. Get back to school. Come down for Christmas and come to the wedding. She'll come around."

Abby stood up and started to pick up all the clothes. Sarah helped. Abby wiped her face. "Thanks, Sarah."

"No problem." She gave Abby a hug. "Now, let's get out there."

"Won't your mom want to see the clothes on?"

"No. For her, it's more about the dollar amount. She just wants to prove she can get you stuff."

There was nothing left to do but check out. Abby left with two full bags of clothes which she graciously thanked Linda for. She actually liked some of the stuff.

When they got home, Craig had the car packed, as promised. Abby took out a new outfit and went upstairs to put it on. She knew she had better wear it. One last gesture of contrition. It was really cute. A black skirt and flowing white top with a modest neckline. Abby could get used to having new clothes from time to time. After saying their goodbyes, they left. The car ride was a quiet one. Craig left Abby alone, and she was grateful.

Chapter 21

Craig woke up the next morning alone. Abby had gone to her room to visit with Kate. He and Abby texted until late, but eventually they both decided to go to sleep. They were excited to get back to the routine of their lives at school. There were a few things to get done before finals. He had a draft of his paper for English, but he had labs for Chem and readings to do for other classes. He also made an appointment to meet with his advisor.

Craig met Abby in their usual seats for biology. She had her hair up and was wearing yoga pants and a new Badgers sweatshirt. The outline notes were ready to go, and after a peck on the cheek from Abby, he settled in for class. He didn't listen much. He was too busy watching Abby concentrate. She looked up at the notes and then down at her computer, and her focus made him laugh. Confident in the material, he preferred to focus on her.

After class, Abby asked if he wanted to get a bite to eat, but Craig said he had an appointment and would meet her later at her place. After that one out-of-place meeting, they fell back into their rhythm. Class, meals, studying, and nights together when they could became their safe zone. The habits of their love came back to them easily, and there was no reason to abandon them. Their gestures of affection sustained them until finals. What more could either of them ask for? Happiness reigned as winter set in. Christmas break was coming. Two weeks at the resort for Craig and a long weekend in Hartland for Abby. They created a happiness together by making each other their most important priority. They needed nothing more.

Craig's Essay

Prompt: In memoir style, explore a moment or place in your life that created meaning. Use the conventions of writing and literary devices we have studied this semester.

Chopping Wood

Before this past week, all of my physical labor displayed itself in the form of a score. Hitting or catching a ball resulted in numbers up in lights on a scoreboard. At the end of the game, after coming out of the locker room, the scoreboard was cleared, and the numbers were written down, becoming one of another endless list of win/loss records. At the end of the season, we cleared the deck and began again. Rep after rep in the weight room or on the track to get that little bit faster or to tip the scales of the record in our favor. Hitting other players and getting hit by them in an endless and meaningless routine of futility. I participated in this charade for most of my childhood.

Now don't get me wrong, there were moments of beauty. A perfectly executed play or a ball hit right on the sweet spot can provide a rush of satisfaction that rivals most anything. However, in the end, the artistic expression provided by both the preparation and execution of each play left me with a hole that I could not fully explain. There was always the car ride of criticism and the video review. The moment could not be left for the expression or execution it was. There was always something more to be done to improve. There was never a time to contemplate a job well done. There seemed to be no meaning, no purpose.

This past week, I experienced a moment of physical labor that contained meaning which needed no video review. A profound sense of accomplishment was rewarded by a clear visual, coupled with the knowledge of how the labor would be used for the benefit of others. I came to a place that was like nowhere I had ever been, because I feel like I may never have really been anywhere. I have gone on vacations and seen beautiful places. However, I have never been to a place where everything felt right, where the people seemed to be an extension of the land. This was a setting where I stumbled to get from place to place, while others, who call this place home, moved with a nimble grace as though every root growing from the ground was set before them in their mind's eye before growing across the path.

My first job in this new world was the simple task of chopping firewood. On the face of it, the mundane routine appeared to be work that was beneath the educated. It was something that should be relegated to the unskilled or should be mechanized in some way. But the first strike dispelled all such thoughts. The wedge was set carefully. The hammer was brought above the shoulder, and then came the pause. The pause was necessary both practically and for a deeper meaning. There was the business of the aim. A partial strike could send the wedge flying off, causing unintentional damage. The deeper moment came from the realization that this violence was creative. The hit was an intense rush exploding like the wood, splintering my previous world and falling anew to the ground of my first real home.

As the pile grew, my only reward came in the form of faint curls of smoke rising from cabin chimneys and the warmth of my own space. It is an accomplishment that, not unlike sports, needs to be repeated over and over again. But this routine is one of creative production. It is a scorecard that does not sit on paper that will curl and rot over time. Instead, it is transformative. My labor provides someone with warmth and others with light to read by when loved ones have gone to bed. It creates a mood in the evenings and a reason to rise in the morning. There is purpose in this task. There is purpose in this place.

Abby: 18, Shopping for Sarah's Wedding Dress with Claire

"This sucks," Claire said, shaking her head. "I'd rather be back at school, working."

"On you senior show?" I responded, looking at the drape and waiting for Sarah to come out with another dress. I think she tried on eight so far. Linda kept vetoing this or that. Sarah is so beautiful, she could wrap herself in a bed sheet and still look good.

"Yeah. This show is going to kill me. So much to do." Claire turned in her chair. "Craig mentioned you take pictures, and your dad hangs them all over the resort. That's cool."

Talking about my pictures embarasses me usually, but Claire really seemed interested. "He does. I really like taking them. I got a new camera for my birthday last year."

"I would love to see them sometime. I mostly take pictures in the city, so it would be neat to see a different setting."

"I'll send you some. I would love to see what you think."

"I will definitely tell you what I think," Claire said as Sarah came out in another dress. "She sure is beautiful."

I looked over at Sarah. "Yes, she is."

"You're coming to the wedding, right?" Claire asked.

"I don't know. I hadn't thought about it."

"You're coming. I'll make sure Sarah sends you an invite."

"Great." I said and smiled at her.

Chapter 22

Craig and Abby found themselves in a familiar atmosphere on the first Friday of second semester. They were at their table, alone, without too much to do other than be with one another. After only thirty minutes, they had given up their studies and were engaged in a conversation that moved from reminiscing about winter break to their current classes. Abby noticed that Craig was being coy about classes. He had astronomy with her and took the time over break to read ahead in Western Civilization so they could talk about the second class in the series, even though he was only in Western Civ 1. Craig could help Abby with her statistics homework because he had taken AP Stats in high school, and math came easy to him. Abby wasn't entirely sure about the rest of his schedule, and he wasn't letting on about much. Actually, he seemed amused by her questioning. All she knew was that they met for dinner instead of lunch and studied in the library four nights a week. Lunch, although it should have worked out according to what Abby knew of the classes Craig was taking, never seemed to.

Over Christmas break, Craig had spent two weeks at the resort falling into the habits of the days. He and Abby had managed to go skiing twice, and despite his boasting, Craig spent most of both days on his ass. John had put the kibosh on the nightly sleepovers by having Craig sleep in the basement bedroom in the family home. Despite the restrictions, Craig and Abby still found time for intimate gestures and longed to get back to the comfort and total freedom of school. When they were at school, they had time for love. There were classes to attend and studying to do, but the nights were for them alone. That's what they thought until Brent decided to break up with his longtime girlfriend. The football season had ended early, and Brent went into a postseason funk. Craig could totally identify with it, but Brent had decided that he wanted to take his depression out on the girl he had been seeing since his junior year of high school. Craig told him that they would eventually get back together, and he shouldn't waste his time. But Brent, being impulsive, insisted that he had outgrown her and needed to move on. The consequence of all this was that Brent was in the room every night, and although he was cool with Abby sleeping over, she was not that comfortable with the arrangement.

However, Brent was going home this weekend. Tonight was the first time Abby and Craig could really spend the night together since they had been back on campus. They stayed at the library longer than they needed to. Abby kept sliding her fingers up and down Craig's thighs as he tried to read. They looked at each other frequently, Craig holding the gaze a little longer than Abby. He wanted to kiss her. He wanted to just stare at her and kiss her for hours, but they waited, talking and reading until eight o'clock.

When they got back to Craig's room, the embrace began before the bags hit the floor. They were almost naked by the time they hit the bed, and they continued to kiss and caress under the covers. Abby wanted to push further, not all the way, but close. She knew what to do next, but was paralyzed by the fear that Craig would stop her as he did at Thanksgiving. They hadn't been so close since that night. Craig too, wanted to touch her entire body, but he didn't want to scare her. They lay thinking the same thought, overwhelmed by a desire for each other that they felt more deeply than anything they had ever known. But still, with the ability to comprehend the consequences, their want became practical. Craig turned on his side, closing the moment. He ran his fingers down her back, feeling its smoothness. "I have a surprise for you tomorrow," he said.

"Really," Abby responded, squeezing him around the waist and burying her head in his chest.

"Yeah. I'm taking you out. We can go on proper date. What do you think about that?"

She looked up at him. "That will be nice. Where are we going?"

"It's a surprise."

"Ok." Abby moved up to kiss Craig. He held his lips to hers for a while and then went back to rubbing her back until she fell asleep.

Chapter 23

Abby didn't know what Craig had in mind, but he had told her to dress up. It was unseasonably warm, temperatures in the mid 40s, so Abby wore one of the dresses Linda had bought for her and did her hair in large curls, hoping Craig liked it. She was excited to be spending the whole night pretending to not be in school. No plans, no routines, just a fun evening.

Craig came to pick her up around six thirty and was awed by how stunning she looked. He wasn't sure why he was always surprised when Abby dressed up, but it made him happy that she always excited him. He was proud to take her out and call her his girl. It was different than it had been with Jen. Craig was proud to be seen with Abby and wanted to introduce her to everyone. He wanted her in every way.

There was almost no activity on campus as they walked to Craig's car. He held Abby's hand with their fingers interwoven, and they swung their arms playfully. He caught her eye and smiled as they hopped off the curb. When they got to the car, Craig helped Abby into the passenger seat and closed the door.

"Where are we going?" she asked softly, putting her hand on Craig's leg as he got situated. She leaned in and kissed him on the cheek. "Tell me."

"Somewhere nice. I have a special meal planned. Don't

worry." They drove off campus.

When they got to The Black Sheep, Abby was confused. "Isn't this the place you came to with your parents?"

"Yeah," Craig replied. "Stick with me." He got out and walked around to help Abby out. "I took care of everything."

They were greeted at the door by an older guy. "Hi, Craig. Good to see you again. I have everything ready to go." He took them to a table that was set at the edge of the dining room where they would be out of the way and have some privacy. There was a lit candle, bread that was still warm, and a relish tray. There was also a pitcher of Mellow Yellow. Abby thought it was perfect. She sat down with Craig helping her into her seat. He sat down across from her and locked in as he always did when they were alone. He often talked about his ability to block everything else out when playing sports or taking a test. He had learned to do this when his father was yelling at him at practices and games. Abby loved how he used the technique with her. She could feel how present he was. Her mind raced.

"Where are the menus?" Abby asked, looking around.

"Don't worry," Craig said, still fully engaged. "I've got something special planned, like I said." He gave her a cheesy smile.

Abby laughed and shook her head.

"What?"

"You think you're so good, don't you? So slick." She looked at him, trying to be serious.

"Yes, I do. You don't even know." He poured a glass of soda for her.

She grabbed a piece of bread, bringing it to her nose. It smelled familiar. She tasted it. "What did you do?"

"You'll see." Craig was giddy.

Abby had no idea what was going on. She didn't like unexpected things. It would have been annoying if it wasn't so damn cute. "This is a nice surprise, Craig. Thank you."

"You haven't seen anything yet."

"What did you do?" Abby repeated, but really didn't care about the answer. 'Stay in the moment and enjoy yourself.' No one had ever done something like this for her. She knew Craig loved her. He never missed an opportunity to show her with some action or gesture. They had gotten into the habit of being affectionate. He was perfect.

They chatted for a while, but nothing had really happened since the day before. Craig asked about Meghan, and Abby returned with questions about Sarah and Claire. The trivial conversation went on for a bit when, out of nowhere, Abby blurted out, "So, where do you go in the afternoons? I've seen you get in your car twice this week. Where are you going?" She saw Craig's face go red and knew he was holding something back but couldn't tell what it was. Craig never broke his routine. "Well?"

"I gotta go somewhere off campus for one of my classes?" he said as if he wasn't sure of the answer.

"Why?"

Craig straightened up and looked past Abby. She turned to see two plates of food coming, held by the man who greeted them when they came in. He set them down saying, "Two special plates just as you ordered. Hope this works for you, sir."

"This looks perfect," Craig said, unfolding his napkin. Before them were plates of crusted lake perch, herb-roasted red potatoes, and garlic buttered asparagus. It was Abby's favorite meal, just like Frank would have made in the kitchen at the resort.

"How did...?" Abby couldn't finish the sentence. She picked up her napkin and placed it on her lap. After a deep breath, fighting back tears, she looked at Craig, who was already eating.

"It's good," he said with his mouth full and another bite on his fork, ready to go.

Abby regained her composure. "How did you do this?" She stared at Craig, unwilling to accept his joking silence.

"I made a few calls," he said with a smile between bites.

"No," she said, still staring at him. She pointed her fork at the food and almost laughed out, "How did this happen?"

"First," Craig said, knowing he had her, "you should eat before it gets cold."

Abby kicked him lightly under the table. "Tell me."

"Ok. So, I called Frank, and he told me this was your favorite meal." Craig took another bite, fully satisfied with himself.

Abby squinted at him and tried to bite her lip to keep from smiling. She couldn't let him win. She felt a tear roll down her face.

"I called around, but then I remembered my dad knew the guy who used to own this place. I gave him a call and asked if he could pull it off. I think he did ok, huh?" Craig was almost done with his fish.

A little annoyed, Abby continued to eat. He called in a favor. That was so the old Craig. On the other hand though, who would go to the trouble of doing this for her? It was just another example of Craig using his charm to get what he wanted. But it was so cute and nice. Abby decided to be happy for now. 'Live in the moment,' as Kate would say.

They ate their meal, and Abby was absorbed in the tastes that brought her home. It was very much the same as Frank would have made. Craig basked in his triumph. He sat back, put his hands behind his head for a moment, and smiled.

The man came back and asked how everything was, and they responded positively. He reminded them that the check had already been settled in advance and told them to take their time and enjoy. Craig indicated that they would be taking dessert with them. "Ok," the man said.

"So now for the real surprise," Craig said.

"There's more?" Abby fanned herself, feeling a little overwhelmed. Craig's face was suddenly very serious. The soft brightness of his eyes was replaced with an intensity she had only seen when he had a task to accomplish. He could go in and out of these moods very quickly when he wanted to. Abby put her fork and knife down to listen. The box with the dessert was dropped off, but they hardly noticed.

"So, the answer to your earlier question," Craig started.

"Which one?" Abby laughed a little, trying to lighten the mood.

"The one about where I'm going in the afternoons." He lowered his voice as though telling her a secret.

"Ok?" She readied herself, still hoping this was a joke.

"So, you know that I came back a little early for second semester?"

"Yes. I assumed it was to hang out with Brent cause he broke it off with his girlfriend." Abby was a little concerned.

"No," Craig said. "I could see him whenever. We live like ten minutes apart."

"So, what then?" There was an edge to her voice.

"I came back to meet with my advisor. Remember, I had that meeting right after Thanksgiving?"

"I think so." Abby took a drink of soda and refilled her glass. She held out the pitcher for Craig, but he waved it off.

"I came back to change my class schedule."

Abby put her elbows on the table and leaned her head on her hands.

"I'm dropping pre-med, and I'm going to finish my degree here."

She half-whispered, "What?"

Craig leaned in with one hand rubbing the sweat from his face. He was taking deep breaths. "I never wanted to be a doctor. It just seemed like the thing to do."

"But you're so smart. What are you going to do, Craig?"

"That's it." Craig smiled. "I switched my major."

"To what?"

"Education."

"Education. What...like teaching?"

"Yes."

"Why would you want to do that?" Abby's eyes sharpened, and her lips puckered a bit. "Why?"

"So, I was thinking I would like to be an English teacher. I really discovered last semester that I like to read and write. I always thought English was stupid, but there's so much I don't know. It's really cool."

"So, that's it?" she said softly. Abby was a bit relieved.

"Not entirely." Craig seemed encouraged by the release of tension. "I want to be a teacher so I can help you at the resort after we graduate. The summer is the busy season, and if I teach, I can help you run the place the whole time and get holidays too. Also, I would have the weekends."

Abby was silent. He lost his concentration momentarily.

"What?" Craig asked. The spark had returned to his eyes. Hers looked like two specks of emerald that were piercing through him. She continued to say nothing.

He tried again. "What do you think?"

"What do I think?" Abby parroted. "What do I think?"

"Yeah."

"So let me get this straight. You totally change your life, give up being a doctor, so you can move to my resort and help me run it?"

"Yes?" Craig was getting nervous.

Abby spoke quietly as not to alarm the other guests. "Are you fucking crazy?"

Craig straightened up and held his arms across the table. Abby didn't take hold of his open hands. He pulled them back, feeling self-conscious, and put them in his lap. "What?" He was confused. "What do you mean?"

"First, we've known each other for less than six months, and, all of a sudden, you're going to change everything? What if we're not together in four years?"

"Why wouldn't we be together, Abby?"

"That's not the point. You can't just go and change your life on a what if?

"Well I don't see it that way. Don't you ever think about the future?"

"Sure, but I don't go changing my life because of it yet."

"That's cause you're the one with the plan. You know what you want to do with your life."

Abby sat straight, her arms by her sides. Her face was

beginning to pale. "But they're my plans, Craig. Not yours. You need to live your life."

"Don't you see me in it? Don't you think I can be at the resort? Don't you see you and me together?"

"Right now, I see you in my life. But you don't get it." Abby could feel herself losing control. She hated the feeling. It was like on Thanksgiving Day. "I want to be with you, but..." She searched for what to say next.

"But what?" Craig was getting angry.

"I don't know if it's my dream anymore."

"What?" he asked. "The resort? It's all you talk about!"

"Is it? Have you actually been listening?"

"What's that supposed to mean? Yes. Since I met you, the resort is all you talk about. Running the resort. Getting home."

"My home," Abby said. "Not yours."

Craig felt like he had just been punched in the gut. He said meekly, "It could be our home." He paused. "What are you so mad about?"

"I don't know if I can run the resort." Abby tried not to raise her voice. "I don't think I can do it."

"Why? You know everything about the place. You could run it in your sleep."

"No. I could run the business, but not the resort."

"You lost me there, Abby."

"I can't talk to people the way my dad does. The way you do. I can run the business, but I can't sell it."

"What?" Craig was red in the face, but still fully focused. The owner came and asked if he could bring anything.

"No!" they both snapped.

"No, thank you," Craig said more softly, holding up his hand to excuse the outburst. The man stared at them briefly, looking puzzled, then left. Craig continued the softened tone, trying to bring the tension level down. "I guess I don't get it. Is this about Thanksgiving, out by the dock? You were just overwhelmed. It was a big crowd."

"No. I watched you the whole week. You're so damn comfortable in every situation. You can talk to anyone."

Craig furrowed his brow. "So? You can too..."

"No," Abby interrupted. "I can't. You can. My dad can. I don't want you to carry me through life. I certainly don't want to carry the burden of you dropping pre-med. I don't need that."

"What burden?"

"You want to change your whole life for me."

"Isn't that what people do when they're in love? Compromise and support each other?"

"Support, yes. Carry, no."

"How do I carry you exactly?"

"You helped me with biology. You help me with stats. Hell, you read ahead in Western Civ so you could help me with that. Now you want to 'help' with the resort."

"Yes. I want to help. What's wrong with that?"

"I need to figure it out for myself, Craig. You need to break free. I can't be all you have."

Another pitcher of soda arrived, and the owner poured both glasses full. "Everything ok back here?"

"Not really," Abby said.

"We're fine," Craig followed. The man left.

"There you go again. Everything's not fine, Craig." Abby stared through him.

He shook his head. "I don't get why you're so angry. I just want to help you."

"No!"

"No what?" Craig asked flippantly.

"I don't need your help."

"Ok. I won't help you with class anymore."

"That isn't it."

"What is it then?"

"I need to figure this out on my own."

"Ok. I'll let you figure stuff out."

"You're not getting me. I need to figure out my life."

"What are you talking about?"

"Everything. I need to figure it all out." Abby paused. "If I want to go home. If I want to run the resort. I need to figure it all out on my own. I don't need your help."

"What are you saying?"

"I'm saying your little plan put me on the spot. I'm not ready for that."

"Ok." Craig didn't know what else to say. "So...what now?"

"I need time to figure this all out."

"The resort? The classes? Fine."

"No. All of it."

"You and me? What are you saying?"

"Yes. You and me. You can't change your whole life for me."

"I did."

"Why?"

"Cause I see my future, and you're in it. The resort. The whole thing."

"Is it me? Or is it the resort you see?"

"What do you mean, Abby? Both!"

"Are you sure?"

"What are you getting at?"

"The resort gives you what you want. Not me."

"What are you talking about? I love you." Craig shook his head. He was trying to shake himself out of this moment.

After a long pause, Abby asked calmly, "What do you love about me?" Her eyes widened, catching Craig off guard.

"I love..." He took a deep breath to give himself time. " I love that you're grounded. I love that you know what you want. Or, at least, I think you do. I love that you know where you're from, and I know that you love me. You make me want to be with you." He said everything all at once, no pauses. After another hard breath in through his nose, he blinked multiple times, and a tear fell down his cheek.

"Did you see what you did there?" Abby said, still calm.

"What?" Craig asked.

"You love what I represent. You said nothing about me. You love that I am what you're not. I have a home. I have a plan. I'm grounded, whatever that means."

"But that is you. That's who you are."

"You're in love with the idea of me. Or the idea of who you think I am."

It seemed to Craig that she had thought this through. She had rehearsed these lines. He didn't understand. "Don't I show you that I love you?"

"All the time," Abby said, reaching for a napkin to wipe her eyes and nose.

"What's the problem then?"

"I don't know."

"Then what are we doing?"

"I don't know. I'm scared."

"Of what?" Craig wiped his own eyes with the back of his thumbs.

"Of you. Of this. Of all of it."

"What about this? We were having a good time." Craig was trying to turn the corner.

"It's always so perfect," Abby said, looking down at the table, unable to look up.

"I think so."

"That's part of the problem." She breathed harder and faster between the sobs.

"How is that a problem?" Craig raised his voice, realizing he couldn't steer the conversation. "What is going on?"

"Take this." Abby looked up and fixed her stare squarely on him. "This dinner. You called Frank, which is nice, so nice...but it's a sham."

"What?" Craig was clearly offended.

"You call in favors. You charm everyone you meet. It's all so easy for you, Craig."

"No it's not. This took a lot of planning."

"It's not just this. It's everything. Everything is easy for you. You can smile and shoot the shit with people and they're yours. You get whatever you want. You got me."

"Is that what you think? I get whatever I want? I don't! Obviously!" Craig threw his hands in the air.

"You're no different than your dad. Everyone wants to be with Craig McLean." With this, Abby looked down. She had gone for the Kryptonite. Craig had nothing, and she knew it. She had hurt him with the biggest bullet she could shoot, and it was over. No going back. "Can you just take me home?" Abby looked up through her tears.

Craig's cheeks had divided into creeks and streams forking one from another. He got up, and she stood as well. He walked to her side of the table, grabbed her jacket, and helped her get it on. Then, he grabbed the dessert and walked out of the restaurant, silently. He opened the car door for her and got in to drive back to campus. When they got to the parking lot by Abby's dorm, Craig parked the car and half-turned to her, "Do you want me to walk you to the door?"

"Sure."

Craig got out of the car. Abby let herself out before he could open the door. She held out the dessert box. "Do you want this?"

"No," Craig replied. "You and Kate can have it. It's apple pie."

Abby started to cry again, softly. It was her favorite. The air outside was cool, but not cold as they walked across the parking lot to her dorm. Craig reached for her hand, and their fingers fumbled together out of habit until she grasped his hand tightly. He squeezed back hard. Abby shuttered with the pain but didn't let go. They didn't look at each other.

When they got to the dorm, Craig asked, "Are we ok?"

"I don't know."

"Are we breaking up?" He began to shake. Abby could feel his hand twitch uncontrollably.

"I don't know. I just need some space."

"So we are." Craig took a deep, labored breath.

"Just let me figure this out. Give me space, ok?"

"Ok." He reached around Abby to hug her, and she squeezed back.

"Bye, Abby."

"Bye, Craig."

They walked away from each other. Abby looked back and saw that Craig did not. She went to her room.

Craig went to their bench. He sat in the cool evening air and looked up at the moonlight. He couldn't tell if it was full or not. Waxing or waning. Everything was unclear. He looked at his phone to see if Abby had texted him. She hadn't. He wrote *I love you* and left it on the screen, wondering if he should send it. After a minute, he hit send, put the phone in his pocket, and walked towards his dorm. A minute or two down the path, he took his phone out. It said "Read" and the response bubble was active. After a few seconds, it went away. Hoping for the message to come through, he stood in the darkness. Nothing came. He went inside. There was no one to call.

Chapter 24

When Craig woke up, he didn't realize that he had even fallen asleep. He looked around for his phone to see if he had any messages. There was nothing. For a moment, he contemplated sending another text, but thought better of it. He rolled out of bed and realized that he was still wearing his jacket. Instead of taking it off, he zipped it up and went out for a walk, leaving his phone on top of his dresser.

There was thick fog over campus. It was a damp cold, the kind that invades your very being if you don't keep moving. That's what Craig decided to do. He was going to walk until he could make sense of everything. He looked down towards the athletic fields at the north end of campus. It looked as if a cloud had descended on them and was starting to rise, so he would soon be in the midst of it.

The path he chose took him south first, and then he thought he would walk the campus counterclockwise in hopes of finding answers somewhere on this frost-covered morning. He was a block or two in when he looked down and saw that he was wearing his dress shoes. His feet began to ache almost immediately, but he continued, looking leisurely at the trees. Their preplanned nature annoyed him. The outdoors wasn't really the outdoors if you didn't have to watch your step. Craig turned east. Every stick on the sidewalk gave him a chance to see how far he could launch it. His lazy pace was the only thing he had found in the coolness of the early morning. He began to focus on the mist that came from his mouth.

When he reached the east side, Craig saw a church just off campus. He paused, trying to remember why this building held significance. It was plain enough, and Craig couldn't immediately recall why it should be special. There had been flyers for events all over the Union, but neither he nor Abby had ever attended one. Then he remembered. Kate went to church here every Sunday. She would be in there. She would have the answers he needed. Craig walked in and sat down at the back of the room. The man who was speaking up front paused to welcome him. Everyone else present turned briefly to look at him, which made Craig feel embarrassed. One head stayed turned when everyone else refocused on the minister. It was Kate. She stared at Craig. He couldn't tell if she was pissed or shocked. She kept staring until he looked down and put his hands in his coat pockets.

When the service ended, Craig continued to sit in the back with his head down. The presiding minister approached him and asked if he was ok or wanted to talk. Craig said no and told him he was waiting for someone. The minister patted him on the shoulder and left. Craig continued to sit until Kate came to him.

"Hi, Craig," she said as she sat down in the row of chairs in front of him. "I suppose you're here to talk to me."

He looked up with his hands still in his pockets. His eyes were watering, but he was determined. "I was actually hoping Abby would be here. Can you help me? How's she doing?"

Kate breathed deeply, her expression unchanging. Craig could see he was putting her in the middle of something and stared back at the floor. "Kate, I don't want you to do anything. You understand?" He refused to meet her eye to eye. "I just want to know how Abby is." A tear broke free. "I just want to know what I did." Craig took his hands from his pockets and wiped his eyes. With wet hands, he reached for the chair Kate was sitting in as if to pull himself up. He didn't stand. Instead, he just pulled himself to the front of his chair. "Can you tell me how she's doing? Tell the truth."

Kate put her hand on top of Craig's, but he switched grips and grabbed her hand. He finally met her eyes. Kate didn't flinch. "She's not doing well. She's torn up and confused. She doesn't know what she wants. In fact, she doesn't know much of anything right now."

Craig kept his eyes fixed on her face as she continued, "She doesn't know if she wants what she's always said she wants. She's struggling with lots of stuff."

"I could help her. Did she tell you that?"

"Craig." Kate loosened the grip, and he let go. She flexed her hand a few times. "She told me all about it. The dinner. All the nice things you did and said. We were up all night."

He could see she was pale, and her eyes seemed heavy. "I just want to know what I did."

"I don't think that's the issue."

"What is it?" He leaned forward, the tears falling from his cheeks uncontrollably.

"I don't know. She doesn't know."

"Should I go talk with her?" His voice cracked over the word 'talk,' and he coughed the last part out.

"No." Her voice was sharp.

"I'm sorry, Kate."

"No." Her tone was softer. "I'm sorry. I didn't mean to snap at you." She moved a little closer. "Just give her time. You'll see her in class tomorrow. She's got to work through this herself. Let her come to you."

"I love her." Craig delivered the line with all the earnestness he could muster.

"I know. And she loves you. Know that. But let her come to you. Promise?" This time Kate grabbed his hand.

"Ok," he said, defeated.

They got up to go. There were two people waiting in the back of the room, and Craig noticed Kate wave them off. She walked him to the door, holding his hand as though she was supporting him the whole way. When they reached the door, she said, "Take care. I'll see you soon, ok?"

"Ok," Craig replied and walked out.

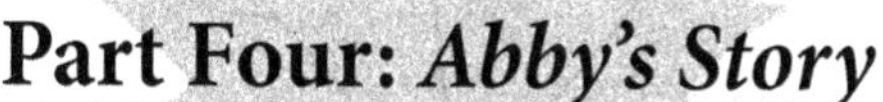

Part Four: *Abby's Story*

Chapter 25

I got to class early so I could sit where I wanted. I wanted to see what Craig would do. With my laptop out, I looked around. Craig was almost always early, but today he didn't seem to be here. I was so tired, having only slept three or four hours since Saturday night. Kate was probably sick of me by now, but she was too good of a friend to show it. Why did I have to fuck things up? Craig's such a great guy.

I looked down at my notes, trying to remember where the professor left off on Friday. Craig and I had made our outline for the week on Friday night. We were supposed to be getting into the origins of the universe today. I loved listening to people talk about the ideas of astronomy, but the math was not my favorite. I hoped it wouldn't be too hard. I wasn't sure how I would get through the class without Craig if the professor started in with computations. Craig is so damn good with math and so damn smart. Everyone we know gets how smart he is, but no one ever talks about it.

He walked in with a hoodie on. Craig never wears hoodies. He has a few, but he told me that the hoods annoyed him. The hood was up on this one, and he walked over to the seats across the aisle from where I was sitting and one row up. He didn't even look at me. I bent my head around to see his face, and when I caught his eyes, he widened them briefly while the rest of his face remained unchanged. A moment later, I turned away. God, I'm an idiot. "You're in love with the idea of me." What the hell was I thinking? Of course he's in love with me. He just doesn't understand. Kate said, "You gotta figure things out, and you have four years to do that. Don't put so much pressure on yourself." She's right. I need to live for now. Why was I thinking I had it all figured out? I don't want to be like my mom. That's what Craig doesn't get. He's like his dad, always at the center of things. I don't want to be like my mom, always behind the scenes, always cleaning up after my dad.

The professor started in, and I tried to listen, but he quickly descended into the physics behind the ideas. Maybe I should drop this class. I'm never going to get it without Craig's help, and besides, seeing him three times a week might start to get uncomfortable. When I looked back again, Craig's hands were moving quickly. He was locked in like he always was with me. Damn it. I know he loves me. Why don't I feel like I'm good enough for him?

Class ended, and I saw Craig packing up his things. I took a deep breath and walked over towards him. "Hey, Craig." He seemed startled. "Can I ask you about some of the math sometime?"

He fumbled with the zipper of his backpack, then swung the pack over his shoulder and turned to me. "Sure thing," he said in almost a pant. "You mean now, or another time?"

"Maybe another time, like up in the library. I don't want to keep you. I know you have a busy schedule." I tried to sound as pleasant as possible.

"Yeah, Abby, I can help you," he said, barely making eye

contact with me. "You know, you can get the old tests on his website. He puts a few of them up there for students to study."

"Oh really." I tried to catch his eye, but he put his hood up. I went to collect my things.

Just as I put my backpack on, I felt a hand around my wrist. "I'll give you the space you need." When he fixed his stare, it excited and unnerved me. "I know you need time to figure things out. But know, I'm right here." He let go before I could answer and walked away.

Kate: 18, Poem she wrote that hangs in her and Abby's room

Is it possible to render life
When reality is broken?
Can we create
A new world
Where things work out
The way we need them to?
No need to search the past
No need to look to the future
We need to remake the now
Take this moment
Explore all its beauty
See people for all their goodness
Try to be a spectator
To our own thoughts
Know what we are going to say
Before we say it
Don't let emotion cloud up
Our mental sky
We will be happy
Because we decide to be
We will not be victims
Of our circumstances
Live for the now
Make the now a place worth living in.

Chapter 26

I'm not sure Kate understood how attached to my hair I was. I don't think she really cared. She tends to get caught up in things and then involve me in them. Locks of Love is a great cause, but I don't see cutting my hair like that again. Although, I do like it now.

I was so nervous. Kate skipped all the way to the Union where her ministry group and a few local hair stylists were sponsoring a "hair drive." I had trouble catching my breath all the way there. Kate was getting her hair cut for the third time. Every time she gets to the point where she can cut ten inches or more, she finds a place to donate. I had been growing my hair since I was ten or eleven. Aside from trimming the split ends, it had not seen a scissors.

"It will be an adventure," Kate said as she skipped a few steps in front of me. She smiled, almost laughing, and beckoned me to move faster. "Come on. Live for the moment." This was one of her favorite phrases. I wasn't entirely sure what she meant by it.

Kate sat in the waiting room, giddy. She was bouncing so much that I couldn't tell if she was more excited for herself or me. "You know this is a good thing. You need a change," she said.

I knew she was right. It had been a week since Craig and I broke up or whatever. Outside of the awkward exchanges in class or quick glances on the paths, I didn't see him that much. He must have stuck with the education stuff because I did see him leave campus a few times. I just can't see him being a teacher. Or maybe, he would actually be perfect at it. He could do anything he wanted. I just don't want to be responsible for holding him back.

"It's our turn," Kate said, and she grabbed my hand. She is such a do-gooder. When we walked into the room, pop music was playing in the background, and hair was all over the floor. It smelled like hairspray, and everyone was energetic and smiley. The whole thing was a bit too cheery for me.

"I'll go first," Kate called from the chair next to mine as she rubbed her hands together vigorously. She was like a kid at Christmas. The woman pulled her hair back in a ponytail.

"Ready?" the woman asked.

"You bet!" Kate yelled. It took all she had to sit still as the woman cut ten inches of hair from her head. "Wooooooo!!!" Kate squealed. She immediately ran her hands through what was left of her hair and shook her liberated head from side to side. Then, she readied herself for the rest of the cut. Kate got a tapered cut, something I could never pull off. It totally fit her spunky personality.

Another woman came up to me. "So, is this your first time doing this?"

"Yes," I answered. "How'd you know?"

"Well, for starters, you look about as jittery as a squirrel, and second, your hair is the longest I have ever seen."

I pulled my hair over my shoulders, and it touched my legs.

My hair was my thing. Craig loved my hair. I think it was his thing too.

"So, are you ready for this?" the woman asked.

"I think so." I tried to sound confident. I was glad my stylist wasn't the super cheery type. Or at least she realized I wasn't into that.

"You have beautiful hair," the woman said as she teased my hair back into a ponytail.

"Thank you," I replied. I was gripping the arms of the chair tightly, and sweat dripped down my cheeks.

"Here we go." And with that, over a half-dozen years and fourteen inches of hair were gone. I reached behind my head, instinctively, to find that my hair now only touched my shoulders, and barely. I shook my head, and it felt so light. "Now let me clean up the lines and style it a bit, hun. You mind if I take a little volume out of it?"

"Sure. Thanks." I didn't want to stop touching it. After a few minutes, she was done and let me look in the mirror. I couldn't help but smile. I ran my hands through it over and over, flipping it back and forth. It was amazing. I felt light and fresh. Kate came over with her hair cut boy short. She looked so cute.

"You look so pretty, Abby," Kate said. She ran her fingers through my hair. She was as giddy as when she came in. We thanked our stylists and got our coats.

As we walked out of the Union, the wind caught my hair and blew it all around. Even tucking it behind my ears didn't help with the new lightness. I turned towards the wind and let it blow my hair back so I could put it in a ponytail. While I walked behind a dancing Kate, I couldn't help but wonder what

Craig would think of it. I half-hoped we would see him as we made our way home.

The next morning I got my answer. After astronomy class, Craig came up to me in the hall. Throughout the lecture, I kept looking at him to see if he recognized me. I even sat in a different seat to throw him off a bit. I didn't mean to play with him, but somehow I knew he would find me easily. When he did walk up, I could feel my heart beating in my throat, and I felt flush and sweaty. He had a curious half-smile, and his head tilted to the side as his eyes narrowed. "Abby?" he said carefully and slowly.

"Hi, Craig!" I replied, skipping over to him. I still felt almost weightless.

He reached his hand up and ran his fingers through my hair. I leaned in out of habit and let him run his hand down my cheek and trace my jawline. It felt so good. "How are you?" he asked quietly and sweetly. "This is new."

"I'm great. And yeah, Kate and I got our hair cut for Locks of Love." I just wanted to lay my head on his chest, but instead, I stepped back. "How are you?"

"I'm ok. Busy," he said, nodding his head.

"How's the field experience?"

"It's fun. I really like it," he said with a smile. "Do you want to get a bite to eat sometime?" The smile abruptly went away.

People were passing all around us as another class got out. I took a step closer to him and put my hand on his chest. "Perhaps," I said without looking up to meet his eyes. I patted his chest with a closed fist and continued, "I'm meeting Kate for an early lunch. I gotta go cause she's got class in about an hour." I looked up. Craig's lips were straight across, and his eyes were wet.

He grabbed my hand gently and said, "Ok. I'll see you around."

I turned to go, but he held my hand for just a moment. "Abby."

I turned back to him. "Yes, Craig?"

"You're beautiful." With that, he let go of my hand and walked off in the opposite direction I planned to go. There was no longer a bounce to his step, and his shoulders were slumped. He put the hood of his sweatshirt up. I watched him until he disappeared. I began to wonder if he hadn't disappeared altogether. I knew I had to figure things out, but Kate was the only one I had to talk to about all of it. I didn't know what to do. Maybe it was time to call Meghan.

Abby: 18, Last time with Meghan before going to college.

"This has been the best summer, don't you think?" I asked Meghan as I looked across the table at her.

"It has been pretty epic. I'm glad I got to work with you all summer. It was more fun than working in the shop." Meghan had her head in her hands.

"I hope we can do this next summer too." I was just so happy. "It was so cool having my best friend around all summer since we're going to different schools soon."

"Yeah. We'll see. I'm just excited to get to Madison. I've been dreaming of going there since middle school." Meghan perked up when she said this.

"Yeah. I know. There was never a question for you."

"Whitewater will be cool."

I was not as excited as she was about school. I was going to Whitewater for the business program, but only so I could get home to the resort. My father told me that someday he would give me the resort, but only if I got a degree. That was the only reason for going to college. "Yeah. I don't know. Sometimes, I wish we were still going to go to school together. Remember the plan?"

"You mean opening a place in Chicago together? I remember that. It would have been fun, but we were kids. I'm still going to move to Chicago, but I think marketing will be the thing. I just love the creative side of that business."

"You'll do great, Meghan."

"Besides, could I really ever tear you away from Wood Lake? You are the resort. It's part of you," she said, finally focusing on my face.

"You're right. I'm just nervous."

"You'll be fine. You'll probably meet some boy who will fall head over heels in love with you, and he will come back home with you, and you will live happily ever after." Meghan couldn't help but laugh at herself a little. She knew I had never had a serious boyfriend and had certainly never been in love.

I played along. "Oh you bet. He'll be a football player and super handsome too."

"I think that sounds about right."

We laughed and told stories for a while longer, and then it was time for her to go. I had to drive to Whitewater on Monday, but she had to be in Madison on Saturday. It was the last time we would be together until Thanksgiving.

Chapter 27

"You did what?!!!" Meghan's voice was shrill coming off the screen. "Are you a complete dumbass?"

"No," I said sharply. "I just need time to figure things out. I don't know what I want right now."

"You want Craig. You want to take over the resort. You want to come home." Meghan was shaking her hands at me. "You never talk about anything else, because that's what you want."

"But you don't understand. I don't know if I can do that anymore. I'm not Craig. Shit. I mean, I'm not my dad." Crap. Why did I say that?

"There you go." Meghan seized on the mistake. "Nice slip. You think Craig's too good for you. Here we go again. You always do the same shit. Something good happens in your life, and you think you don't deserve it."

"That's not true," I pleaded, not fully convinced of my own words.

"Of course it is," Meghan continued. "You did the same thing with Troy. He said he liked you, and you went out a few times, and then you drove him away because you thought he couldn't be interested. Your dad buys you a new boat for doing such a good job working through the summer, and rather than having fun, you only use it for work because you don't think you deserved it. Now Craig. You want me to go on?"

"Do you think that's really true?" I asked.

"Hell yeah." Meghan was staring through the computer screen and through me as well. "Think about it, Abby. Has he done anything other than be great to you?"

"No. Not really," I replied sheepishly. "It's just that…" I couldn't put it together.

Meghan jumped in. "It's just that what?"

"It's just that he jumped in on my dream. He's so much better than me at meeting people and selling the place. He doesn't know what he wants from life so he inserted himself into mine. He doesn't even know who he is!"

"Really?" Meghan sounded suspicious. "I've only known him for a little while, but the one thing I do know is that he loves you. Sure, he loves the resort. Who doesn't? Sure, he loves that you have a dream and a purpose, but that's who you are."

"No, Meghan. It's part of who he thinks I am. It's not me."

"Well, Abby, it seems to me you're the one who doesn't know who she is. All I know is that he wants you. He wants to be with you because he loves you. Not what he thinks you are, but what he knows you are."

"How do you know?"

"He called me and asked me. That's how. Pull your head out of your ass and figure this out cause I've never seen you happier than I did this fall. He makes you happy. Don't throw that away."

She hung up. I laid my head down on the pillow. He loves me. I didn't even care how he got Meghan's number. Why couldn't I believe I was worthy? A tear came down my cheek, and I rolled to the side to wipe it away. There was homework to do, and normally, I would be with Craig on a Friday night up in the library. I wondered if he was up there. I wanted to go find out, but decided against it. I couldn't do that tonight.

Even though we were just partners on a project, sitting across from another guy in the cafeteria felt weird. However, it was nice to talk with someone besides Kate. Mark was like the guys I knew back home. He was from Hayward and loved being outdoors. We could talk fishing and hunting, and he knew what it was like to live in a town largely dependant on making a living from people visiting from outside of it. His parents owned a restaurant on Main Street. They lived outside of town in the woods, on a lake, and I found out that he had grown up just like me. We got along well enough and worked efficiently on our stats projects, but I could never like Mark as more than a friend. He wasn't Craig. He asked me to go get a bite to eat, and I said yes so we could talk about homework. I hoped he didn't think we were on a date.

"So, how are we going to get all the data we need when the acquisition we want to study won't be complete until the summer?" I tried to get things started with talk about class.

"I'm not sure," Mark replied. "We might have to choose a different subject."

"Perhaps." I looked around the cafeteria. It wasn't quite full, but almost. People were walking everywhere, but then I saw them. Jen and Craig were sitting over by the window. Mark kept talking, but I was no longer listening. Between people passing by, I became fixated on Craig. Why was he eating with Jen? They hadn't spoken, as far as I knew, for months. I knew they went way back, but was he seeing her again? I could see him giving her his full attention. He was smiling and laughing between bites. I hadn't seen him smile like that in weeks. We had barely even spoken in almost two weeks. Was he moving on?

"Abby?" Mark said. "Abby?" He looked behind him.

"Oh, yes," I said returning to the table. "What?"

"Where'd you go? Whatcha looking at?" He looked back at me.

"Oh. Nothing."

"You were staring at that couple by the window."

"They're not a couple," I said sharply.

"Looks like it to me," he said calmly. "Do you know them?"

"Yes." I looked down and pushed the remains of my salad around.

"Ok," Mark said slowly. His face was blank. "Well, I guess I'll see you around." He started getting up to go.

I reached across the table. "Mark," I said. "I'm sorry I snapped at you. The guy's my ex-boyfriend." I couldn't believe I said it.

"Oh. That's ok. I'll see you around."

"Sure. Sorry. Bye."

"Bye." He walked away. I looked back, and they were gone. I started to pack up my things, but someone sat down across from me. Hoping it was Craig, I looked up smiling. It was Jen.

"Hi, Abby," Jen said, perky as always. She was always so damn happy. I guess that's how you get when everyone thinks you're so pretty and you get whatever you want.

"Hello, Jen," I said as nicely as I could. "How have you been?"

"I've been great," she replied. "So you and Craig are taking a break, huh?"

"Is that what he's calling it?" I was getting annoyed already. What the hell did she care?

"Listen, it's probably not my place, but Craig is my friend. He's all torn up over this. He wants nothing more than to get back with you."

"Really?" I tried to sound sarcastic.

Jen remained unfazed. "Yes. Really. Listen." Her instructional tone really bothered me. "Abby, Craig was never happier than he was with you. He certainly was never as happy with me as he was with you. I think you made him better. He's a great guy, but somehow, you made him better."

I didn't quite know what to say. I muttered, "Thank you." But that was all I could get out. I felt like I was going to cry.

"I don't all know what went on with you guys, and it's really none of my business, but Craig is wrecked. You made him happy, and I'll bet he did the same for you. Just think about it?"

"Ok. Thanks."

She got up and walked away. I was left a bit speechless. Craig had deployed everyone. Or maybe everyone could just see for themselves. Maybe I was wrong. Maybe he did love me for me. "I made him better." The words played over and over in my head. Could that really be possible?

Chapter 28

Craig came to pick me up on a Wednesday evening around eight. We had to do a lab for astronomy class where we went out to chart the stars and identify a few of the planet formations. We had considered getting new lab partners but decided we could handle it. We had to send time-stamped pictures to our professor and use the app we downloaded for the class. It was a cool and clear night. I put on my winter coat and a hat, which had become a habit ever since I got my hair cut two weeks before. It had been almost four weeks since we broke up. I had said it a few times in my head and was beginning to settle into the thought, even though I still wanted things to work out. I just needed him to understand that I was scared. I needed to figure things out for myself. The resort was a dream of mine, but everything was so overwhelming. I needed him to get all of that, but how could I even begin?

I saw Craig walking up from a distance. I was excited to see him, but when he saw me waiting and our eyes connected, I was suddenly really nervous.

"Hi, Abby," Craig said cheerfully.

"Hi, Craig," I said, giving him a smile. I couldn't tell if he was trying to be happy or if he was really over us. It was all just too confusing.

"So...are we going to do this thing?"

"That's what you're here for, I guess." I heard the awkwardness of that answer immediately after uttering it.

"Where do you think is the best place to go?" Craig asked. This struck me as surprising because he usually had a plan to get things done as quickly as possible.

"I'm not sure. North of the athletic fields maybe? There might be less light over that way."

"Sounds good to me," he said. "You lead."

As we walked, I could see the spring in Craig's step that I was used to. He was almost skipping out in front of me the way Kate always did. I didn't know what to make of it, but his mood was fine by me. It certainly was better than him frowning around like he had been the last couple of weeks. I guess who could blame him though?

"Come on," he called from a few steps ahead.

"What happened to me leading?" I asked.

He laughed, and I broke into a jog to catch up to him. The stars became clearer as we walked the path to the north side of campus. We found a good spot between lights to make our first observations. Craig brought his tablet with the app so we could get started. The assignment was more a matter of appreciation than work. I was beginning to feel the same way about Craig. We pointed to different places in the sky, and he would take pictures as I took down notations on what we were seeing. We made a good team.

After only a little while, we finished all our observations and gathered the pictures we needed. Craig emailed me the folder so I could annotate the pictures with my notes and finish the assignment. It was eight forty-five, and I told him we should probably head back. It was getting chilly outside.

As we walked back, Craig asked, "Are you cold?"

"Yes," I said. "A little."

"Can I put my arm around you?" he said quietly.

"That would be nice." And he did. "Thank you."

We walked past the fields and past my dorm and just kept on walking. I had a feeling that he would keep walking all night, so I suggested we find a place to sit down.

"Sure. Why don't we go to our bench?"

"Craig," I said a bit more sharply than I wanted.

"No," he said, surprised. "Just to sit and talk. It's right around the corner."

He wasn't lying. It was only a ten-second walk. We found it and sat down.

"Soooo, how's it going?" Craig asked, putting his arm on the back of the bench behind me. I moved away an inch or two, and he pulled his arm back.

"Fine," I said pensively, looking at him with my eyes narrowed. I wasn't sure where he was trying to go. "I'm fine, Craig."

"Neat," he said cheerfully, fidgeting with the strings if his sweatshirt. Again, I couldn't tell if he was really in a good mood or just trying to be. If it was the latter, I appreciated the effort.

"How have YOU been?"

"Up and down. You know. Getting a bit better, I think. I'm really busy." His eyes met mine. It felt a little weird seeing him without his usual intensity. He seemed a bit distracted and distant. I longed for him to lock in. It was one of the things that made him so attractive.

"How's the field experience going?" I must have asked the

right question, because his eyes lit up.

"Oh it's great. I actually get to lead some small groups and interact with the kids. It's been fun so far." He was animated and leaned in, pulling closer. 'There's the Craig I love.' I couldn't believe I was thinking that.

"You actually work with the students?" He was really excited, so I kept the conversation going. I was really enjoying just listening to him talk.

"I was supposed to be observing, but I love working with them. I'm at a middle school, so it's younger students. They're really cool. I'm helping with a math class right now." He began to focus unwaveringly on just me. I think he could tell I was listening, and I could feel the bubble closing in a little. He put his arm back around me.

"Well, that's right up your alley," I said, laying my head on his shoulder just for a moment. It was just what we did. I don't think he noticed.

"Yeah. It's been fun. I think I might have found my thing. I look forward to it every day." I smiled at the intimacy. "But," he added, "it's early."

I lifted my head and looked directly in his eyes. "Hey, Craig," I said softly. "Can I ask you something?"

He turned his head to the side to meet my face better. "Of course." His voice was sure and true.

"I don't know how." I looked away for a moment.

"You can ask me whatever. Don't worry about it."

"Ok...Did you call Meghan?" I wished I hadn't asked the question as soon as I did. I could see Craig's smile straighten to shock or surprise, but then it returned.

"Yes." He straightened up. "Yes. I didn't know what else to

do. I didn't mean to piss you off or anything."

"No. She Skyped me and was all pissed at me. She thinks I made a big mistake." I could feel myself welling up. I didn't want to cry. I took a deep breath.

"You just need time. I kinda threw a lot on you. It was dumb of me not to talk with you about my plans."

"It's not just that. I saw how you were at the resort. It's like you fit perfectly, and you are such a natural at…" I couldn't finish the sentence.

"A natural?" Craig said. "At what?"

"At everything," I spat out.

He laughed. "I wish."

"But you're good at everything you try. You're smart, and you get along with everyone."

"Really? You really think that?" He continued to chuckle.

"Yes. You're always helping me and everyone. You can talk to anyone. I just wonder. I always wonder." I paused again.

"Wonder what?" he asked, taking his arm from around my shoulder. He took my cold hands in his and began to gently rub them. I looked up, but the stars were obscured by the light from the street lamps.

"I wonder why me? Why did you choose me?" I lowered my gaze to engage him again.

"What are you talking about?"

"I was just so scared a few weeks ago. What makes me someone you would want to change your life for?" I stood up. The feeling of fear I had a month ago started to flood back in, and I shivered. I didn't know if it was the cold or that I was just upset.

"Hey," he said. "Stop."

"What?" I was biting my lip and trying not to lose control. I didn't want to cry, but it was inevitable.

"I chose you because you're my best friend. You're the only person I've ever met who I could really talk to. You don't expect me to be anyone. You listen to me and just allow me to be me. All those other people are just falling for my bullshit. You're the only person I can really be myself with."

I grabbed one of his hands, unwilling to go further with the conversation. "Can you walk me home?"

"Yes," he replied. "Of course. Just one more thing."

"What?" I said quietly. I was so tired.

"I just want to be your friend. Can we just be friends?" He had so much sincerity in his voice. I squeezed his hand tightly.

"Yes," I said. "That sounds nice."

"Let's get you home. You've got our homework to finish." He winked at me.

I laughed through the last of my tears and breathed deeply. He was just too damn cute. We walked back to my dorm, and I gave him a hug. "Thanks for a fun night." I half-expected him to kiss me, and I would not have pulled back. Instead, he tapped my nose.

"No problem, friend." He had a sly smile on his face and turned to go. "Don't watch me walk all the way home now." He never turned back, but I watched him walk away until he was out of sight.

"Wow. You were out late on a school night," Kate said sarcastically from behind her desk. "What gives?"

I put my jacket on the hook and my hat into my pocket. Then, I went over to my dresser to get a towel to wipe my face.

I sat down on my bed and opened my laptop. Kate slid out from behind her desk, stood up, and came over by my bed. She leaned her head down between me and my laptop. She made a funny face and said, "Abby. Abby. Abby. Abby. Tell me what's going on." I couldn't help but laugh. She straightened up.

"I have homework to do, young lady," I said in a stern voice, but I couldn't hold it together. After a moment, I sat up and took a deep breath. Kate was still waiting, wide-eyed.

"What?" she asked. "Did you kiss him?" She made a smoochy face. I couldn't tell if she was excited for me or if she wanted to live vicariously through me.

"No!" I replied. "We took a walk. That's all."

"Boring!" she yelped. "So are you guys a thing again or what?"

"We're friends," I said flatly.

"Friends, smriends. What did he say?"

"He told me he wanted to be friends."

"Really?" Kate sat down in her chair and spun around slowly. "He said that?"

"Yes."

"What did you say?" She planted her feet and stopped spinning.

"I said sure." I tried to act like I was going back to my work. Kate didn't buy it.

"You said sure?!"

"Yep." I smiled a tight smile. "That's what I said."

"You're killing me. He asked you to be his friend, and you said 'sure.' You guys are the boringest couple on earth."

"We had a nice talk. We told each other the truth. I think it was good. No offense, but I just need him as a friend," I said.

"Why would I take offense? I get it. Come on, though, that's it?"

"That's about it. I just need a bit more time to think things through. I needed my friend back."

"Well, good for you," Kate said and rolled her chair back to her desk. "Now you get that homework done, young lady." Then, she broke out laughing.

Chapter 29

Over the next two weeks, I saw a little more of Craig. We started sitting next to each other in class, went out to lunch a few times, and even studied in the library on a Friday night, although we now sat across from each other. We started to laugh and smile as we talked about our days. He was always excited to tell me about his field experience. He loved talking about the kids, and it struck me that he had never seemed so happy. His drive and purpose seemed to have returned. Education was a subject he wanted to stick with, although he hadn't told his parents yet. We lived in the now of our days, and things were good. Every night we could, we took a walk around campus. There was never a hint of him trying to hold my hand or put his arm around me, although I kinda hoped he would. The weather was often cold and damp, but our bubble was returning slowly.

Then, I got a call. It came out of nowhere. I let the phone ring and saw a voicemail from the caller. The message was from Sarah. "Hey Abby. It's Sarah. Just making sure you're coming to the wedding next week. You didn't RSVP so I thought I'd check. Call me." I had totally forgotten she'd invited me, and I never got a formal invitation. I called her right back.

"Hello?"

"Hi. It's Abby. I didn't recognize your number."

"Oh, Abby. Hi. Thanks for calling me back. I have a list of calls to make."

"So...about the wedding."

"Yeah. So you'll be there right?"

"Well, Craig and I aren't together anymore."

"Really?"

"Yeah. We're still friends and all, but we aren't a couple."

"Wow. He didn't say anything."

"So, I don't know. It would be weird if I come, I think."

"Oh no. I want you to come."

"But..."

"But nothing. You came to my fitting, and I had so much fun getting to know you over Christmas. I know my parents would love to have you come. And Claire would love it too."

"Ok," I said awkwardly.

"Cool then. Did Craig give you the invitation?"

"No. He didn't."

"That little shit."

"Well, we're not together, so…"

"Well, get it from him. It has all the information on it."

"Ok."

"Great. So we'll see you next week?"

"Sure."

"Ok. Bye, Abby. Thanks."

"Bye." I was about to hang up the phone when I heard, "Wait! Wait!" I put the phone back to my ear.

"Yes?"

"Chicken or steak?"

"What?"

"Do you want chicken or steak? We need to get the final count to the venue this weekend."

"Steak."

"Great. Bye."

"Goodbye." I hung up and texted Craig. *Your sister just called about the wedding.* Several minutes passed before a response came.

Oh shit. Sorry.

So, I'm going.

Really?

Sarah didn't give me much choice.

That sounds like her.

We should probably talk logistics.

That would be good. Tonight? Library?

Sure :)

;)

You're a goof.

Yep.

Part Five

Chapter 30

Both Craig and Abby decided that she would go to Madison on Saturday. Craig had to go to the rehearsal dinner on Friday, and she had no interest in that. Kate would drive Abby up to Madison before going to Milwaukee to catch a plane to go on her mission trip with her church group. Craig told Kate to drop Abby off at the Monona Terrace, and then he and Abby could run up to the room to change. All through the ride, Abby was nervous.

"Abby," Kate said. "You've barely said a thing. What's up?"

"I'm just nervous. I'm not sure about this weekend." She looked out the window.

"You'll be fine. Craig will be there."

"I know, but…it's weird. I don't think his parents like me."

"Forget them." She looked at Abby and reached to touch her leg. "Remember, enjoy the moment. It's a beautiful day. Dance with Craig, eat some good food, and have some fun."

"I know."

"You'll be home tomorrow. What can be better than that?"

"Thanks, Kate."

As they pulled up to the Terrace, Abby could see Craig waiting for her. It was still morning, so he was dressed in normal clothes. She was thankful he wasn't in his tux yet. It would have made her feel like things were getting too real too fast. Craig was an usher, but he had assured Abby that he would be sitting at her table. She said goodbye to Kate and went to get her bag, but Craig had already grabbed it from the back seat. He gave her a half hug, and they walked towards the hotel. Their room was on the eighth floor.

"I'm really sorry about the room," Craig said before opening the door.

"Did you mess it up already?" Abby said, surprised because Craig's side of his dorm room was always impeccably clean. It was Brent who was a slob.

"No, that's not it." He let Abby go in first. She walked through the room to the open shade and looked out the window at the beautiful view of the lake. She was excited to see open water.

"I'm not sure what the problem is, Craig. This is a really nice room."

"Turn around."

Abby turned to seeing him standing next to one bed, king-sized. She had walked right past it. "I think Sarah did this on purpose," Craig said. "I'm sorry. I tried to get it changed, but they're packed."

"That's fine. I'm sure we can manage."

"Really?" Craig said. "I thought you'd be pissed."

"What's the point? And like you said, Sarah probably set it up. If there's nothing we can do, who cares? Just stay off my side," Abby responded, wagging her finger and smiling. "When does this whole thing get going?"

Craig laughed a bit and said, "Two o'clock. I have to be at the ceremony on the Terrace at one to start seating people."

"What time is it now?" Abby asked, looking around for a clock.

"Eleven, I think," Craig replied. "Want to get some lunch?"

"Sure."

They went downstairs and walked out on a beautiful, early spring morning. The day had blessed them. With a mild winter, so far spring was following suit. A person could get away without a jacket. They found a place to get a quick meal and headed back to the Terrace. Sarah was to be married in the Terrace ballroom with the view of the lake as her backdrop. There would be pictures after the ceremony, and cocktail hour started at five. Abby planned to go upstairs during pictures and take a quick nap.

The wedding space was immaculate, as Abby expected it to be. They were using the same room for the ceremony and reception. Everything was done with purple accents, and with the lake in the back as they were married, it was a scene out of a magazine. 'Just the way Linda would like it,' Abby thought to herself.

During the ceremony, Craig had Abby sit near the back so he could sneak in after everyone was seated. After greeting his parents and thanking them for having her, Abby took her seat. Claire was a bridesmaid. Her hair was done nicely, but she had dyed it purple to match the decor. She had succumbed to convention for the weekend, almost. Abby caught her eye when she came in, and Claire gave her a wry smile and a wink, which made her laugh. Sarah was gorgeous of course. There was not a hair out of place. As Craig had explained, this whole weekend was Linda's big show. Sarah played along as she always had; being perfect was a habit of hers. It seemed to be the thing to do in the McLean family. All the children seemed to hate it, but they all accepted the perks.

Craig sat down next to Abby as the ceremony began. He took her hand in his, and she touched her head to his shoulder for a moment. "Sarah's really beautiful," she whispered.

"Yeah. She sure is. Brad's a good guy too. I'm really happy for them," Craig said, looking up at his sister.

The ceremony was religious in nature, but not overly so. There were readings and a message from the minister, but no communion, thankfully. Abby didn't want to have to walk up front. When it was over, Sarah saw Abby as she walked out. "Thanks for coming," she whispered as she was swept out the door.

"I gotta go," Craig said. "You going to be ok?"

"I'm a big girl, Craig," Abby responded. "You go on." He kissed her on the forehead and went off.

Abby waited until the room cleared out a bit before walking out on the Terrace deck. She found a place to sit for a while and thought about how familiar Craig was getting and whether she was ok with it. He was such as good guy. He treated her well, and it seemed that he was always thinking about her. Craig was always in her mind as well. Sometimes, when she should have been listening in class, Abby found herself thinking about something funny Craig said or a goofy face he made, and it made her chuckle aloud. More often, she thought about Craig holding her at night and how content that made her feel.

All of these thoughts and feelings were churning around when she forced herself back to the moment. A sailboat was out on the water. It was the only boat out, and Abby supposed it was because the water was still very cold. She watched as it moved across the lake. With little wind, the pilot had to work hard to make it go. Abby imagined that he was just happy to be out on the water. There was a freedom in being out there. There was no time to think, just react. "Be in the moment," she said out loud. She was starting to understand.

Back up in the room, Abby took the bags off the bed, and a piece of paper fell out of Craig's bag. She picked it up to put it back, but when she turned it over, her legs went numb, and she sat back on the edge of the bed. The paper was in fact two pieces of wax paper, and between them were three leaves. Craig had placed the leaves together and ironed them into the wax paper just the way she described when talking about some of the art projects they did at the resort. When she examined them closer, she noticed one of the leaves had a date on it. It was the day of their first official date. He must have picked it up down at the lake. The other two leaves had writing as well. One said "Wood Lake" and had a quote from one of her favorite Jason Isbell songs, "Stockholm." It read, "I traded those lessons for faith in a girl." The other leaf said, "I choose her." Abby began to breathe heavily. This gesture said everything about them all at once. She decided to put the paper back into Craig's bag. He had obviously meant her to have it at some point, but she didn't want to ruin the surprise. After placing it in the bag, she just lay back on the bed and smiled at the ceiling. She wiped away a tear.

Abby had actually managed to fall asleep for a little while. When Craig came up to to get her for cocktail hour and dinner, he woke her up by sitting next to her on the bed and running his fingers through her hair. "Hey," he said. "Wake up, sleepy. We've gotta get going." He kept his voice low. Abby didn't want to open her eyes. She just wanted him to stay in the room and keep talking to her.

"Ok," she said, stretching. "I gotta look at my hair and makeup."

Craig watched her walk to the bathroom. He hoped he could soon call her his girlfriend again. It would be weird to introduce her without that phrase, but he didn't want to ruin what they were creating. He just wanted to touch and hold her as he had done before.

"Ready to go?" Abby asked in a cheerful voice. She had styled her hair with soft curls and done her eyes smoky, which make the flecks of blue and green in them jump off her face. She had on a black dress, which Craig had hardly noticed before under the sweater she had worn to the ceremony, and she was actually wearing heels. Not high ones, but heels nonetheless. He didn't say anything. "Babe," Abby said then quickly closed her mouth. "Sorry, Craig." Her face was red.

"You can call me babe," Craig said, smiling and getting up. He recognized her embarrassment. "You look very pretty. You're right, we need to go."

"Thank you," Abby replied. She was nervous about the reception. She didn't really want to talk to Linda and Mike, but she steeled herself for the inevitable encounter. Craig offered his arm ceremoniously, and she took it. They were off.

During the cocktail hour, Craig got Abby and himself two glasses of red wine. She mostly followed him around and was introduced as a friend, though she supposed that many people were making their own assumptions. She did her best Craig impression, smiling and making small talk with relatives and those friends close enough to call aunts and uncles. More than a few times, Craig rolled his eyes and puffed his cheeks in an exhausted way. Abby could tell that he was being honest when he said it was all bullshit. All you really had to do was answer the questions being asked and reflect those questions back, pretending to be interested. It became easier when everyone had a few drinks in them. The wine was top notch, but Abby knew well enough not to drink too much. She had no intention of letting things get out of hand as they almost did over Thanksgiving. When Craig brought her a glass of water without asking, she knew he was thinking the same.

Dinner went off without a hitch as Abby let Craig do most of the talking. The steak was amazing. The spice was just right, and Abby had another glass of wine. Craig marveled at her ability to hold her own. She had returned to the confident, forward-looking girl he had fallen in love with in the fall. She was sure of who she was and confident with what she planned to do with her life. There were a few times he found himself lost in watching her, especially when Claire stopped to chat. They seemed to get along so well. This made Craig happy. The crowd of familiar people drew his attention away from her at times, but Abby would bring him back into focus with a wink, a smile, or a pat on his thigh.

Glasses rang out, and toasts began. Jim and Mike propped each other up through a drunken thank you, and the best man and maid of honor spoke. Craig was happy he had been excused from a sibling toast, telling Abby that Claire had smashed the idea. Linda was not happy.

Music started, and there were the traditional dances and a wedding march that Craig had to attend. One of his "uncles" slid down into the seat next to Abby.

"So what's the name of that place your folks own in Eagle River?" He was certainly not sober.

Abby turned to him and smiled. "Wood Lake Resort."

"I think I stayed there once. Small place? Nice lodge? Good fishing?" His face was red, and he leaned in a little too much for her liking.

"Sounds about right."

"What's his name? The guy that runs the place?"

"John Whitworth...my father," Abby answered.

"Yeah, John. He's a good guy. He took us on a fishing tour early one morning. I caught a good one. There was this other guy who cleaned it for us and cooked it up for lunch?"

"The fish?" Abby inquired sarcastically. "That would be Frank."

"Yeah, Frank!" the man said, slapping the table a bit harder than he probably intended. "Great place. Your family owns that place?"

"Yes, sir," Abby said, nodding her head.

"Great place. I need to get back there." The man stood up. "I'm going to get a drink. Need anything?"

Abby held up a half-full glass of wine. "No. I'm fine."

"Suit yourself."

Abby took a drink and looked for Craig on the dance floor. He was being goofy, jumping around more than dancing. She laughed to herself.

When the wedding march and introductions were over, Craig came back and sat down, taking off his coat and hanging it on the back of his chair. He put his arm around Abby's chair and watched the father-daughter dance.

Abby leaned over to Craig and tapped him on the chest. She pointed and whispered, "Sarah looks so beautiful. She's in her element."

"She does," he agreed, not taking his eyes off his sister. "She's a really good sister."

Abby appreciated him being able to say this. This vulnerability had been one of the things that she appreciated at the beginning of their relationship.

The dance ended, and the floor was open to requests. Abby and Craig were paralyzed by the fear of being the first one to break. They both wanted to dance, but neither wanted to be the first to ask. Before either could talk, Linda came and sat down at their table.

"Hello there, you two," Linda said a bit too loud. "Thank you for coming, Abby."

"Thank you for having me, Mrs. McLean," Abby replied in a calm, confident voice. Craig looked at her and smiled.

"So, Craig tells me he switched his major to education," Linda started in.

"Mom," Craig said. "Don't."

"You're going to let me talk, Craig," she retorted.

"That's what he tells me, Mrs. McLean," Abby said.

"Well Mike and I think it has something to do you with you and that damn resort."

"Is that so?" Abby added a bit of sarcasm to her answer that she was sure wine had clouded from Linda's understanding.

"Yes. We don't want him to become a teacher. He's going to be a doctor."

Abby looked sternly at an emasculated Craig, whose eyes were wide but his mouth was mute. "Well, it seems to me that Craig can do what he likes. He seems to love it. And besides, my mother is a teacher."

Craig was struck by how calm Abby was. She didn't show

the slightest sign of being frustrated. He took his arm from the back of her chair and put it at his side. Abby grabbed his hand and squeezed it hard.

"Well all this change is too much for us," Linda said. She took a gulp of wine and looked at Abby with wild eyes.

"I would agree. Change is hard." Abby looked at Craig and smiled. "But today is a good change, right?" She looked back at Linda. "Let's enjoy today." Linda's face went blank. Abby continued, "Do you want to dance, Craig?"

He looked at Abby, surprised, and then to his mother and back to Abby. "Sure?" he almost asked. They stood up. Still holding hands, Craig led Abby through the tables to the dance floor. They faced each other, and he said, "Holy shit. I'm so sorry about that. You were great."

Abby snorted and slowly shook her head. "Fuck her. I'm so sick of people ripping on teachers. It was less about you and more about that." She looked up at him with a half smile and continued, "Thanks for the help." Then she put her hands on Craig's shoulders. "Dance with me."

After a few songs, one that Abby knew very well came on. She stopped and gently pushed herself away from Craig. "You planned this." She was smiling.

"No," Craig said. "I swear. Sarah's a country girl, so I told her about them, and she liked it. She must have put this on."

It was "Keep Us" by Peter Bradley Adams, one of Abby's favorites. The last verse played as they swayed to the melody,

There's a lesson in the rain that change will always come
let us ride this wave and then greet the sun
and though the ground may shake and we'll think

we've had enough
we must raise our flags for the ones we love.

She put her arms around Craig's waist and pulled him close, resting her head on his shoulder. He put his arms around her shoulders and squeezed her. "Thanks for coming today."

"You're welcome, Craig."

They danced out the song and then went back to the table, poured another glass of wine, and watched others mill about. There's something about a wedding as it drifts into the late evening. People gravitate into clusters. Ties loosen, and dresses are fluffed. Abby and Craig let the rhythms settle around them. From time to time, their hands found each other, and it was followed by a smile or gentle touch on a leg. They danced a few more times. There was no need for talk. They were with one another, and it was all they needed at that moment.

When they eventually got up to the room, Abby went to the bathroom to change. She came out in sweats and a T-shirt, and Craig was dressed much the same. He went to the bathroom, and when he came out, Abby was almost asleep. He turned out the light and slid into bed carefully. While lying on his back and staring at the ceiling, Craig was startled when Abby rolled over and laid her head on his chest. He propped himself up on his pillow a bit more and hesitantly put his arm around her until she fell into her normal spot. She draped her leg over his. "I just want to see how it feels," she whispered.

"It feels pretty good to me."

"Me too. Goodnight, Craig."

"Goodnight, Abby."

Chapter 31

When they woke up in the morning, Abby was still tucked up to Craig, who had rolled to his side to face her. She waited for him to wake up. The first thing he saw when he opened his eyes was her smiling at him, her beautiful eyes shining in the muted sunlight.

"Good morning, sleepy," Abby said. "You better go the bathroom so I can take a shower. There's not going to be any sneaking in like at home, you hear?"

"Sure thing. I gotta pee anyway." Craig jumped out of bed and scampered to the bathroom while Abby got ready to take a shower. She gathered her things and quickly undressed, wrapping herself in a towel from the closet. When she heard the sink running, she went in and put her things down on the counter.

"Shoo now," she said as Craig looked her up and down. "Get out," she continued playfully. Right as he went out of the door, Abby dropped her towel, and their eyes met in the mirror for a moment. She winked at Craig and closed the door, locking it. Craig just stood for a minute, then went to lie down on the bed. He looked up at the ceiling and laughed to himself.

Later, after breakfast, as they were packing up the room, Abby came up behind Craig and popped him on his butt.

"You're taking me home right?"

"Wait, what?" Craig said as he turned around.

"You're taking me home, right?" Abby asked again.

"To the resort? In Eagle River?"

"Where else?"

He was confused. "Ok, but..."

"How else am I supposed to get home, Craig?" Abby stated in the same clear voice she had used the night before. "Besides, what else are you going to do for spring break?"

"Nothing, I guess."

"Right. No one is going to be home at your place," Abby pressed.

"Yeah. Everyone is leaving Monday."

"Correct. Let's go to your house and get your things and head north. We can come back for Claire's show at the end of the week."

"Wait, are you sure?"

"Yes. I'm sure."

"Does this mean?"

"That I want my best friend to come home with me? Yes."

"Cool," Craig said and packed the rest of his stuff.

Craig left a note for his parents, who expected that he would be home, telling them that he had gone up north for the week, and they should have a nice vacation. He texted Claire telling her the plan and asking for the details of the art show the following Friday. She texted back immediately, *Good for you!! Have fun!! Friday at 6. I'll send you directions.*

He gathered some clothes and his boots. The car ride with Abby was filled with laughter and sharing songs and stories from the wedding and their time apart. They went over Linda's speech from the night before and laughed it off as the raving of a drunk woman, although Abby was secretly concerned that Linda's disapproval of her would continue to be a thing. They stopped in Stevens Point for lunch and then pressed on the rest of the way to the resort, arriving in time for dinner.

Craig noticed how Abby's shoulders relaxed and she closed her eyes when they pulled into the parking lot. She took a deep breath as though taking it all in. When she got out of the car, she was transformed. The spark in her eyes, which Craig had only seen intermittently over the past few months, was back in full force. She reached up in a stretch and spun around on her toes before getting her bags, and they headed to the house.

John emerged from the garage in work pants and a heavy flannel. He took off his glasses to clean them, and Craig caught his eye. "Welcome home, you two," John said loudly.

Craig was struck by the thought that he was home. This place felt more familiar to him than the white walls that had surrounded him for the last ten years of his life. He looked up at the canopy of pines and took his own deep breath. The smell made him smile.

After giving Abby a hug, John said, "Boy, am I glad to see you, Craig." They shook hands, and John continued, "One of my normal hired cleaners is off on vacation skiing in Colorado this week. I could use a hand."

"Happy to help, sir," Craig said as he picked up his bag.

"Well, good. Not sure Abby told you, but the resort is shut down for the week, so we're doing a lot of cleaning and maintenance. Snow's melted, and there's still ice on the lake. Don't get much business anyway, so it's a good week to catch up on things and get ready for later in the spring."

"Sounds good, sir. I'm ready to work."

"I know you are, son. Abby didn't tell me you were coming, but you can get yourself fixed up in Grandma's room downstairs. I think supper is almost ready."

"Thank you," Craig said, and they went inside.

Dinner had an intimate feeling to Craig. Everyone helped with preparation and cleanup, and the jokes and laughter were easy and frequent. There was nothing even resembling the discomfort and tension of the night before. Abby described the wedding in such detail that Craig was amazed at all she observed. Taylor was interested in the wedding discussion but played on her phone the rest of the time. They drank a bottle of wine and lit a fire. Craig sat and listened to John outline the week while Abby unpacked. There was a lot of work to be done, but Craig was excited. The prospect of purposeful routine invigorated him. When Abby returned to the living room, she asked, "Craig, do you want to go surprise Frank? Say hello and stuff?"

Craig jumped up. "Yeah. Sure. Excuse me, Mr. Whitworth."

"No problem, kids. He'll be thrilled," John said.

They set off to find Frank. As soon as they got out of the house, Craig asked, "Does Frank ever take time off?"

"No," Abby answered. "Ever since Rita died, he just works. He always said living here is like a vacation. He takes a day every now and then, but for the most part, he's just here. He's part of the place, you know?"

"Yeah. I guess. Just wondering," Craig said.

They scampered through the woods to the lodge, and Craig let his feet find the way. The lodge loomed, quiet and dark. Without people, the resort took on life of its own. It was a character in its own story, rather than just a place. Craig couldn't quite wrap his head around it.

Abby enjoyed these weeks. Twice a year they closed down for repairs, and she loved the way the resort looked when they were done. There was a freshness to the place, and the routine gave them a chance to begin anew.

They made their way to the cabin road and then down the path that led to Frank's place. There was a little moonlight in the forest to guide them. Abby knew the way, but Craig was unsure on this path. When they got to the door, she knocked, and Craig pretended to hide behind her. They could hear Frank shuffling to the door. It opened.

"Abby!" Frank said with open arms. Abby took a step forward.

"Surprise!" Craig yelped as he hopped up.

"Craig!" Frank said and moved to give him a hug. "Well this IS a surprise. Come in!"

The living room of the cabin was small. There was a love seat against the right wall with side tables, and an easy chair that looked worn in and a huge carved coffee table in the center of the room. National Geographic magazines and dog-eared books were strewn about. The walls were bare save for some of Abby's pictures and one, a picture of Frank and his wife, right above the couch. The lake was in the background, and Frank looked much younger. Craig stood staring at it until Abby tapped the seat next to her and he sat down.

"Can I get you two anything?" Frank asked.

"No, thank you," Abby responded as she looked at Craig, who was shaking his head. "We're fine."

Craig took hold of Abby's hand and held it in his lap. Feeling tired, Abby leaned on his arm, smiling to herself. The fire was going in the two-sided fireplace that split the living room and the kitchen. It was the only internal wall in the front of the cabin. The rest was open. Frank went to the kitchen and emerged with a small glass of what looked like whiskey or brandy. He set the glass on a side table and fell into his chair. "So, how was that meal I sent you the recipe for? Not as good as mine, I'm sure." He took a sip from the glass.

"No, Frank, it wasn't as good as yours. But it was a nice gesture," Abby said, taking a quick look at Craig.

"And how'd your announcement go, young man? Big news."

Craig gripped Abby's hand a little tighter, and she brought her other hand over his. She whispered, "It's ok. You can tell him. It's Frank."

"Well, it didn't go so well. I think I scared Abby a bit." Craig looked at her, and she nodded. "We actually broke up."

"Well, I figured it was too big a gesture. Girls get scared by that. Right, Abby?"

"It was a bit much," she replied.

"Let me tell you both a little story," Frank said. He took another sip from his glass. "I asked Rita to marry me twice. The first time, she said no."

"Really?" Abby asked.

"Yep. She said no. See, I planned out this whole thing. Had the ring ready and had some friends over. I did it up nice. Cooked her favorite meal. We were out at the campfire, and I asked her in front of everyone."

"She said no in front of all your friends?" Craig said, surprised.

"You bet. That was Rita. Told me that a proposal was something between me and her. It was not for everyone. See, the big gestures are not what gets them. It's the little stuff." Frank paused and lowered the foot rest on his chair so he could lean forward. "So, you guys are fine now?"

"Actually, we're just trying to be friends first," Craig said because he thought that's what Abby would want to hear.

"Yeah," she concurred, but Frank cut her off.

"Ha! Who you fooling?" Frank spouted out. Abby and Craig looked at each other. He continued, "You guys have been holding hands since you sat down. Abby's got her head on your shoulder. You keep looking at each other. Friends my ass."

Abby straightened up, taking her head off Craig's shoulder. They kept holding hands.

"You guys are full of shit. Ha!" Frank swallowed the rest of the contents of his glass in one gulp. "Now, Rita and I were friends. Best friends. But you know…" Frank paused and took a deep breath. "It's the little things. Let me tell you a secret. Emotions come and go. There are going to be days you love each other. Can't keep your hands off each other. There'll be other times you're at each other's throats. But you can't forget the gestures, like holding hands, a kiss in the morning or at night. You have to look one another in the eye when you talk to each other. You have to listen, you know. Really listen, and remember. Those are the things a relationship is built on. You two got that going for you. Anyone can see it." He paused and took another deep breath, more labored this time. "It's time for you two to go." He looked straight at Abby. "Now, you report to me in the kitchen first thing in the morning. We're going to clean that thing top to bottom, and we're going to get that place done before you move on to your dad's list, you hear?"

"Yes, Frank," Abby said as she stood up. Craig followed her, and as he stood, he looked back at the picture of Frank and Rita. Their smiles seemed so genuinely happy. Frank stood straight and tall while Rita's hand was intertwined in his. For just moment, Craig saw himself in the picture, standing with Abby, filled with pride.

Abby and Craig put on their coats and walked into the darkness. "Bye, Frank," Abby called from the steps.

"Night, y'all," Frank responded and closed the door behind them.

Turning into the cool night air, they stopped at the bottom of the steps. "Wow," Craig said. "That was intense."

"Yes," Abby agreed. "It was."

They made their way carefully through the woods and onto the cabin road. The light in Frank's cabin was out, and only the glow of the fire showed in the window. Before them was darkness, but they found each other's hand. Abby kicked the ground as she walked. She swung their arms gently as she swayed side to to side. For just a moment, they stopped and peered at the bench on the dock. They gazed at each other, and then walked on to the house.

Chapter 32

"Rise and shine, sunshine. You're mine today." The lights flickered on and off, and Craig couldn't figure out what was going on. When he opened his eyes, John was standing in the doorway. "Abby's off to work with Frank all day, and we are going to cut some fresh trees. Sound good?" He waited for an answer.

"Sure thing, sir," Craig replied as he rolled to a sitting position.

"Good. Get yourself some breakfast, and we'll be off." John disappeared.

"Great," Craig said to himself. He looked at the clock, which read six thirty. "Shit." With that, he got up and got dressed, putting on the Carhartt work pants he got for Christmas, much to his mother's dismay, and a long-sleeve shirt and an old hoodie. He ate a bowl of oatmeal with brown sugar, greeted Vickie, and went out to a running truck where John sat, waiting. They drove to the land north of town. Mostly, it was a quiet ride.

"So, we have two large trees downed and trimmed. We're going to cut them into sections to put in the truck, and then you can chop them up later," John stated in a very matter-of-fact tone.

"I can do that," Craig said, still a bit sleepy.

"I know you can. We also have to turn all the piles over this week."

"What do you mean?"

"Every cabin has a pile right?"

"Yes, sir."

"Well, we need to stack the new wood on bottom to dry out and get the old stuff up top so it gets burned first. It's a big job."

"Got it," Craig said, nodding.

"Good." John patted him on the shoulder. "I'm going to leave you in charge of that project."

"Ok." Craig was looking forward to the work. The fact that John was going to trust him with his own project gave him pride and a goal on which to focus.

When they got to the land, there were two trees that had already been dragged to the parking area. John was going to use a chainsaw to cut them up into manageable sections for Craig to load onto the truck. Craig started by selecting branches that had been stripped that had enough wood to be made into firewood. John got to work on the trunks. When he had several cut, he paused and called for Craig, who had to roll the cut pieces up a ramp into the truck. It was hard work. Very little was said aside from direction, and Craig tired quickly. He hadn't worked out since he and Abby broke up. He was surprised how fast he wore down.

Finally, the first tree was loaded. Craig leaned against the truck, drinking water that John gave to him. John drank coffee. Craig watched as John picked up a few logs and threw them towards the truck. He never seemed to tire. 'Old man strength,' Craig thought to himself. That must be it. He had heard of these guys, who never saw the inside of a weight room, but could lift just about anything. After working so many years on the resort, it made sense. 'That would be something,' Craig thought.

"Break's over," John called. "I want to get this load back home by lunch so we can get it chopped up by the end of the day. The Northwoods is fooling with us. There's still plenty of cold nights ahead, and I want to be well stocked."

"Sure thing," Craig said and got back to work. He tried not to think of the soreness that was setting in and, instead, just focused on the task at hand. John joined in after the cutting was done. He took two logs and tossed them on the pile, skipping the ramp altogether. Craig just shook his head and got into the cab.

Later, after a bit of chopping, Craig found Abby. She was sitting at the bar eating a sandwich with only the kitchen lights on. He came up behind her and rubbed her shoulders. She turned and smiled saying, "You can keep doing that." Craig squeezed her one more time and sat down next to her.

"How was your morning?" he asked.

"It was fine. Frank works me hard, but I love it. He makes it fun. And yours?"

"I'm beat," Craig said, putting his head in his hands. He was covered in sawdust and twigs.

"You look it," Abby said with a laugh. "And you stink too."

"Thanks," Craig said, giving her a punch on the arm.

"Hey." She punched him back. "You want me to make you a sandwich?"

"That would be great."

Abby hopped off the stool and went to the kitchen. Craig laid his head on the bar.

From the kitchen, Frank called, "John kicked your ass

pretty hard this morning, huh? Might be too soft for this life." He laughed loudly.

"He might be," Abby said and winked at Frank.

Craig just waved one hand without raising his head.

When Abby came back out, she went behind the bar and poured Craig a Mellow Yellow and set his sandwich down next to his head. She ran her fingers through his hair and tickled the back of his neck to wake him up. "Hey," she said quietly. "Here's your food."

Craig woke up and stretched hard and loudly. "Thanks, babe." Neither of them batted an eye at the phrase. He took a bite from his sandwich. "Good. Thanks," he said with his mouth full.

"What's my dad got you doing today?" Abby asked as she began to finish her own lunch.

"He put me in charge of the wood. I have to turn over all the piles and make sure the stock is up at all the cabins and the lodge." He took another huge bite of his sandwich and drained the soda. Abby filled his glass again.

"That sounds like a big project. I guess I won't see you until tomorrow night."

"Possibly." He finished his sandwich and drank the rest of the second glass of soda. "I should probably get moving again." Craig reached his hands across the bar. Abby took them and gave them a squeeze.

"Be careful."

"Thanks. See you at dinner?" Craig reached back to grab his plate.

"I got it, babe. No worries." Abby cleaned up his plate and glass.

"Thanks," he said and shuffled off.

The chopping went well. Craig found a pace that suited him. When he needed a break, he loaded some wood and took it to a cabin. No need to stock it yet as he had to turn the piles over anyway. By the end of the afternoon, every cabin had enough wood, and he began to figure the allotment he needed for the lodge. John told him to steal a little from the cabins to finish the lodge for now, a task he got done happily.

After a long day of work, Craig and Abby freshened up before heading to the dinner table. Dinner was quiet save for Taylor sharing her day at school. Abby, Craig, John, and Frank were all too tired to be much in the way of conversation. Taylor and her mother cleaned the table while the rest planned out the next few days. Craig would finish his wood project while John and Abby moved on to the cabins. Frank would do inventory.

Decisions made and plans laid, Abby and Craig decided to watch a movie and turn in early. They found the latest Bourne film on Netflix, and Craig lay down on Abby's lap. She rubbed his head, making him fall asleep within minutes. She kissed him on the head and turned off the movie. When Craig woke up the next morning, he found himself on the couch with a pillow under his head and a blanket to keep him warm. He smiled and got up for work.

Tuesday was much like Monday with Craig working like a dog, but now, with every pile he flipped, there was an end in sight. He ate lunch with Abby again, barely conscious, and went to bed early with the promise of the next two days being less intense so he could spend more time with her.

Abby had watched Craig work and wondered if he loved it as much as she did. The routine was all she hoped it would be, and the rhythm of the familiar was what she needed to ground herself and forget about the past few months. She could focus on each task in the moment and execute it as she always had. This was why she loved the resort. There was a comfort in the known, and the realization that Craig was part of that known was beginning to settle upon her. She was not yet prepared to tell him, but she was ready to love him again. She had never really stopped.

The next day, Craig was reintroduced to the Abby he met at Thanksgiving. They were cleaning cabins, but not the way they had done at Thanksgiving or Christmas; that was just turning them over. This was get-down-on-your-knees cleaning. They used heavy duty cleaners and went over everything twice. Abby even brought out paint to touch up some areas, making everything seem new.

Craig just followed Abby's lead and did as he was told. They turned on music, and, at first, he dove into his tasks, but always found himself falling behind. Abby was locked in to what she was doing. Craig began to see that he was slowing her down, despite her insistence that he wasn't. He also noticed that she had the ability to drift off into her work. She would do this from time to time, singing to a song or swaying to a music all her own. At these times, he would just watch her and smile. He loved her, and he knew she would always be enough.

They knocked out three cabins the first day and set the goal of four for the next day. Craig was confident they could get it done. He talked at supper about how the skills he was learning would come in handy when he had his own place. Abby was not amused. Despite her growing affection for Craig, she was still reluctant to speak of the future. She was just walking in the now. What Frank said had really sunk in deeply. Relationships were work, and she didn't want to take moments with Craig for granted. For all his intensity, he drifted into the past and the future at the expense of the now. She loved his enthusiasm for life, but worried about him getting off on too many tangents or getting too far ahead of himself. They were only nineteen years old.

Vickie and Craig did have some nice conversations about teaching. He was interested in any advice she could offer. However, she did warn him about how policies in Madison had affected the profession. Being a teacher in Wisconsin was not what it once was. Craig appreciated the perspective, however, he believed the kids made it worth the trouble. Vickie readily agreed.

Taylor, in all her juvenile impetuousness, asked if Craig and Abby were getting married. That question silenced the table until Abby said they were just good friends. Taylor's sour face displayed that she was not convinced, and Abby's parents didn't press the issue. Shortly after supper, Craig and Abby went to bed early, mostly to avoid any further inquiry, and also because they wanted to meet their goal. Thursday was their last day at the resort.

Thursday evening, having finished four cabins, Abby and Craig decided to treat themselves by going out to Butch's Pizza. They just wanted some time to talk things out and be by themselves after a week of hard work. They ordered a large, knowing it would be too much food, but they were too tired to care.

"So," Craig started, "we need to be in Chicago around six. It'll probably be about an hour to get through the city, so I think we should leave at ten or so?"

Abby took a deep breath and sat back on the bench. "Ok," she muttered. "At least we can sleep in a bit."

"Yeah," Craig said, leaning his head in his hands. "I'm so tired, Abby."

"I know. Me too. But I like the work."

"Me too," Craig replied.

"Really?" Abby sat up, putting her head in her hands as well and looking at Craig expectantly.

Craig straightened up, leaving his hands on the table. "Yeah. I like that I can see what I've done. There's that sense of purpose, you know?"

"I suppose," Abby agreed. "I think that I like it because I feel like I'm contributing to the family...I feel like I'm contributing to the future of the business. Away at school, I don't get that feeling."

"I get you," Craig said. "I'm glad you included me this week. I'm happy I came up here."

"This is the real work of the resort, Craig."

He took time think about her comment. He looked off to the kitchen area and then back at her. "How do you mean?"

"My dad might seem like the front man, but he has a mental list a mile long all the time. He works twelve to fourteen hours a day, seven days a week. He never takes a break. He's given us a good life and all, but…"

"He's a good man."

"Yes, he is. I guess I just don't want to let him down."

"How would you do that, Abby? You're great."

"You know what I mean. It's weeks like this where I see him fixing this and that. He knows how to do all this stuff. I feel like I don't know anything." Abby's voice was rough and quiet. "I don't even know if I can learn everything he knows."

Craig offered his hand, which she took without looking. "I don't know what you want me to say."

"I'm not expecting you to say anything. Just listen," Abby said. She rubbed her eyes with her free hand.

"Ok," Craig said. "I'll try."

The pizza came, pepperoni and pineapple, salty and sweet. For almost ten minutes, nothing was said. They ate and drank their fill, nearly finishing the pizza. Breathing heavily, Abby said, "Holy shit. I'm tired."

"Yeah. Me too," Craig agreed.

They just stared at each other for a another minute and said nothing. Craig broke first, smiling and laughing. Abby shook her head and laughed softly as well. He thought about what he wanted to say. He didn't know if this was the right time but went for it anyway. "Abby?"

"Yeah." She looked up, smiling.

"What are we doing here?"

"Eating. What do you mean?"

"You and I. What is this?" He spoke softly.

"Right now?" Abby asked. "Right now, you're my best friend, Craig. There's no one I would rather be with. What else would there be? I'm just too tired to think about it beyond that, ok?"

Defeated, Craig gave up. "Ok."

"I'm sorry I can't give you more."

"That's fine. You're my best friend too."

"I know." Abby smiled. "Can we go home?"

"Home?"

"Yeah," she said confidently. "Home."

Abby: 19, Revision of Poem for English

When the leaves on the trees begin
To bud and the flowers bloom
When the school year grinds
To its end and the water opens
When the visitors return
With stories of the outside world
The dock goes in
The cabins reopen
The buzz is all around
The birds come back from the south
And the fish rise again
Then I am home
There I belong.

Chapter 33

Abby slept all the way to Madison. As he drove, Craig thought about what Frank had said to them. He realized he had made a mistake and had come on too strong. He had basically proposed to Abby after knowing her for four months. The change to an education degree, although spurred by his love for her, had actually turned out to be the best thing. Craig could see himself working with kids for the rest of his life. He never felt like that about medicine. Abby's mom had not deterred him even though she had brought up things he hadn't considered. In reality, he just wanted things to go back to the way they were. He wanted to spend every night with Abby and wanted to kiss her again and run his fingers through her hair. When she slept, her face was so peaceful. Her lips were relaxed and full; she looked free from worry. Craig had not slept that peacefully in almost two months.

When Abby woke up, Craig was running his fingers over her shoulders.

"Good afternoon, sleepy," he said.

"Where are we?"

"Just south of Madison."

"How long until Chicago?"

"Not sure. But we're making good time, so I think we'll get

there early enough to grab a bite to eat."

"That's . . ." Abby yawned loudly, ". . . good. I'm going to be hungry."

"Well, I'm sure there will be places around campus to get something," Craig said, trying to sound like he knew what he was talking about. Truth be told, he was nervous about finding the campus and, even more importantly, finding a place to park. It was Friday, and people would be out.

Sensing his lack of confidence, Abby asked, "Do you know where you're going, Craig?"

"Sure," he said, striking a hopeful chord. "No problem."

"Ok." Abby made no attempt to hide her sarcasm.

"Let's just have fun tonight."

She looked at him, puzzled. "Ok. Why wouldn't we?"

"I don't know. I can be a drag sometimes."

"True," Abby said with a laugh.

"You think you're funny, huh?" Craig said, squeezing her leg and poking her in the side.

"Hey," Abby gently slapped his hand away. "I agree. Let's have fun. I'm really looking forward to Claire's show."

"Me too," Craig agreed. "We've seen some of her photos and sketches, but she's always kept her other work secret. I don't know what to expect."

"It should be cool."

When they got to the city, Abby's head turned all around. "This place is amazing."

"Haven't you ever been here?" Craig asked. "I thought your mom was from Chicago."

"I came here with her when I was little, but for the last ten years or so, people mostly come up by us. There really are no weeks off. If we do come down, it's to see family in the suburbs. No one is really interested in going into the city."

"It's pretty neat," Craig said. "I hope I can find this place."

Abby noticed that he had both hands on the wheel. "Do you need me to navigate?"

Relieved, Craig replied, "That would be great."

They made it to campus and parked the car. It was only four thirty, so there was plenty of time to eat before going to the art center. They found a place to get Chicago dogs and sat down at a table overlooking the river, taking in the brilliant sights of the city. Abby looked up much of the time, while Craig did his best not to spill on his shirt. She was amused by the pains he took, putting a napkin on his lap and leaning way over the table. He licked his fingers between every bite.

Craig ate quickly and spent the rest of the time watching Abby. She was beautiful. He had been sitting at tables with her for over half a year, and she just got prettier every time. Even when food fell from her mouth, and she quickly brought a napkin to her face, he thought it was cute as hell. Her skin was so smooth, and her eyes sparkled in the late afternoon sun. She caught Craig staring. "What?"

"You're beautiful."

Abby smiled at him with relish in her teeth.

Craig laughed.

"What?" she asked, licking her teeth. "Oh." She wiped her mouth with a napkin and began to laugh herself. "You're pretty cute yourself, Craig." She finished her last bite and watched Craig watch her. He smiled and crossed his eyes to make her laugh. As Frank said, it was the small things, the gestures, that made all the difference. Craig was the master of the small things. True, he had made the grand gesture, and it scared the hell out of her. However, he made all the small ones too. It came naturally to him, and she loved him for the way he loved her. She wanted to tell him she loved him again, but she didn't want to move too fast. She wanted him but was scared he'd go big again and send her running. The words of Meghan, Kate, and Frank echoed in her head, and she knew she was good enough for Craig. He was lucky to have her, and she was lucky to have him too.

They made their way to the Logan Art Center. When they went in the main gallery, they were both struck with the beauty of the place. The building was a piece of art itself. There were high ceilings and punches of color on white canvases hanging in the main hall. Craig had texted Claire that they were in front of the art center, so she met them as they were coming in. She greeted Abby brightly with a hug. Craig was happy to see that they had made such a strong connection. Claire gave him a half hug and led them on their way. She explained that she had chosen a studio space to have her show because it represented where she believed she was as an artist. The pieces she was presenting were finished, but *she* was a work in progress. Craig nodded in agreement. The metaphor resonated with him. He, too, had a lot of work to do.

Claire had arranged her work by medium as far as Craig could see. There were drawings on the left wall, followed by multimedia pieces along the back. On the right were her photos. She had always shared her pictures with him, so it was these pictures that he had known. She had taken pictures of all the family events, so consequently, she was often not in the family pictures, but she had always occupied a space of her own. Craig hung back as Claire showed Abby the way to view the pieces.

Claire drifted back to Craig. “Thanks for coming, little bother.” She gave him a little squeeze.

“Of course,” he replied. “Not a problem. Always good to see what my little sister has been up to in the big city.” He laughed. Although Claire was older, she had always been the shortest in the family. She took after her mother in size, but in no other ways.

“Craig!” Abby called, beckoning him.

“What?”

“Come here.”

Claire and Craig walked over. Abby was looking at a pencil drawing that was so realistic it looked like a photo. She looked back at them with wet eyes. “Is this me?”

Claire put her arm around Abby’s shoulder. “Yes.”

The picture was black and white with only her eyes colored, light blue and green with flecks of brown. The face was slightly averted, and the mouth was smiling, but closed. It looked like she was right at the point of laughing.

“How did you . . .” Abby stopped short and looked back at the drawing.

“That was the picture of you I had in my mind from Thanksgiving dinner. I just couldn’t get it outta my head, so I drew it.” Claire looked at Abby and continued, “You have beautiful eyes. You know that right? They’re so strong. Hard to forget. Craig sent me a picture of you last fall, after Thanksgiving, and I used that to get the details right.”

Abby turned and hugged Claire. “Thank you,” she said through the tears.

"Of course. No problem, Abby. You guys look around. I'll catch up with you later. And thanks again for coming." She walked off to greet others who were coming into the room. There was a mix of people, older and younger. Some were obviously Claire's friends and others, Craig and Abby assumed, were professors.

They followed the wall displaying all the sketches to the multimedia projects. Craig was drawn to a collage that looked familiar. The figure, when you stood back, was a football player running with his right hand extended. Arrows, both curved and straight, were painted over the figure. Craig realized the lines were a football play, one he often ran as a receiver. It was a play that depended on speed to make the edge. As he moved closer, he saw that the entire collage was made up of tiny pictures of him playing football through his high school years. The title was "Movement." The explanation read: *"My little brother was always moving. I could never get him to sit still long enough to even take a picture. So, I decided to make him stop the only way I could, by capturing him in motion."*

Abby came up behind him. "Is that you?"

"I suppose it is. I never knew how talented she was. I mean I knew, but I didn't."

"It's really hard to know someone fully, I guess."

"I guess so," Craig said, still staring at the picture.

"Come look at this one," Abby said with a tug at his sweater.

They came to a piece that was difficult to define. Parts seemed drawn, while other elements seemed painted or photographed. It went from left to right, and the beginning was like a blueprint of a house. This gave over to perfectly defined landscaping and bright colors. In the middle, the colors seemed to fade, and the house started to disappear. All the way to the right, there was a cloud of colorless dust.

After looking at the piece for several minutes, while Abby commented on the techniques, Craig realized it was their house. It dawned on him that this whole room was Claire's journey. The work after the house was all photographs, mostly of Chicago. She had abandoned the suburbs for the city. The elements she hung onto were the people, but the city had captured her heart. Claire had paid homage to her upbringing, but she was now beyond it. They looked at the rest of the work and even peeked at a couple of professors' clipboards to get a sense of how things were going for her. Generally, well. Craig saw himself in the questions Claire was grappling with. She was questioning who she was becoming. He still had no clue of who he might become.

When they got back to the entrance, Claire was still talking with people. One of her friends said, "Is this your little brother, Claire? He's a hottie."

Craig blushed a bit as Claire replied, "He's not bad. But he's with his girlfriend, so watch out." She smiled at Craig and Abby.

Abby saw his red face and chuckled a bit. She reached out to grab his hand. He squeezed it out of habit.

"So, what did you guys think?" Claire asked.

"It was all so great," Abby said, letting go of Craig's hand and giving her a hug. "You have so much talent."

Craig agreed. "It was really good. I'm glad we came."

"Me too," Claire said, smiling. "Let me walk you out."

Claire and Abby continued to chat about the work as Craig hung back, looking around the art center. Before him were two of the most important girls in his life. Sarah and his mother were important as well, but Claire had always understood his struggles. The All-American boy was dead. Claire, and now Abby, always knew he never really lived outside the lines. But now, he longed to strike a new path free from boundaries. He watched Abby walk ahead with her whimsical and carefree gait, swaying side to side and fully engaged in conversation with Claire. The more he learned about Abby, the more he loved her. She was all he wanted now. As they approached the entrance, he took a few jog steps to catch up. "What are you two chatting about?"

"Craig," Claire said seriously. "I haven't told Mom and Dad yet, but I applied for graduate school, and I got accepted."

"For art? Here?"

"Yes," Claire replied. "I'm going to get my Masters and maybe my Ph.D."

"What do you think Mom and Dad are going to say? They aren't going to be happy." Craig was sure of that answer.

"Well, I got a scholarship, and I'm going to TA, so it won't cost them a thing. I guess, it's not their decision anymore."

Craig smiled. "Well, I'm happy for you." He reached out and gave her a big hug, lifting her from the ground for a moment.

"And I've got some news," Abby said.

Craig looked at her, confused.

She continued, "I've invited Claire to come to the resort for the summer as an artist in residence. We've been talking about it since Christmas."

"You did," Craig said. His eyes darted back and forth between both girls.

"Yep. She doesn't start school until the fall, and my dad said it was fine. He likes having artists around. We've hosted a couple of writers over the years."

"I'm going to teach some art classes for the guests, and it will be so good to be in a new environment for the summer. Time to clear my head and all," Claire said.

Craig shook his head, feeling a bit bewildered. "Well that sounds really cool."

"Great," Abby said with a clap.

"Well, you guys should get going. Traffic's a bitch on Friday nights around here."

They said their goodbyes, and Abby and Craig walked out into a beautiful spring evening. Craig went over to a tree just outside the entrance and plucked a new leaf. Abby watched him with a smile, closing her eyes and holding onto the feeling of the moment.

"I don't want to go home yet," Abby said. "Do you want to get a cup of coffee?"

"Sure," Craig said. "We've driven a lot today. I could use some coffee."

They walked a few steps and stopped to look back on the art center and the campus. "This is quite a place. Downtown is like a forest of buildings," Abby said, taking a spin.

Suddenly, Craig pulled her close and kissed her. She hesitated for a moment, then returned his kiss with more passion, and they stayed close to one another for several moments. People walked past, but they were fully focused on each other, the world disappearing around them. When they finally pulled themselves apart, Craig said, " It was really cool of you to invite my sister to the resort for the summer."

"It will be fun."

Excited, Craig pressed on. "Maybe I can come up and work

for the summer as well? Maybe…"

Abby put her finger over his mouth and then moved in to kiss him gently. "Shhh, Craig. We're here now."

Craig looked at her with narrowed eyes. "What are you saying?"

Abby said plainly as she could, "Let's not talk about the future. No big gestures. Let's just take a walk for now. Find some coffee." She grabbed his hand and led him down past the campus. They didn't know where they were going, but it didn't matter. They found a place called Hallowed Grounds that felt more like a pool hall than a coffee shop, but it had a nice vibe and suited their mood. They ordered coffee. The Weepies' "Happiness" was playing. Abby swayed as they walked to a table.

Craig was confused about what he should say, so he waited for Abby to speak first. He reached his hand across the table, and she placed hers in his. The leaf lay between them.

Abby looked at the leaf and finally spoke. "This is a nice place."

"Yes it is." Craig said impatiently. "What were you saying outside, Abby? I didn't understand."

Abby took a breath and knew she had to go all in. She said, "I love you NOW." She hesitated, waiting for a reaction but was met with a blank stare. "Do you get what I'm saying?" She held him in an intense spell. He stared back at her very deliberately, but she never broke.

"I love you," Craig said, trying to kiss her from across the table.

She backed him off. "I know, but let me talk," Abby continued slowly. "I love you right here and right now. Will I love you tomorrow? Yes. Will I love you next week? Yes. Will I keep loving you? I sure hope so. But let's just be here with each other right now, ok?" She looked down and saw Craig rubbing the back of her hand with his thumb.

"Ok," he said. "I can do that." He took a sip of his coffee, set it down, and then reached out his other hand. Abby grasped it tightly.

"Is this enough?" she asked, looking at him like she did the first time they were in the library together months ago, with a mixture of desire, intrigue, and hopefulness.

"Yes. This is enough. This is all I need." For Craig, at that moment, there was only her, and the world faded around them. "Do you believe me?"

"No," Abby said calmly as she picked up the leaf and twirled it in her fingers. She held the leaf close to her face so only her eyes showed above it. "I don't need to believe you, Craig, because I already know. I think I've always known."

Benjamin R. Nysse is foremost a husband and father. When he is not teaching English and Creative Writing at Hamilton High School in Sussex, Wisconsin, he can be found on the sidelines of a track or cross country meet, at a football or soccer game, or sitting in the audience listening to his youngest daughter sing. This is his first novel.